She finally met his eyes. "I'm too cold."

He reached across and felt the skin of her forehead. She still felt like ice.

He pulled the remainder of the pack toward them and gently pushed her head down on it until she was lying down. Then he undid his blanket and lay down behind her. Covering both their bodies he pulled her close toward him. He could feel the rigid set of her shoulders through the two layers of fabric that separated them. He'd already assured her that he wouldn't hurt her, so he just kept still and hoped that his actions would speak louder than any words he could say.

Gradually, over the space of a thousand heartbeats, he felt her muscles relax and her breathing grow heavier as she drifted into sleep.

All his instincts were roaring at him to remove the blankets between them and press their flesh together. It would warm her faster; of course it would. While he lay there fighting the impulse he admitted to himself that her warmth was not the only thing at the forefront of his mind.

He wanted to slide his hands over every inch of her perfect body and for her to welcome his touch.

She trusted him and so he didn't move.

Author Note

Thank you for choosing to read *The Warrior Knight and the Widow*. I've loved this story ever since Braedan strode into my mind, brandishing his sword and threatening to destroy anyone who tried to harm my feisty heroine.

Ellena has grown up in a man's world and has suffered badly for it. I love how she's still determined to control her own destiny, even if that sometimes makes life hard for her. These two characters have been with me for over a year and I've spent hours in their world. I hope you enjoy being there with them, too.

I love to hear from my readers. Please get in touch with me on Twitter, @ellamattauthor.

ELLA MATTHEWS

The Warrior Knight and the Widow

HARLEQUIN
HISTORICAL

If you purchased this book without a cover you should be aware that this book is stolen property. It was reported as "unsold and destroyed" to the publisher, and neither the author nor the publisher has received any payment for this "stripped book."

HARLEQUIN® HISTORICAL™

Recycling programs for this product may not exist in your area.

ISBN-13: 978-1-335-50544-6

The Warrior Knight and the Widow

Copyright © 2020 by Ella Matthews

All rights reserved. No part of this book may be used or reproduced in any manner whatsoever without written permission except in the case of brief quotations embodied in critical articles and reviews.

This is a work of fiction. Names, characters, places and incidents are either the product of the author's imagination or are used fictitiously. Any resemblance to actual persons, living or dead, businesses, companies, events or locales is entirely coincidental.

This edition published by arrangement with Harlequin Books S.A.

For questions and comments about the quality of this book, please contact us at CustomerService@Harlequin.com.

Harlequin Enterprises ULC
22 Adelaide St. West, 40th Floor
Toronto, Ontario M5H 4E3, Canada
www.Harlequin.com

Printed in U.S.A.

To Matthew, Annabella and Jacob.

Chapter One

As the group began to descend yet another endless hill, Ellena turned in her saddle and caught a last glimpse of her home. She could make out the flags fluttering atop the turrets of Castle Swein before it finally disappeared from view. She slowly turned around in her seat and gripped the pommel tightly. The conviction that she'd made a terrible mistake hardened in her stomach.

Ferocious-looking warriors boxed her in on every side. The solid mass of men and the clinking of their weaponry served to make her feel like a prisoner. Not one of them had so much as turned to look at her or speak to her since they had set off at dawn.

Through the wall of chain mail that surrounded her she could just make out the leader of the group and the reason she was in this uncomfortable situation. Sir Braedan Leofric. He was right-hand man to her father, the Earl of Ogmore, and known locally as 'The Beast'. Sir Braedan had convinced her to return to her father's estate when all reason had argued that it was a bad idea.

Her stomach growled, reminding her that she'd not eaten anything since her evening meal the night before.

She nudged Awen into a faster trot. At first the animal was reluctant to pass the leading horses but Ellena persisted. Although the men wouldn't want her to pass, her rank was higher than theirs and she was nominally in charge.

'I don't like riding surrounded,' she told Braedan as she pulled up alongside him.

'It's for your own safety,' he said, without turning to look at her, his dark eyes constantly roaming the upcoming countryside.

The long fingers of his left hand curled round the hilt of his sword and the sun glinted off his chain mail. His warriors were fearsome enough, but this man's broad chest and muscled arms made him a force to be reckoned with.

Ellena shivered, despite the warming sun. She'd been foolish to think she could trust him. He'd no doubt keep her safe, but he wouldn't tolerate her questioning his demands. She'd been in charge of her own destiny for so long it was going to be hard to lose control—even if it was only for the five days they'd have to travel together.

'No one would be so foolish as to try and take me when I am riding with so many armed men. And I'm no use to anyone dead,' she pointed out reasonably.

'I don't think Copsi needs you alive. He only needs your body. Now, get back into the centre of my men,' he demanded. 'Please,' he added as an afterthought.

'No!' She would show this man she was not afraid of him.

Braedan gripped the front of his saddle and finally turned to look at her. A thrill ran down her spine as his dark eyes glared at her.

'Why do you find it so difficult to obey orders?' he ground out.

'I'm not one of your men. You are not in any position to give me orders. In fact I would say that it was the other way around, wouldn't you?'

Braedan's lips twisted into a sneer, emphasising the scar that slashed through them. 'I take orders from your father only.'

'Well, I take orders from no one,' she replied.

He stared at her for a long moment. She gripped her reins tightly to stop her fingers from visibly shaking.

'Is that so?' he asked eventually, with something akin to laughter lacing his words.

She nodded defiantly.

'Men—fall in,' he barked, without taking his gaze from her.

As one, his band of men rode past them to form a protective barrier once more.

If she'd been standing she'd have stamped her foot. As it was she settled for muttering curses underneath her breath. She'd allow him this victory, but she was determined to make it his last over her.

'I didn't know a lady knew such words,' said Braedan, the corner of his mouth tilting slightly in what might have been the first smile she'd seen from him.

She was surprised he didn't immediately push his way to the front, to take point again. But at least she had someone to talk to now that he was cocooned within the group. She'd settle for company even if it meant spending time with the most frustrating man she'd ever met.

'I have brothers,' she explained.

'Yes, I've met them. I'm surprised they would swear in front of you.'

Of course he'd met them. He'd grown up as one of her father's many trainee knights. She hadn't noticed him then. Her days had been spent preparing for her own adulthood, when she would marry and form a good alliance for her family.

It was only later, after the fall of his family's good name, that Braedan had arrived back at her father's castle. She'd already left to marry Lord Swein. That had been eight years ago.

'They'd have been whipped if my father had known about it,' she confessed. 'But knowing the words has come in useful over the years.'

He nodded thoughtfully.

They rode in silence for a few moments. Braedan seemed intent on the countryside once more and Ellena took the time to study him. Two scars ran across his face. A long silvery one stretched from beneath his left eye to cut through his short dark blond beard. She couldn't see his right side, but she knew that a thicker scar ran from his ear to his jaw.

Ellena's newest maid was frightened of his face, saying the damage made him look inhuman. Ellena didn't understand that sentiment. To her the scars spoke of a hard life, but also a fascinating one. One very different from her own.

'Are my scars interesting to you, my lady?' he asked, breaking the silence that stretched between them.

Heat flooded her face. He'd seemed to be concentrating so intently on their surroundings that she hadn't realised he was aware she was looking at him. She turned and focused attentively on the tree line far away in the distance, hoping she was hiding enough of her face to cover her blushes.

'You've had a few lucky misses,' she commented, when she could bear the silence no longer.

'It is not luck, my lady. It's the amount of time I've spent training that has saved my life on several occasions.'

She turned back to look at him. 'If you were that good surely you could have prevented more than one person from slashing your face?'

This time his mouth erupted into a full smile and her stomach whooshed in response. She pressed her hand over the sensation. No man had ever caused that reaction—certainly not Lord Swein, nor any man since his death. She shuddered. She did not want that response to any man, let alone her father's guard dog.

'Perhaps you can give me some pointers, Lady Swein, being as your face is free from any blemish?'

He turned to look at her and her eyes got caught in his dark brown gaze.

'I am not so foolish as to fight at all,' she said, her tart words coming out far softer than she'd intended.

'Then you are the lucky one,' he said.

She nodded slowly and the sounds of the others around them faded away, leaving only awareness of the man riding next to her. Her heart rate increased and she pulled her gaze away with effort.

'When will we stop for something to eat?' she asked, her stomach growling again.

'Soon,' he said. 'After the next hill is a good spot.'

She tried not to groan at the thought of traipsing up another steep incline before she could have some food.

She was determined not to appear weaker than the men who surrounded her, but some sound must have escaped her lips because he asked, 'Are you tired, my lady?'

'No.'

He raised an eyebrow.

'A little,' she confessed.

Absolutely everything ached—even her little fingers. She wasn't used to riding for long periods, but she was damned if she was going to tell him that.

She took her hand off her reins and used it to wipe the sweat from her forehead. Although they were entering the cooling season the sun was still warm, and she was beginning to regret the thick cloak she'd put on when they'd left early that morning.

'Would you like to remove your cloak?' Braedan asked, as if reading her mind.

She glanced across at him, expecting him to look annoyed at this sign of weakness, but instead his eyes were soft. For some reason that frightened her more than any of his steely-eyed frowns had done.

'Do we have time to stop for that?' she asked sarcastically.

'No, but we can remove it as we ride.'

Before she could ask how he'd nudged his horse closer to hers, until their knees were touching. She gasped at the uninvited contact but she didn't move away.

This close, she could see that his dark brown irises were flecked with yellow.

'Unclip the brooch.'

'What?' she said stupidly.

He pointed to the fastening by her throat.

'Unclip it and I'll pull the cloak away from you.'

She swallowed. Here she was, becoming transfixed

by the colour of his eyes, and he was trying to help her cool down.

'I'll take the reins while you do so,' he said.

He leaned across and his fingertips brushed the back of her hand. She shivered as a tingle raced down her spine. Awen skittered beneath her and Ellena momentarily lost her balance. Firm fingers gripped her elbow and pushed her upright. She quickly regained her seat and shrugged him off. She could still feel the imprint of his fingers after he'd let go.

'Thank you,' she muttered, unable to look at him.

He didn't comment.

She swiftly undid the clasp and he pulled the material of the cloak away from her. Without slowing down, he folded it and draped it across the back of his own horse.

'I can—' she began.

'Sir,' said Merrick, Braedan's second-in-command. 'There are men up ahead.'

'Are they armed?' called Braedan, the grip on his sword tightening.

'I can't say for sure.'

The intimacy of the last few minutes disappeared as if it had never been.

'Our position is best here. If we go further down the valley we will be vulnerable,' he said, with calm steel running through his voice.

As one, the men slowed and stopped.

Aldith, Ellena's maid, was hustled into the centre of the men as well. The girl had gone very white and Ellena smiled at her.

'It's probably nothing,' she said, but she could tell at once she hadn't convinced her.

Ellena didn't blame Aldith for being frightened. Only

yesterday Bronwen, Ellena's previous lady's maid and closest companion, had been mistaken for Ellena herself and attacked. Her leg had been broken during the ordeal.

Up until that point Ellena hadn't believed her father's assertion that there was a threat to her life, but seeing her maid and friend lying crumpled in the dirt of a mud track had broken something inside her, and she'd agreed to return to her father's estate—for a brief visit only.

She would inform him that she had no intention of remarrying. She would appeal to him for soldiers to be sent to her home to protect her from the men who wanted marriage with her in order to get her small but prosperous lands, some of whom were becoming more forceful in their demands.

Swein wasn't a grand estate, compared to most but it had the advantage of sitting on a wide, shallow bay, which was ideal for making trade of highly desired goods easy. The rich soil was also fertile, and under her guidance the region had prospered, making it appealing to local landlords keen to add the area to their own estates.

She'd found offers of marriage easy to turn down, but she wouldn't be able to protect herself if someone decided to invade. Her men weren't as well-trained as her father's elite warriors. All she wanted from her father was the offer of more protection.

Next to her, Aldith's horse skittered and Ellena turned away to hide her irritation. Bronwen hadn't been able to travel with her because of her broken leg, and now she was saddled with a woman she didn't know well.

Ellena suspected the only reason Aldith had volunteered to come with her was because she had her eye on Merrick; she'd been sending him longing looks all morning, which Ellena had found amusing to begin with. Other than providing her with that degree of entertainment, she hadn't been any company for Ellena so far.

From her position at the centre of the group, Ellena could only just make out the advancing men. They appeared to be at least double their own number. Her palms felt slick and she wiped them on her tunic.

Aldith whimpered quietly.

The men finally stopped a few paces away.

'Sir Leofric,' said the obvious leader.

'Lord Copsi,' was Braedan's clipped response.

Lord Copsi didn't look like much of a threat. His wispy beard clung in patches to a florid face and small eyes peered out over a bulbous nose. It was hard to believe that this man was her father's greatest enemy.

The pair had been at loggerheads over land for as long as Ellena could remember. And one of the Earl of Ogmore's most grievous insults, in Copsi's eyes, had been to marry Ellena to Lord Swein.

As part of the marriage agreement Copsi had been forbidden to travel on Swein's land, meaning he couldn't easily access the sea trade routes. Even Ellena had thought the decree was a bit harsh, but the more she'd learnt about Copsi in the years after her marriage the more she'd understood her father's position.

In earlier years Copsi had been privy to the King's ear, advising him on matters of state. It had only been when Copsi had begun to benefit financially from a couple of suspicious deaths that he'd fallen from favour. The Earl of Ogmore had then married the King's youngest sister, and had risen in power and influence. A situation Copsi had bitterly resented.

Ogmore's land abutted Copsi's in various places, and

skirmishes between the two men's soldiers had broken out several times. Ogmore was holding his position but Copsi wasn't conceding defeat.

After Swein's death Copsi had sent a couple of emissaries to Ellena. The hints had been subtle, but it had become clear that he was trying to broker a marriage between her and himself.

Even if she had been tempted to remarry, it would not have been to a man whose two previous wives had died in suspicious circumstances, both of them only a short twelve months after marrying him. Her first marriage had been bad enough, but at least she had survived it. She wouldn't put herself under another man's mercy again.

'What are you doing in this part of the country?' Copsi asked Braedan.

'I'm on the Earl of Ogmore's business,' growled Braedan. 'You are straying dangerously close to the border,' he added.

Copsi ignored Braedan's comment and let his eyes blatantly roam over the group. When he caught sight of Ellena a faint smile crossed his reptilian lips.

She shuddered and tasted bile in her throat, the thought of that mouth anywhere near her body making her feel sick. For the first time since leaving her castle she was grateful for the solid wall of warriors that surrounded her.

'Well, it is good to see you again, Sir Braedan. I won't keep you. I know Ogmore doesn't like you to keep him waiting.'

Ellena was shocked by Lord Copsi's patronising tone. Rumour had it that no one spoke to The Beast like that and expected to get away with it.

Braedan's jaw tightened but he said nothing.

Copsi looked at him for a long moment, and then turned to his men and motioned that they should proceed.

Braedan and his men held their positions until Copsi had disappeared from sight.

'I'm afraid we won't be stopping to eat, Lady Swein. I want to make Nerdydd by late afternoon,' said Braedan.

'But…that wasn't that threatening,' said Ellena, dismayed at the thought of having to continue riding until they reached the first stop on their destination. Copsi might have a bad reputation, but he looked as if a strong breeze would push him over.

'We have some men in Copsi's court who are loyal to your father,' said Braedan as he nudged his horse into action. 'They have reported that he has become increasingly obsessed by the thought of making you his wife. It would serve the double purpose of disrespecting your father and getting hold of Swein's land. We had hoped to take you to Ogmore before he was aware of it, but he obviously has spies of his own in your father's court. He will now be determined to take you before you reach your father's lands. Today's meeting was about checking how much manpower we have. We would be foolish to underestimate him. Come—we must ride quickly.'

Ellena's muscles protested as the horses fell into a steady trot, but she didn't argue against Braedan's point despite her growling stomach. The quicker she returned to Ogmore, the quicker she could convince her father that there was no need for her to marry again. She was content at Castle Swein and she had no intention of being married off.

She shuddered, despite the warmth of the day. Her

marriage had been the stuff of nightmares. She would not enter into such a union again—especially not with Lord Copsi, a man who reminded her too much of her vile late husband.

Chapter Two

Braedan would have preferred to camp outside in the woods, where the acrid smell of spilt ale and the relentless babble of strangers would be replaced by the soothing sound of the wind whispering through branches. But as his latest mission meant he was charged with the safe return of his liege's only daughter, he could hardly expect the gently born lady to camp under the stars.

Besides, it was unlikely that Lord Copsi would mount an assault here. There were too many people around. He would wait until they were camped out—which they would have to do at least once before they reached the safety of Ogmore Castle. Braedan was sure they would find trouble at that point.

He took a long draught of ale and was surprised by its fruity tanginess. A serving maid appeared by his right elbow to top up his tankard. She'd been sending him smiles all evening, causing his men to smirk and make ribald comments, but he had no intention of taking her up on what she was clearly offering.

He covered the top of his cup with a hand and shook

his head. He needed to stay alert, and drinking too much ale wouldn't help.

He downed the rest of his drink and dropped the tankard on the table as he stood. He'd make another circuit of the grounds and check for any signs of Copsi and his men.

He strode out of the tavern, ignoring the plaintive face of the maid. He'd made no indication that he might return her interest, and he doubted she had any real desire to bed him anyway. He might have been passably attractive when he was younger, but years of campaigning for Ogmore's interests had left his face disfigured and he knew that he repelled most people.

Even his own mother struggled to look him in the eye any more—but that might not be solely down to the scars covering his face and have more to do with her disappointment over the way life had turned out for their family. She was not living the way she would have expected when she'd married his father, an eminent and wealthy landowner.

If women showed him any interest he knew it was his reputation as The Beast that drew them to him, and he'd long since tired of achieving pleasure on that basis.

The tavern door closed sharply behind him and the sounds were immediately muted. He breathed a sigh of relief and stepped away from the inn. A fine mist coated his hair and beard and he turned his face to the heavens, relieved to be outdoors once again.

The sun had set and the streets of Nerdydd were quiet and cool. A lone man scurried past, his head bent and his cloak wrapped tightly around him. Braedan watched him as he made his way down the street but he didn't once turn towards the inn so he was probably harmless.

Even so, Braedan kept a tight grip on the hilt of his sword as he slowly made his way around the inn. At the side he glanced up at the window he knew to be Ellena's chamber. The shutters were tightly clamped together but he thought he could just make out the flicker of a candle burning somewhere deep inside the room. He wondered fleetingly whether she had finally shed the veil that covered her hair; he was almost desperate to know whether it was the same dark colour as her long eyelashes.

He pushed the thought aside.

His job was to make sure she arrived back at her father's estate in one piece. He should not be thinking about how beautiful she looked, even when she was fixing him with that haughty gaze she used whenever she wanted to put him in his place.

Thoughts of trailing his fingers over the soft skin of her neck kept pushing into his mind when he was least expecting it. It was irritating, because not only was she above his touch but she was also the most stubborn woman he'd ever met. He'd prefer not to think of her at all.

He was returning her to her father so that the Earl could find her a suitable husband and keep her away from his sworn enemy, Copsi. It was nothing to do with Braedan who she married—although he was glad it wouldn't be Copsi.

His hand tightened on the hilt of his sword and he thought of her horrified expression when he'd told her that Copsi was determined to wed her before she reached her father's fortress. Copsi was a man no woman should be subjected to. Braedan's spies in Copsi's court revealed a man who took pleasure in tormenting women.

He thought women existed solely to give him pleasure, and thought nothing of taking a woman against her will.

Braedan would fight tooth and nail to make sure that Ellena stayed out of Copsi's hands while she was in his care. And once she was married to someone else she would cease to be of use to Copsi, who would turn his attention to some other poor woman.

He hoped for Ellena's sake that the Earl of Ogmore would choose someone who matched her in intelligence and strength. Almost anyone other than Copsi would be a better partner for the elegant Lady Swein, whose light blue eyes watched him with a mixture of regal disdain and intelligent understanding.

The one emotion he'd never seen cross her face was fear. Unlike most people, she wasn't afraid of him. *Yet.*

Braedan smiled. Ellena had made no secret of her desire to remain widowed. But the fact that his wilful daughter didn't want to marry again wouldn't matter to a man like Ogmore, who was keen to spread his influence across the country and not averse to using his family members to achieve his aims.

He would like to be a fly on the wall when father and daughter met again. Both were as stubborn as each other, although he was fairly confident Ogmore would win in the end. He usually did.

It was nothing to do with him whether or not she remarried.

Braedan knew he was a bully for taking her away from her home, but she had to remarry anyway, and a new husband would allow her to have children of her own. What woman didn't want that? And there were plenty of contenders for Ellena's hand. Many men wanted to form an alliance with her influential father, and marriage to his daughter was one of the best ways to secure his protection.

The most likely contender was the Earl of Borwyn, whose land was close to Ogmore's. He was reportedly a decent and handsome man.

Braedan's fists curled as the urge to punch someone rushed over him. He took a deep breath and loosened them—what was wrong with him?

The stables were at the back of the inn and he made his way towards them. He would check that Stoirm was settled for the night before turning in himself. He had scheduled his watch for the early hours of the morning. He found it hard to sleep for more than five hours anyway, and he preferred to be busy rather than just lying there remembering all the people who depended on him and were now waiting for him to let them down—as his father had done before him.

Soft, whispered noises were coming from deep within the stables. He paused on the threshold and tilted his head, listening.

A grunt which sounded suspiciously like Merrick reached his ears, followed by a soft, feminine moan, and he smiled ruefully. Perhaps the barmaid had persuaded his friend to sample her delights.

From his vantage point at the stable entrance he could see that Stoirm was contentedly munching through the hay provided for him, and that was enough for him. He'd leave without intruding.

He quietly stepped backwards, so as not to disturb the lovers, but before he could go much further the woman giggled.

He knew that sound. It was Ellena's tiresome maid—

the one who had been making eyes at his second-in-command all day.

If she wasn't with Lady Swein then Ellena was all alone.

Someone was supposed to be with her constantly.

He raced back to the inn and practically ran over a stable boy who got in his way.

The two guards he'd stationed outside her room were still there.

'Has anyone been in or out of this room?' he demanded.

'No, sir,' they both replied as one.

Without pausing to knock, he pushed open the door and strode inside.

There was a squeal and a flurry of bedclothes as the door slammed shut behind him.

'What...?' spluttered Ellena as she struggled to untangle herself from the bedcovers.

Braedan stood frozen in the centre of the room. He'd been right about Ellena's hair. It was a rich chestnut colour and her locks fell in waves loosely around her face and down to her navel.

His eyes followed the tresses and he realised she was wearing only a white chemise. Although this was tied up to her neck, he could still make out the curves of her figure beneath it.

'What are you doing barging into my chamber?' she demanded.

Heat flooded his face as he realised he was staring at her like some sort of young page who was seeing a woman other than his mother for the first time.

He cleared his throat. 'Aldith isn't with you. Anyone

could have barged in here and taken you. Why were you so foolish as to let her go?'

She frowned, and he fought the urge to rub the crease away with his thumb.

'You have men guarding my chamber and the shutters are locked from the inside. What on earth did you think would happen?'

'You are not meant to be left alone,' he repeated stubbornly.

Why must she always question what he said or did? His men obeyed him out of loyalty and others did so out of fear. But *she* never backed down from him. Her response was both an annoyance and a thrill.

She threw back the covers and slipped from the bed. For a moment he was treated to a glimpse of a slim, pale ankle before she dragged on her long cloak, robbing him of any sight of her skin.

He tried hard not to feel disappointed.

'I'll be honest,' said Ellena. 'I was quite happy for Aldith to go out for a bit and enjoy some company in the tavern. We don't have much in common, and after five minutes of talking to her I realised that I should have chosen anyone else in the castle to accompany me on this journey. I was enjoying spending some time on my own.'

'It is not the company in the taproom she is enjoying,' said Braedan.

He didn't know why he had said that. It wasn't right to talk about pleasures of the flesh in front of gently bred ladies, and it would have been kinder to everyone if he'd let Ellena carry on believing Aldith was sharing a cup of ale with the men downstairs.

'What do you...? Oh, I see.'

A pink blush stole across her high cheekbones and

Braedan took an involuntary step towards her. She didn't seem to notice, and he managed to halt himself from moving any further before he did something inappropriate.

As the daughter of an eminent earl, and niece to the King himself, she was so far above his touch that to reach out to her would surely be his downfall in more ways than one. Besides, he had enough dependants relying on him. He didn't want or need another one.

And even if neither of those problems existed he was pretty sure she couldn't stand the sight of him—and for once it was nothing to do with his many scars. She didn't like taking orders and she seemed to think she had the right to give orders to *him*.

He supposed he didn't blame her—despite his irritation at her refusal to take his instructions seriously. He'd taken her from a comfortable existence at Castle Swein and thrust her into a dangerous situation with an unknown outcome.

'Do you think she'll be long?' Ellena asked, breaking him out of his thoughts.

He chuckled in spite of himself. 'I guess that depends on Merrick's stamina.'

She turned an even deeper shade of red and turned slightly away from him.

He realised he could see her toes peeking out from under the hem of her chemise and his gaze became locked on that tiny piece of skin. He wanted to slide his hand along the length of her foot and let it continue further up her long legs…

'I don't understand why she'd bother,' was her unexpected response.

Braedan felt his own skin begin to burn with embarrassment—or perhaps it was the overwhelming lust that had hit him out of nowhere. He wasn't sure.

He opened his mouth to respond, but then clamped it firmly shut before he could say any more to offend her. It would be best for him to wish her goodnight and leave. But for some reason his feet were refusing to obey his mind's orders and they stayed exactly where they were.

She'd inadvertently revealed something of her marriage that perhaps it would have been better if he hadn't known. She hadn't enjoyed intimate relations with her husband.

That wasn't entirely surprising. The man had been thirty-four years older than her when she'd married him at sixteen. No young woman would enjoy lying with a man older than her father. But that could not have been the whole reason. The revulsion on her face spoke of experiences worse than just lying with a man she didn't find attractive.

He clenched his fists to stop himself from taking those final steps towards her and showing her exactly why Merrick and Aldith had taken themselves off to the stables.

As if finally realising what she'd revealed, he saw her back stiffen and her neck lengthen as she stood taller and gave him the regal look she always used when she wanted to remind him of her status.

'When you return downstairs please ask someone to send up some warm water. I asked Aldith to fetch it, but it appears she has forgotten.'

And that put him in his place.

Here he was, imagining running his fingers through her thick hair and over other parts of her body, and she was treating him like the errand boy she clearly thought he was.

'I'll see it's done and I'll return Aldith to you,' he growled.

She pulled a face of displeasure before masking it under a cool nod.

He left without saying another word.

Pulling the door firmly shut behind him he glared at her two guards. 'Do not let Aldith leave her alone again. Not even for Merrick,' he barked at them.

The two men had the grace to look shamefaced.

He stomped back downstairs and found someone to take warm water up to Ellena. Then he went in search of his friend.

But tearing a strip off Merrick for following his cock instead of his training still didn't make him feel any better, and it took a while for sleep to come to him that night.

Chapter Three

Ellena didn't know what was worse: the pain in all her muscles or the damp, soggy weight of her hair, which was causing water to soak through her cloak and freeze her to the bone.

After three days of riding this was the first night they were going to sleep in tents, and the weather couldn't have been worse. A fine mist this morning had turned into a downpour as the afternoon had dragged on. She began to long for a pair of shears to hack the weight of her waterlogged hair off.

As a child, she'd waited impatiently over many summers before her hair had reached the coveted waist length. Whenever she had been allowed to, she had unplaited her hair and revelled in running her fingers through the rich strands, loving the way the sunlight picked out the different shades.

She hadn't done that in years.

After her marriage her hair had been another way in which her husband could hurt her, using its thickness to pull her about whenever she displeased him. Before illness had taken over his life she'd displeased him almost every day. Her failure to get pregnant had been the worst of her transgressions, and his increasingly violent efforts to make her so had given her a desperate fear of the marriage bed.

Using her hair to drag her to his bedchamber had been one of his most humiliating punishments. After his death she'd tried hard to find joy in its thick length again, but the urge to cut it all off still pulled at her every now and again.

The horses squelched through rivers of mud as they followed Braedan through a densely packed forest. El-lena frowned at his broad back, the hard muscles en-cased in chain mail. Since he'd barged in and out of her room three nights ago they'd barely exchanged a word. She'd heard him yelling at his man Merrick and at Aldith before Aldith had slunk back into the chamber they'd shared, but apart from some sullenness on Aldith's part the incident might never have happened.

After an interminably long time they finally reached a patch of land, surrounded by trees on all sides, that appeared to meet Braedan's satisfaction and the horses pulled to a stop. Ellena allowed her body to slide off Awen, rejoicing when her feet hit the floor with a thud. For a long moment she clung to the side of her horse, allowing the animal to keep her upright.

She closed her eyes and tried to imagine the hot bath that would be awaiting her at her father's castle in only five days' time, but ice-cold rain dripped down her face and seeped beneath her clothes, chasing the fantasy away and making her shiver.

The sounds of men moving about gradually pene-trated her musings and she opened her eyes to see ev-eryone busy at work. Everyone, that was, apart from herself and Aldith. Aldith was still sitting atop her horse, surveying the scene before her, her lips twisted into a grimace of horror.

Ellena looked around. They were sheltered by the trees but the ground was still a boggy mess. It was not going to be a comfortable night's sleep.

Aldith had barely spoken to her apart from the occasional, 'Yes, my lady,' since the unfortunate incident of Merrick and the stable, so she didn't bother to address the maid. She wouldn't be a great deal of help in this situation anyway—it was an experience outside their usually comfortable living standards—but at least Ellena was willing to try and improve their situation. Aldith would wait until somebody helped her.

It wasn't Ellena's fault that Braedan had been so monumentally angry at her being left alone for a brief period. She'd heard the row he'd given the two lovers through her shuttered window—although why he hadn't yelled at them before he came to check her room was beyond her. Surely he could have sent Aldith up to her and spared them both that embarrassing scene? She'd practically discussed her sexual relationship with Lord Swein and for the life of her she couldn't fathom why she'd done it.

There was something about Braedan's dark eyes that drew her in and made her say things she wouldn't say to another person. But really—what had made her talk to him about intimate relations with her late husband when that was something she was very keen to avoid thinking about at all costs? The humiliation and the pain were things she never wanted to revisit.

She wished she could take back the comment she'd made about sex not being worth the effort. He'd probably thought her ridiculous.

She gave herself a little shake. It didn't matter right now. All that concerned her was getting out of the relentless deluge of water. She led Awen over to the rough shelter where the other horses were gathering. She made sure the mare had her share of oats before leaving her in the capable hands of Nilson, one of Braedan's men, who seemed to have a gifted touch when it came to horses.

All around the clearing shelters were being erected with a speed that suggested they'd done this many times before. Very little was being said as the men concentrated hard on their tasks.

Out of the corner of her eye she could see Aldith sliding off her horse, and she wondered whether she would expect someone to deal with it for her. She snorted. Aldith sometimes acted as if she was royalty.

'Your tent has been erected, my lady,' said Braedan from behind her.

She turned towards him. He was pointing to a circular structure in the centre of the enclosure but he was looking directly at her. Rain ran down his face and dripped off the end of his nose. She smiled at the sight and for a second he smiled back at her. Her heart stuttered strangely at the sight.

'Where's the food tent?' she asked, pulling her gaze away from his face and focusing instead on a point just behind his head.

With that, his smile vanished and his customary scowl appeared.

'Eluard is dealing with the food, my lady, but it will be awhile before it is ready.'

He stalked away from her, his boots making large prints in the mud.

'I guess I'll have to find the food tent by myself, then,' she muttered under her breath.

She squelched around the clearing until she found Eluard attempting to light a fire under a sheet of canvas, its sides held up by thick wooden poles. The youngest of Braedan's men, Eluard seemed to be given less physical jobs than the others, and she found it quite sweet that the men, for all their gruff exteriors, seemed to treat him like the son of the group.

He jumped up when he saw her approach and a deep blush spread across his ruddy complexion.

'I'm…sorry. It…it's not ready yet, my lady,' he stuttered.

Ellena glanced at the bag by Eluard's feet, which appeared to hold a lump of unidentifiable red meat.

'I can see that.' She smiled. 'I've come to help.'

She couldn't have startled him more if she'd told him she'd grown an extra arm.

She suppressed an amused smile; she didn't want to upset him by laughing at his expression. She sensed it would hurt his feelings.

'You see to that fire,' she said, 'and I'll see what other provisions we have.'

They might be far away from anywhere, but she wasn't about to eat a lump of meat with nothing to go with it. She'd been riding all day and she was starving.

She rummaged around in a large canvas bag and found a few sad-looking carrots and a couple of leeks. She set about chopping them into a large stewing pot.

'I don't suppose there's any wine?' she asked as she neared the end of the vegetables.

'No, my lady.'

'That's a pity. This is going to be very dry otherwise.'

'There is some ale…'

'You fetch that, then, and we'll add it to the pot.'

'I'm not sure Sir Leofric will like—'

'Let's not tell Sir Leofric,' said Ellena, and was re-warded with a shy smile.

'Don't tell me what?' demanded a deep voice from the edge of the shelter.

Eluard's face flooded with colour again and he im-mediately turned his attention back to the carcass he was attempting to chop.

Braedan looked curious rather than angry, so El-lena said, 'We're attempting to make this stew edible. I thought a slug of ale might improve the flavour. That is all.'

Braedan couldn't move. Of all the things he'd been expecting to see when he'd found that Ellena wasn't in her tent, the sight of her chopping carrots into a stewing pot hadn't featured once.

He'd thought when she'd asked where the food tent was that she was demanding to be fed, but he should have known better. Over the last three days she'd rid-den long hours and not complained once. He'd known *men* who couldn't last as long as she could in the saddle.

Instead of hiding away in her tent, like her irritating maid, she had made herself useful. How many other highly born ladies would know what to do with a bag of uncooked vegetables past their best?

'I don't mind a drop of ale going in,' he commented.

Anything to make the food more edible was good in his eyes, although he did wince when he saw how much ale she was pouring into the pot. He hoped she knew what she was doing and was not wasting precious drink.

Eventually the rest of the men were trudging in, and helping themselves to ladles of the rich-looking stew. Ellena sat on an overturned log and spooned food into her mouth. Her maid stayed on the other side of the food tent—relations between them seemed strained—but young Eluard sat near her, speaking shyly to her now and then.

Braedan was pleased she'd found someone to keep her company, because her maid wasn't much good, and of course he was pleased it was Eluard. It wasn't as if Braedan could keep her company himself...

It was essential he maintained a certain distance, because he was the one in charge and all his men looked to him to set an example. If he appeared to be over-familiar with her then the rest of them would follow, and the Earl of Ogmore would not be pleased.

It was annoying, though, the way his gaze kept seeking her out, and how a hard knot of jealousy seemed to be forming in his stomach because *he* wanted to be the one to make her smile.

He threw another log on the fire. 'Move closer to the warmth, Lady Swein,' he said. 'It will help to dry your clothes.'

She raised one of her arched eyebrows at him.

'Please,' he added.

She smiled then—the first proper smile that had been directed solely at him.

His heart stumbled and he took a quick step backwards. She was beautiful, but her smile made her breathtaking, lighting up her blue eyes and making him want things he would never get from her.

He strode quickly from the tent and back out into the

rain. Breathing heavily, he made his way to the edge of the camp and leaned against a tree.

She was forbidden. He knew that. In fact it was probably *because* she was denied to him that he was finding her so damn attractive and muddling his mind. He'd always wanted things he couldn't have, and she was no exception.

But if she didn't hate him now then she definitely would when she found out about his reward for returning her to her father.

He rubbed his eyes and pulled himself upright. Enough of this distraction—he would find his men on watch and see if they had anything to report.

The woods were silent, apart from the rustling of creatures in the undergrowth and the cawing of a bird overhead. He trod softly around the encampment but found nothing untoward. He returned to find that Ellena and her maid had retired to their tent.

His mind once more turned to her unbound hair and the way her chemise had clung to her body. She'd be sleeping in all her clothes tonight, but that didn't stop his thoughts from taking a turn he was desperate to avoid.

He stalked away from her tent before he did anything foolish.

'What is it about this journey that has you so jumpy?' asked Merrick when Braedan joined him by the fire.

'I'm no different from normal,' said Braedan as he stretched his fingers out to the warmth.

Merrick snorted, but didn't comment any further. Their usual camaraderie had been strained since Braedan had yelled at his friend for enjoying Aldith's company. He didn't regret it. Ellena must be kept safe at all costs.

He hadn't told Merrick that this mission was different from every other one he'd ever taken. That this time there was so much at stake. If he was successful then the last eight years of hard graft would finally be rewarded and he would be able to repair some of the damage that had been done to his family's name and fortune by his father's treasonous acts.

He sat by the fire long after Merrick had turned in. The logs spat and hissed, turning black as images of his father teaching him to ride his first horse flickered through his mind. He hadn't known it at the time, but that had been his last taste of sublime happiness.

He hadn't thought about the big, burly man who'd raised him in a long time. As a boy he'd idolised him, but just as he'd reached manhood everything had been destroyed. His father had been executed as a traitor and his lands and wealth stripped from the family he'd left behind.

Braedan had taken his mother and two distraught younger sisters with him to the Earl of Ogmore. Braedan had done his knight's training under Ogmore's supervision, but even so it had been beyond humiliating to kneel before him and beg him to take in the three women.

In return Braedan had sworn his allegiance to Ogmore and he'd been doing his bidding ever since, rising to be his chief of guards and earning himself the nickname The Beast because of the ruthless way he squashed Ogmore's enemies and the way his face had been disfigured while doing so.

Now, in return for years of service, Ogmore had promised him stewardship over Castle Swein so long as he safely returned the Earl's widowed daughter to his care. Stewardship there would finally give him a certain status in the world, and allow him to build up enough wealth for his sisters' dowries.

Ellena had been refusing her father's entreaties to return for nearly a year. Two emissaries had been sent and had failed to return with her. She was apparently every bit as skilled at manipulation and dissembling as her wily father.

Ogmore's patience had finally worn thin and he had dispatched Braedan to do the job.

Braedan felt a stab of guilt every time he thought of how he had finally got her to agree to leave her precious castle. He had told her that she needed to negotiate her freedom to act as steward of the castle with her father directly, and that hiding in Castle Swein was the coward's way out.

He'd seen enough of her stubborn nature to know that she wouldn't like to be branded a coward, and he'd been right. It didn't sit right with him that he knew something she didn't, but that castle meant more to him than simply another home. It meant the restoration of his family to their rightful place in the world and the safety and welfare of Katherine and Linota, his two sisters, who had been so badly damaged by their father's actions, and who would never make good marriages if they were forced to continue living as they were currently.

If that meant betraying the beautiful Lady Swein then so be it.

The first watch returned to camp and he heard the second group of men fan out in the forest. He stood from his place by the fire and stretched. He ought to get some rest, as it would be his turn to stand sentry soon enough.

It felt like only seconds later when he was awoken by

shouting. He grabbed his sword and was running before he'd left the shelter of his tent.

'What's happening?' he shouted to Merrick.

'A warning's been sounded. There are men approaching.'

'Stay with the women,' he commanded as he raced to the edge of their encampment.

Behind him he could hear the panicked braying of the horses, and in front the sound of men engaged in sword fight.

He dispatched his first opponent within seconds of joining the fight.

He was on to the next one before the first had dropped to the floor.

Soon the metallic smell of blood filled the air. The tip of another opponent's sword had grazed his neck, but it was only a light cut and he soon had his vengeance by adding his body to the growing pile of their enemies.

The fighting was intense, but they were gaining the upper hand, and before long he heard the welcome sound of his enemy retreating.

'Make sure they've all gone,' he barked to his men.

He turned on his heel and raced back to their campsite, muttering a prayer that they'd done enough to keep Ellena safe.

A watery sun was just beginning to peek through the trees when he burst back into the opening.

Merrick stepped forward to greet him. 'Is it all over?'

'For now,' said Braedan. 'Are the women safe?'

'Yes, but I'm afraid—'

Braedan didn't wait for him to finish that sentence. He pushed past him and rounded the corner of the tent.

There he found Ellena kneeling in the mud. Eluard's

head was resting in her lap and even from this distance he could tell that the boy was badly injured.

She lifted a tear-stained face to his and his gut wrenched at her expression.

'He shouldn't have been fighting but he insisted—' Her voice broke as she bent over the boy. 'Why would someone hurt a young man just to get to me? Couldn't they see he was little more than a child?'

Braedan crouched down next to her. Her whole body was shaking and he resisted the urge to pull her into his arms.

'Will you take him to my tent?' she asked, turning her pale face to his.

He opened his mouth to protest—it wasn't appropriate for her to have a man in her tent, even a young one—but she forestalled him with a soft, 'Please,' and he found himself nodding instead.

He lifted Eluard, who moaned softly but didn't wake, and carried him to the bundle of blankets she'd been using to sleep on. Eluard weighed virtually nothing, and he cursed himself for bringing the lad on this mission.

He gently settled the boy on her makeshift bed. Over the coppery smell of the boy's blood he could sense Ellena's delicate fragrance in the air, the soft scent of lavender and something else he couldn't identify but which he thought of as uniquely her.

Staying this close to her was dangerous. Being alone with her was too much of a temptation.

'I'll send Aldith in,' he said to her, before striding out of the tent and away from the enforced intimacy.

Ellena had cared for her sick husband for nearly four years as illness had gradually taken his life. She'd seen everything the human body had to offer and had quickly got over any squeamishness.

She took a deep breath and began to remove Eluard's tunic. Blood had soaked through the fabric. She shuddered, but carried on. No matter how bad it was for her, it was worse for him, and she didn't want him to be frightened by waking up and seeing a look of horror on her face.

The tent flap opened behind her, but she didn't look up. She didn't want to see her maid right now. She had been useless when the attack had happened. If it hadn't been for the sake of propriety she would have sent her maid back to the castle, but she knew she was stuck with the tiresome woman—at least until they arrived at Ogmore.

'Merrick tells me you tried to protect Eluard,' said a gruff voice behind her.

She jumped at Braedan's words. She hadn't expected him to return.

'I probably did more harm than good,' she murmured, remembering her very brief battle with a blond-haired stranger. 'I merely used Eluard's sword to block the man from striking Eluard again. Merrick took over before I really knew what was going on.'

He didn't respond but neither did he leave the tent.

She heard him inhale as she finally exposed Eluard's wound—a deep, long cut across his chest.

'Here,' said Braedan, handing her some strips of fabric.

His callused fingers brushed hers as she took the offered material. She ignored the tingle the contact made and pressed the cloth to Eluard's wound.

'Stitch him up as best you can,' said Braedan abruptly.

'We're leaving as soon as the tents are packed up. It won't take long.'

Ellena stood quickly and turned to face Braedan. Only a whisper of air separated them in the confined space of the tent. She knew she wanted to argue with him but his proximity had momentarily robbed her of coherent thought.

She took a small step backwards and cleared her throat. 'We can't move him.'

'We must. We can't stay here. Copsi knows where we are and he'll attack again once his men have rallied.'

'Then you'll have to fight them off again. We cannot move Eluard now. He will surely perish if we do.'

'If we stay here then more of us will die.'

Braedan turned to leave but Ellena grabbed his arm, stopping him in his tracks. The tight band of his muscles moved beneath her fingers and she quickly let go as a strange heat seared through her.

'I will not leave,' she said.

'Yes, you will,' he answered, and he swept from the tent, that gentle side of him vanishing as if it had never existed.

Chapter Four

Ellena stood next to her horse, gripping the animal's reins tightly. The skin on her face was a worrying shade of pale but her back was ramrod-straight and her blue eyes flashed angrily.

Braedan rubbed his forehead. She hadn't so much as glanced in his direction since her tent had been dismantled and Eluard had been strapped to a makeshift stretcher. And if she was angry now then her mood was going to be a lot worse when she found out where he wanted her to travel for the next part of their journey.

Copsi had fallen back, but he knew their location and he knew their direction. They would have to move quickly as they were especially vulnerable right now.

'I've decided we need to split up into two separate parties,' he said, the sound of his voice cutting across the low rumble of his men's voices and reducing them to silence. 'Tanner and Walden, you will take Eluard to the nearest town. Seek a medic; I don't care what it costs.'

Out of the corner of his eye he noticed Ellena twitch in surprise and she finally turned her head towards him.

'Aldith, you will swap cloaks with Ellena and ride

with Merrick on his horse. Instead of following our planned route we will cross the River Burcoed and take a more circuitous course to Ogmore's land. It will take us longer, but it will give us the element of surprise. Ellena, you will ride with me. Nilson will take care of the riderless horses.'

He heard Ellena's gasp of surprise but didn't turn to look at her. He knew she would hate being in such close proximity with him, but he wouldn't be swayed on this matter.

'Won't Copsi and his men expect Lady Swein to be with you? It would make more sense if she rode with me,' Merrick argued. He was the only one of his men brave enough to contradict his orders.

Braedan nodded. That did make more sense, but he would be damned if Ellena sat between Merrick's thighs—besides, he was the one who had sworn to keep her safe. He was better placed to do that if they were close.

'Yes,' he said. 'But I hope we'll throw enough doubt on the situation to split their forces. We've already depleted their numbers so there can't be many of them left.'

Merrick nodded, although he was clearly unhappy.

No one else raised any objections and he was pleased that Ellena hadn't argued. He'd half expected to deal with her strenuous objections and he didn't want to put her down in front of his men. She deserved their respect after the way she had treated Eluard. Not many noble ladies would put a young orphan's safety and comfort before their own, kneeling in the mud and carefully dressing his wounds.

'We leave now. Lady Swein, please swap your cloak with Aldith's.'

The two women didn't glance at each other as they exchanged clothes, the transaction allowing Braedan a brief glimpse of Ellena's hair. Her dark locks were tightly bound in an elaborate plait that was gathered at the nape of her delicate neck.

Ellena pulled the rough woollen hood of her maid's cloak over her head, while Aldith fixed Ellena's veil over hers. It wasn't the best of disguises—Ellena was much taller than Aldith—but it was better than nothing. Her rich dark green cloak clearly marked her out as a noble-woman and made her an obvious target.

The rigid set of her shoulders suggested she wasn't happy with him. He sighed quietly. If only she was as soft and as gentle with him as she was with Eluard his life would be a lot easier.

The image of her tending to him while he lay in bed sprang suddenly to mind and he pushed it away force-fully. That would never happen.

'Lady Swein.' He held out a hand towards her, hop-ing that because she hadn't argued she would be willing to join him on his horse.

'I don't think this is necessary,' she said, turning to face him.

'You'll be safer if we ride together.'

'No... I...' She looked around the group of assem-bled men, who were already on horseback and watch-ing their exchange.

Although none of them betrayed any emotion at her obvious distress, he could sense a subtle shift in their allegiance. These men had willingly followed him into many battles, but by helping Eluard she had gained their support. They would defend her to the death—possibly even against him. Luckily he meant her no harm.

'Please,' he said, trying to soften the demand, despite the fact he had no intention of letting her ride by herself. He would tie her up and throw her over the back of his saddle if he had to.

She nodded quickly and the muscles in his back relaxed. If anyone tried to get to her they would have to come through him—and he wasn't easy to kill.

He swung into his saddle and then pulled her up to join him.

He immediately regretted his decision.

It had been torturous, imagining what her curves would feel like against his body. The reality was far worse. As they began their brisk trot through the trees the saddle pushed her thighs against his and every movement Stoirm made jolted their bodies together.

By the time they'd cleared the forest all his focus was on the parts of his body that touched hers. He should have been concentrating on the surrounding countryside, but nothing could distract him from the direction his mind was taking him.

He wanted to tug the hood of her cloak from over her hair and unbind the pins that held her plait in place. He wanted to run his fingers through the long tresses and touch his lips to her slender neck. He imagined her sighing with pleasure as his beard tickled the sensitive skin there, until she relaxed against him and allowed him to touch his mouth to hers. His kiss would be soft and gentle until...

'Sir,' said Nilson, bringing him back into the moment. 'There's a small group of men following us.'

Braedan twisted in his saddle. Behind them a tight group of riders followed at a brisk pace. He cursed under his breath; he'd hoped they'd get further than this before Copsi's men caught up with them.

Once their pursuers realised they'd been spotted they nudged their horses into action and flew towards them, quickly raising their bows and pointing them in the direction of him and his own men. With Ellena in front of him he wouldn't be able to reach his own bow and arrow.

Braedan kicked Stoirm into action. 'Hold on tight!' he yelled to Ellena as an arrow hit his chain mail and bounced harmlessly off.

His men rode hard next to them, providing a protective shell around Ellena. He heard Aldith squeal, but Ellena remained silent.

More men appeared at the top of a rise to the right of them. Copsi and his men must have been following them more closely than he'd realised.

The new group began to charge towards them, their weapons drawn. He had only a split second to make a decision.

'Men!' he shouted. 'Hold them off. You know the route I plan to travel. Meet with us once you've drawn them off our trail.'

He pushed Stoirm into a faster gallop and they flew away from the scene. Behind him he heard the sounds of a battle taking place but he didn't look back. He needed to get Ellena to safety, whatever the cost.

Chapter Five

Ellena held tightly to the saddle as the wind whipped past her face and the countryside passed by in a blur of greens and browns. She wanted to know if they were being followed, and if their companions were safe, but she didn't dare turn round or distract Braedan. One false move at this moment would bring death to either one of them.

Stoirm ate up the distance, but even so she was surprised at how quickly the wide River Burcoed came into view.

Through the layers of fabric that separated them she felt the rumble of Braedan muttering something, but she couldn't make out what over the noise of the rushing river.

'What's wrong?' she called out, and then clarified, 'Apart from us being attacked and chased, that is.'

'The bridge is down.'

'Is there another one?'

'Yes, but we'll have to go into the village of Ferwalt to cross it.'

Her legs trembled with exhaustion. She wanted to

lean back and shelter against his comforting solid body, but she forced herself to remain upright. She was still humiliated at the way he had ignored her request to stay at the encampment and tend to Eluard, and the way he had insisted she ride with him. It was frustrating that once again she had so little control over her own life, even if she knew his actions had saved her life.

'What of your men?' she asked, schooling her voice to remain calm despite her growing panic.

'We must assume that they have lost and that Copsi's men are not far behind.'

Her heart gave a thrill of fear. 'But your men are the best fighting force in the land. We cannot give up hope.'

'I am sure that they will defeat Copsi, but without seeing it happen I must act as if they have failed. If they do not catch us up then we will regroup before we reach Ogmore Castle.'

Ellena twisted round to look at him. 'You mean we are alone now?'

A muscle twitched in his jawline. 'For the time being, aye.'

She turned her attention back to the path in front of her. She could *not* be alone with this man. Not for an afternoon, let alone for the four days it would take to get to her father's castle. Her reputation would be ruined and she'd be forced to marry him.

And that couldn't happen.

Not because he was The Beast, but because she wouldn't remarry. He'd expect things from her she wasn't willing to give, and she never again wanted to be a man's plaything. She would fight for her independence with every resource that she had or she would die trying.

'No one need ever know,' he said roughly, as if he'd read her thoughts.

She nodded once and said nothing. She would ensure that they didn't. Being forced into marriage was not something she was going to let happen.

He pushed Stoirm back into a gallop and they raced along the river's edge.

They passed a crofter's cottage, and then shortly afterwards another one came into view. Ellena felt Braedan's muscled arms tighten around her as he brought Stoirm into a gentler trotting motion.

'It won't do for us to enter the town as if we are on the run. We'll only draw attention to ourselves. In fact...' He tugged a signet ring off his right-hand little finger and pushed it onto her ring finger—one she'd deliberately kept clear of any adornment since the end of her marriage. 'We'll say we're a married couple.'

'Do we really need to go to such lengths if we're just passing through?' asked Ellena, looking down at the large ring that hung loosely below her knuckle, the metal still warm from contact with his skin.

'Stoirm will need to rest. I've pushed him hard today. We'll also need to get some provisions, as most of the food was in Nilson's saddlebags.'

As the village came into sight Braedan brought Stoirm to a complete stop. He climbed down from the saddle and pulled a long dark cloak from one of his packs. He slung it around himself to disguise his chain mail and they set off again, with Braedan leading the horse rather than riding behind her.

Ellena felt horribly exposed, so high up on Braedan's horse, and she surprised herself by missing the comfort of his solid presence.

'Can I get down too?' she asked.

He glanced up at her, his expression unreadable. She thought he was going to argue, but then he held up his hand to help her down.

The touch of his rough palm against the smooth skin of her own caused her to inhale sharply. She'd never touched a man this way. Not even Lord Swein, who had used his clammy hands only to touch parts of her body she would rather have kept to herself.

Braedan's hands were warm and dry and surprisingly comforting. She longed to cling to them, to feel their reassuring strength for longer, but he released her as soon as her feet touched solid ground.

She shook herself. She must remember that although he wasn't her enemy, he certainly wasn't her friend. He was The Beast—a man who worked tirelessly for her father's best interests. He was not, and never would be, someone she could trust.

She straightened and walked alongside him.

She needed to remember that.

They didn't speak until they reached a tavern at the centre of the small village.

'We'll stop here to eat,' said Braedan.

He tied Stoirm up to a post and untied the packs strapped to his side.

Inside, the tavern was dimly lit, but comfortingly warm and dry. Ellena stripped off the rough woollen cloak, glad to be rid of the itchy fabric even if she did feel exposed in her long, deep red dress and without her customary veil. She touched her hand to her plait, relieved to feel it was still in place even if a few strands had worked free.

Braedan strode to the bar and addressed the landlord.

'My wife needs some wine while I see to our horse,' he said. 'Then we'd both like to eat. Is there somewhere private we can do that?'

Coins were exchanged and the two of them were taken to a small room with a dining table and some surprisingly comfortable-looking chairs.

'Lord and Lady like to eat in here when they come,' said the landlord, by way of an explanation. 'I'll bring the wine through in a minute.'

He closed the door behind him, leaving them alone.

Ellena stepped nervously towards the unmade fireplace. No one knew she was here and no one would come to her aid if Braedan turned out to be not as honourable as her father believed. Swein's reputation had been good, after all. She'd had no way of knowing he would turn out to be a monster.

Ellena swallowed and closed her eyes. For a moment she was back in her marriage bed, with Lord Swein's cold fingers pulling at her skin, his muffled breath panting in her ear as he roughly took his pleasure while she prayed for the ordeal to be over so she could return to her own room.

Once he'd finished he would push her from the bed, finding amusement in the way she hit the ground. He would only give her a few minutes to dress before forcing her from his room. Occasionally his attentions had hurt her so badly she had only been able to hobble the short distance to her own bedchamber.

She raised trembling fingers to her hood. Perhaps if he couldn't see her face and her hair she wouldn't prove a temptation to Braedan. She tugged on the fabric but nerves had made her hands weak and she couldn't lift the fabric.

'It will all be all right, Lady Swein. You are safe with me and I will get you back to your father's lands.'

She opened her eyes and looked at him.

His steady expression as he stood and breathed evenly in front of her reassured her.

'Thank you,' she said quietly, taking her hands away from her hood and dropping them down by her sides.

'I will check on Stoirm and then I will be back. Lock the door after me. I will tell the landlord that I will bring the food to you, so only open the door if you are sure it is me.'

The floorboards creaked as he strode out of the room. She heard him wait in the corridor as she pushed the bolt across, sealing the room from the inside.

She took a seat at the table and waited.

Only a week ago she had been safe in her castle and now she was here, in this strange room, fleeing for her life. She had made some bad decisions in the past, but leaving Castle Swein was possibly the worst. She should have stuck to her instinct and stayed in the home that had given her so much comfort since the death of Lord Swein.

Since she'd been acting as steward it had become a place where she was respected and loved in equal measure. She had swept away years of bad management and created a safe place where the people flourished. She might have been under threat from the likes of Copsi, but she had known that her tenants would rather lay down their lives than let her be taken by a man whose reputation was every bit as unpleasant as their previous lord.

She folded her hands in front of her. She hadn't wanted them to do that, knowing that her father could send men to protect them from the threat of invasion.

She had to keep reminding herself that this was why she was going to her father's castle. She wanted to protect her people and he was the man who could help her do it. She might have to put up with him suggesting she should marry again, but she was a far stronger woman than the sixteen-year-old girl who had married Lord Swein.

She'd been raised knowing that it was her duty to make a good alliance through an advantageous marriage and she had accepted it. She'd married the elderly Lord Swein not with any excitement but with a feeling of pride that she was helping her father's dynastic ambitions. Aligning Swein's lands to her father's had given the Earl a reach far greater than any of his peers—and, as she'd later found out, helped him win a strategic battle against his old enemy Lord Copsi.

Their marriage had been childless—which in the early years had been a source of pain to her. She'd been so desperate to please her husband and provide him with the heir he wanted so badly. She'd also wanted a child for herself. A child who would have helped stave off the loneliness she'd felt so far away from home.

Later, when she'd come to fear and despise her husband, she had felt glad she hadn't brought any of his children into the world. There was no doubt in her mind that Swein would have beaten his small son if he had displeased his father in any way. He'd had no compunction about beating *her*, no matter how small the infraction. She couldn't have borne it if she'd brought a vulnerable child into their volatile world.

Now she was glad that there was nothing left to remind her of him. She'd had all trace of him swept from the castle the day he had died. His clothes had been burned and his golden jewels melted down and handed out as coins for the tenants who had suffered so badly under his management.

As part of her marriage agreement, after the death of her husband, the land and the castle now belonged to her father—the infamous Earl of Ogmore. But Lord Swein had been ill for four long years prior to his death, and lazy before that. Ellena had taken on the management of the estate and she was good at it. She was not going to give that up—even if it meant going against her formidable sire.

She had hoped that her father would see the prosperity of Castle Swein and leave her to run things. He benefitted from her careful management, after all. Her mourning period had passed and her father had left her alone. She'd begun to believe that he would allow her the unusual honour of running the castle herself. But she'd been mistaken.

Two envoys had come before Braedan. Both of them had tried to persuade her to return to her father's lands. He'd had offers of marriage for her and he wanted to consider with her who would be the most suitable match. Those envoys had been easy to evade. A little bit of gentle manipulation and they had returned to her father's lands without her.

She stood abruptly from her chair and began to pace around the small room.

If only her father hadn't sent Braedan.

As soon as she'd seen him approaching Castle Swein astride his giant horse she'd known he was going to be a daunting foe. He dwarfed her own soldiers, and as he'd strode through the corridors people had scuttled out of his way—scared, perhaps, by his reputation, or even by the way he looked as if he'd fought a thousand battles.

As for her, she wasn't frightened of him as such. His dark eyes did send a thrill through her whenever he fixed her with his piercing stare, but for the most part she didn't think he would hurt her. He was an honourable man beneath his gruff and slightly menacing exterior—nothing like her vile husband, who'd dressed in the finest clothes and never looked as if he would lift a hand to hurt anyone.

Looks could be deceiving.

She tiptoed to the door and pressed her ear against the wood. In the distance she could hear the sounds of people talking and laughing in the taproom. It was a normal day for them. She could probably stroll among them almost unnoticed and no one would stop her if she walked out and left the building.

But if she made a run for it now how far would she get? And, more importantly, who would catch her?

Braedan's wrath might be bad, but marriage to Copsi would be worse. And besides, Braedan was right. She did have to negotiate with her father at some point. Surely once he could see how well she was managing the running of Castle Swein by herself he would stop this ridiculous notion that she needed to remarry.

She moved away from the door and sat back down at the table, before standing up again and making another circuit of the room. Doing nothing felt unnatural; she was used to constantly being needed by someone—either to solve a conflict or make a decision.

She began to pace back and forth.

She jumped when a knock finally sounded on the door.

'It's me,' said Braedan's muffled voice.

She opened the door cautiously and he waited patiently while she checked he was alone. When she was sure, she pulled the door fully open and let him in.

In his hands he carried two bowls of stew. The scent of the meat and herbs hit her as he passed and her stomach growled in response. He set the bowls on the table and handed her a cup of wine. She took a long sip and felt the fruity liquid rush over her tongue.

'Is Stoirm all right?' she asked as they both settled at the table.

'He's going to need a long rest,' said Braedan as he picked up a spoon and began to eat.

Ellena's appetite fled at the news and she pushed the bowl away from her.

'What are we going to do in the meantime?' she asked.

Braedan kept his concentration on the meal in front of him. 'We'll have to get a room here.'

Ellena half stood and then sank down again. 'Two rooms,' she clarified.

'Do you have any coins on you?' he asked gruffly.

'No.'

'Then it will be one room.'

He went on spooning the food into his mouth. Ellena waited for him to say something else, but when he didn't she picked up her own spoon and tried a small mouthful.

The dark meat melted on her tongue. She took a bigger spoonful, this time adding some of the thick, rich sauce. Her appetite resurfaced and she began shovelling the food in.

'Won't it be obvious?' she asked when she was nearly halfway through her meal. 'I mean, Copsi's men will be looking for a man and a woman travelling through here. We're probably the only ones to arrive today, and on a horse that is clearly exhausted. They'll know exactly where to find us and we'll be easy to catch.'

Braedan scraped around the edge of his bowl with his spoon and then settled it back on the table.

'We'll take the room for this afternoon only and take it in turns to rest. We'll leave once night has fallen. The bridge is only accessible from the village and I've paid the landlord a hefty amount to inform me if there are any other strangers around. If there is any sign that someone is on the bridge we shall leave the village and cross at the next point.'

Resting separately sounded good to Ellena. At least she wouldn't be expected to share a bed with Braedan, but still... They were going to be in a room together, alone, with a large bed in it. Would he...?

She shuddered and dropped her spoon.

'Lady Swein?'

She looked up and met his steady gaze.

'You have nothing to fear from me. I will keep you safe.'

She nodded, even though her heart stuttered in fear— or in some other emotion she couldn't identify.

She picked up her spoon and forced the rest of her meal down. Although she was no longer hungry, she didn't know when she would next get to eat.

Despite his reassuring words, she was trembling as he ushered her into the bedchamber and locked the door behind them. The room wasn't large. A dressing table stood under the thin window and two sitting chairs were arranged in front of the unlit fire. And, just as she'd feared, a large bed took up most of the space.

What man *wouldn't* think of bedding with such a large reminder in front of him? And there would be nothing she could do to stop him if that was what he decided to do; experience had taught her that.

'If you're cold I will ask the landlord to light the fire,' said Braedan, dropping his satchel onto the dressing table.

'I'm quite warm, thank you,' said Ellena, keeping her back to the door and staying as far away from him as she could manage in the confined space.

'But you're shivering,' he said, gesturing to her arms, which wouldn't stop shaking.

She unwound Aldith's cloak and wrapped it tightly around her body. 'I'm fine.'

Braedan watched her as he took off his weaponry and laid it next to his satchel. He began to unstrap his chain mail. Each piece thudded to the ground as he dropped it.

Her shaking intensified. *Why was he undressing?*

'Is it me?' he asked quietly, his gaze dropping to the floor in front of him, where the pile of discarded metal lay.

Even without the protective suit he was still alarmingly large.

'What do you mean?' she asked, startled.

'People are frightened of me because of this.' He gestured to his face. 'I've been told my scars make me appear less than human. Some people find it hard to be in close proximity to me.'

His gaze flicked up to her face and then back down to the floor.

'No,' she said, taking a step towards him, her arm outstretched, her fear briefly forgotten. 'Whoever told you that needs to be whipped. You look as human as the next person.'

He smiled briefly, but kept his gaze to the floor. This

was a side of him she'd not seen before. She doubted he let many people see that he felt vulnerable about his appearance. Her heart ached a little for him.

It was true, his scars made him different from other people, but he was still an attractive man. She had noticed the way women's eyes followed his impressive body when he entered travelling inns on their journey, so she was not the only woman who noticed the way he looked. But just because she could appreciate him, it didn't mean that she wanted to lie with him.

She was never going to do *that* with a man ever again.

'I...you see...it's not...' She cleared her throat. She owed him the truth—and who knew? Perhaps it would avoid any awkward misunderstanding between them. 'Some widows have a reputation for being loose with their favours.' She gestured to the bed. 'I'm not one of them.'

To her surprise, his face flooded with colour, the redness of his skin emphasising the white of his scars.

'It hadn't crossed my mind that you were, my lady. You take first rest. I will keep watch.'

He gestured to the bed and then turned away from her, pushing the table towards the door and pulling up one of the chairs. He opened the shutter slightly and sat down, resting his forearms on his legs. Not once did he glance in her direction.

Ellena shrugged off her cloak and crawled onto the bed in a sea of misery. She'd embarrassed them both completely unnecessarily. Of *course* he wasn't interested in her—only men who wanted an alliance with her father ever had been.

With her long, thin body her brothers had often likened her to a young sapling. Lord Swein had often told her she reminded him of a boy and that he was only lying with her to get an heir.

Like most men, Braedan probably preferred women with a chest. And really that shouldn't matter—she didn't want him to have those sorts of thoughts about her, because it meant he would leave her alone, but really... Couldn't he have at least pretended not to be horrified by the idea?

She turned onto her side, facing away from him. She pulled the covers over her and squeezed her eyes tightly shut, thinking that sleep would be impossible...

But it was dark when Braedan woke her.

'Is it my turn to take watch?' she mumbled.

'No, it's time to leave.'

She sat bolt upright.

'You were supposed to rest,' she said, shocked that she'd slept so deeply with a man in the room.

'I am used to staying awake for days at a time. There is not much sleep on the battlefield. You needed the rest more than I did.'

'I am not weak,' she protested, struggling out from under the bed covers.

'I know you are not, but I am more used to it. Come on. We must go.'

He waited while she straightened her clothes and pulled her cloak on. His chain mail was already in place.

'Did you see anything suspicious while you were watching the street?' she asked quietly as he moved towards the door.

'No,' he whispered. 'Not much is going on outside tonight but we must still be vigilant.'

He slowly unlatched the door and stepped out into the corridor. When he was satisfied there was no one around he gestured for her to follow him. She caught a hint of his outdoor woodsy scent as she stepped in close behind him, quietly following him down the corridor.

A stair creaked beneath them and they both froze. But the taproom remained quiet and they continued on their way.

Ellena shivered as they stepped into a small court-yard at the back of the tavern. She pulled her cloak tighter around her. The temperature had dropped since their morning flight along the river's edge, but at least it wasn't raining.

The light of the half-moon cast eerie shadows around the yard as they made their way to the stables. Stoirm nickered softly at their approach. Ellena rubbed his nose as Braedan tied his saddlebags to the horse's side.

Ellena followed as he led Stoirm out of his stall and into the courtyard. He gestured that they should take the horse onto the main thoroughfare before getting on and she nodded her understanding.

She was glad they didn't have to speak. Her stomach curled in embarrassment every time she thought about what she'd said to him before falling asleep. She stumbled over a stone and suddenly gasped. In her misery, she'd completely forgotten about the others. Why hadn't his men caught them up yet? Were they all dead?

'What is it?' Braedan's voice rumbled close to her ear.

'What about everyone we left behind earlier?' she whispered. 'Should we wait for them?'

'No. If they survived their meeting with Copsi's men then they will have tried to draw them off in a direction away from us. We'll meet them at the castle.' He paused. 'Hopefully just *before* we reach the castle,' he clarified.

He didn't have to explain why. The scandal of the two

of them arriving at the castle together would ruin her reputation completely.

He seemed so sure his men were still alive, but was he just telling her that to relax her? They'd be safer in greater numbers, so surely it would be better to back-track and find his men.

He helped her into the saddle and then swung up behind her. She tried to lean forward, away from the warmth of his body, but the soft leather made her slide towards him until she was resting between his hard legs again. She hated it that her body enjoyed the sensation.

'We're going to ride quietly through the village,' he murmured over her hair, 'and then we'll race across the bridge. On the other side we'll head straight to the edge of the forest. If anyone's watching us we'll lose them in there.'

She nodded against his chest and breathed deeply, try-ing to relax. Every time they passed a deep shadow her fists tightened as she imagined someone leaping out to grab her from the dark. Behind her, Braedan stayed alert.

The streets of the village were deserted and there was only the noise of the houses creaking under the wind as they made their way to the edge of the settlement. The muscles in her neck gradually relaxed the further they travelled; they were going to make it.

'I think we're being followed,' said Braedan quietly.

'I can't hear anything,' she said, gripping the pom-mel tightly.

He brought Stoirm to a halt. 'Listen.'

She heard the faint thud of a large animal walking, before it too stilled.

'Do you think it's a horse?' she asked quietly.

He nodded. 'At least two, I think.'

She turned slightly to look at him. He was concentrating fiercely on the horizon, his jaw locked and his dark eyes blazing. He seemed to reach a decision.

'Hold on!' he called, and he set Stoirm into a fast gallop.

Stoirm thundered onto the bridge. Ellena heard a faint cry of surprise behind them before all sound was drowned out by her pounding heartbeat. She hadn't realised that the river would be so far below them, or that the crossing would be so long.

They were only halfway across when she realised they were being followed.

Ellena had a second to be terrified before arrows filled the air around them. She screamed as one grazed her cloak.

Braedan pulled her tightly towards him, protecting her with his body, but he didn't slow.

'Why are they shooting arrows at us?' she yelled. 'I thought Copsi wanted to marry me.'

'It's me they're trying to kill, not you,' he shouted back.

Ellena clutched the pommel in front of her, her hands slippery with sweat.

'If something happens to me,' he yelled over the rush of water and the stomping of hoof beats, 'keep riding.'

She opened her mouth in a silent scream.

Braedan seemed so large and unbeatable that she couldn't imagine anything happening to him. Without him she wouldn't be able to control the large animal beneath them, let alone direct the stallion to her father's castle.

They cleared the river and began to race for the safety of the treeline. No arrows were reaching them now, so they must be outstripping their pursuers—either that or Braedan had been hit and they knew all they had to do was wait.

There was no way for her to check.

They entered the relative safety of the trees and Braedan brought Stoirm to a canter.

'Are you hit?' she gasped.

'No,' he ground out.

'Then why are we slowing?'

'Stoirm,' was all he said.

She looked down to see an arrow had pierced the horse's flank.

'No… Is he…? He's going to be all right, isn't he?'

Braedan didn't answer.

Stoirm came to a stop. Braedan lifted Ellena off the horse and quickly joined her on the forest floor. Stoirm limped forward a few paces before falling to his side.

'Do something!' said Ellena, as the great animal's breathing became laboured.

'I'm sorry, Ellena, there's nothing I can do.'

He began stripping several of the saddle bags from Stoirm's side. Sweat coated the animal's body and the eye Ellena could see was wide with pain.

'How can you be so calm? He's dying and he's doing so because of us!' screamed Ellena, beating her fists against Braedan's solid chest, scraping her hands against his chain mail, causing the skin to burn.

He grabbed her hands and pulled her towards him. Her body was crushed against his side and his face was a hair's breadth from hers. Only her husband had ever been this close to her, but unlike all the times she'd been near Lord Swein she didn't feel afraid.

'I have to be this way,' he ground out as his breath

brushed against her skin. 'If we don't keep moving I will die and you will be caught. It will be worse for you, I think. But don't think for one second that I am not affected by Stoirm's death, because you are wrong.'

Beside them Stoirm's breathing slowed and then stopped. Her anger died at the same moment and was replaced with an unending sorrow.

'I'm sorry…' she whispered.

He nodded and released her, his fingers trailing down her arm. Her skin tingled in their wake, despite the many layers of clothing that separated them.

'Can you carry that?' he asked, handing her one of the bags that had been strapped to Stoirm's side and snapping her back to the moment.

'Yes—and something more if you need me to.'

Her fingers felt cold and stiff, but she held out her hands to receive another package.

'Sir Leofric!' called a voice from beyond the edge of the trees. 'I know you can hear me. Hand over Lady Swein to me and no one needs to be hurt.'

Braedan signalled to Ellena that she should start walking into the forest.

She shook her head fiercely. She was not leaving him. What if something happened to him and she never saw him again? Her heart pounded painfully in her chest. She wanted to throw her arms around him and cling to him.

He gave her a little shove and she stumbled. *Go*, he mouthed at her.

Tears pricked her eyes as she leaned down and bent down to stroke Stoirm one last time. She took another look at Braedan, who nodded firmly. She turned and quietly made her way in the direction Braedan had indicated, her heart pounding frantically in her chest.

'If I hand her over to you, what guarantee do I have that you won't kill me instantly?' called Braedan.

Ellena swung round sharply.

Braedan shook his head and gestured for her to carry on.

'You have my word as a gentleman. In fact I would handsomely reward you for doing so. Come over to my side and I will reward you far better than that old goat ever has. What is Ogmore paying you for this? It cannot be enough to lose all your men.'

Ellena's legs faltered, but she kept going. Braedan was buying her time to get away and she mustn't fail him.

'You lie!' called Braedan. 'My men would never be beaten by that untrained rabble you ride with.'

'Then why are we here and not them?' said the voice, a hint of laughter creeping into the words.

Ellena stumbled over a log and grazed the skin on the palm of her hand. She pulled herself back onto her feet and kept moving, all the while straining to hear what was being said behind her.

'Come, Sir Leofric, there is no way out of this for you. If you surrender now you have my word that I will be kind to the girl. I am not a monster.'

Ellena was too far away to hear Braedan's reply, but whatever he said brought the sounds of fighting through the forest.

Tears stung her eyes as she plunged her way blindly forward. Strong, stubborn Braedan was putting his life in danger for *her*.

The clang of metal hitting metal gradually faded. She stopped and rested her hand on a tree trunk, the rough bark anchoring her. She tilted her head, hoping the sound of Braedan following her would reach her, but she could only hear the sound of the wind rustling the leaves above her.

She tapped the wood with her fingers. What should she do now?

Braedan had told her to go on, and for now she would follow that instruction. She needed to put distance between her and Copsi, because if Braedan had failed then there was nothing to stop Copsi taking her.

She tugged her cloak tighter around her and began to trudge onwards. As she stumbled over twisted roots and abandoned logs Ellena rubbed the spot above her heart. It hurt with the memory of Stoirm lying amongst the tree roots, without anyone to keep him company.

Her thoughts strayed to his rider. It was easy to think of Braedan as The Beast, someone without feelings, but there had been no mistaking the haunted look in his eyes as Stoirm's life had slowly ebbed away. The fact that Braedan had cared so deeply about his horse reordered the way she thought about him.

Tales of The Beast had spread across all Ogmore lands, until he had become the stuff of children's nightmares—a cruel, hard creature who carried out her father's orders with ruthless efficiency. But she'd seen the way he was with his men. Yes, he dished out orders, but his men followed him with respect, not with fear. He'd looked after Eluard and made sure the boy reached safety when her own husband would have abandoned the boy in the woods once he was no longer of use.

She couldn't ignore the way he'd treated her either. Men, she knew from experience, sometimes took what they wanted from a woman, without thinking about the consequences. She'd been completely in his power and yet he'd let her sleep while he watched for danger. Those weren't the actions of a monster.

She needed to stop thinking of him as the enemy. He was the man who would keep her safe until she reached her father's castle.

As she walked she bargained with God. If he kept Braedan safe she would obey his orders without fighting him any more. She would be compliant until she reached the safety of Ogmore.

She walked until the sun began to rise on the horizon and then she fell to the ground. She could go no further. She rolled into a ditch and pulled some leaves around her. It was the best she could do.

Her eyes fluttered shut as the sun rose above her, bathing the area in a soft golden light.

Chapter Six

She awoke to the crackle of fire and the scent of roasting meat.

Her arm protested at being slept on for so long and she tugged it from beneath her. Slowly she pulled herself upright and looked for the source of the smell.

A little way from her sat Braedan, his head bowed over an open fire as he turned a makeshift spit.

'You're alive...' she croaked, and she flung herself at him, the need to feel for herself that he was really there robbing her of her normal reticence.

He caught her with one arm and surprised her by pulling her tightly to his side, as if he also needed physical reassurance.

Instead of pulling instantly away, she nestled her head in his neck and breathed in the musky scent of his skin. She brought her fingers up to trace the edge of his jaw and his short beard prickled her skin. She felt his intake of breath, but for once she didn't care if she'd shocked him.

All through that endless walk last night she'd pictured his lifeless body and the depth of her anguish had surprised her. She didn't want to dwell on why that might be. She hoped it was because she didn't want to be alone out here, but she feared she was developing some sort of attachment to him.

Right now the reason didn't matter; she only wanted to reassure herself that he was still alive.

'What happened?' she asked, unable to let him go.

'I fought with Copsi's men. Unfortunately I didn't kill Copsi, but I did wound him enough that that they will need at least a day to regroup.'

'How did you find me?'

'I followed your trail through the woods,' he said. 'We need to work on your ability to move without leaving a trace.' He smiled against her hair.

She allowed herself to cling to him for a long moment, and then she pulled away. Up close she could see purple shadows beneath his dark eyes.

'You must be exhausted,' she said softly.

'I rested for a bit when I found you, and then I thought you might be hungry.' He raised an eyebrow.

'I can take over with this,' she said, lightly batting his hand away and reaching for the spit.

'I think it is ready, my lady.'

She stilled. 'Last night you called me Ellena. I think, under the circumstances, you can continue to call me by my given name.'

He didn't answer, and for a moment she worried that she'd overstepped some sort of boundary. That this new feeling of attachment might be one-sided.

'Thank you,' he said eventually. 'You can call me Braedan.'

She nodded, but didn't turn to look at him. 'I think

you're right. This is ready. Shall we eat? And then you must rest.'

They ate in silence. Ellena devoured the meat straight from the bone, peeling it off with her teeth and her tongue. She was glad no one from Castle Swein could see her now. She was about as far from ladylike as it was possible to be. But she didn't feel bad about it. She was just glad to be alive and free.

After they'd finished eating Braedan lay down and fell asleep immediately. His face, softened by sleep, looked younger. She wanted to trace his scars with her fingertips, but managed to suppress the strange urge that kept compelling her to touch his face. He'd think she'd gone crazy if he awoke to find her stroking his skin.

She shook herself. She didn't normally have the impulse to touch men—Swein had killed off all feelings of desire during their marriage. It must be the relief of finding Braedan alive and knowing that she wasn't alone that was giving her these strange thoughts and feelings.

To keep herself occupied, and away from his sleeping body, she went through the bags they had saved. She found some blankets and threw a couple over Braedan, being careful not to look at him for too long as she did so.

Braedan woke slowly. For a minute he stared at the grey clouds he could see through the network of branches above him, unable to work out where he was. Every muscle ached, and the temptation to close his eyes and return to oblivion was almost overwhelming.

He turned his head and saw Ellena poking the fire with a log. Flames crackled into life as she did so and she smiled, clearly pleased with herself.

He watched her for a moment as the light from the fire

danced over her delicate features. He'd had only a vague recollection of Ogmore's daughter from when he was younger. She'd been kept away from the young pages training to gain their knighthoods, but he'd glimpsed her on feast days. Even as a young man starved of female companionship he hadn't spared her much more than a passing glance.

She'd been thin and tall, rather like a weed, and he'd not thought much about her after she'd left Ogmore's castle to marry. Her reputation around the castle had been as a plain, docile little thing, but either she'd changed in the eight years since she'd left her father's home or no one had really known her back then.

She was passionate, fiery, practical and loyal. She was kind-hearted. And even with streaks of dirt covering her face there was no way she could be described as plain. From the moment he'd seen her, defiantly watching him approach her castle, he'd been aware of her core of strength. As he'd come closer he'd been struck by her light blue eyes and long, graceful neck. Her willowy figure had filled out, leaving her with soft curves and an alluring walk. But her beauty didn't stop at the surface; underneath all that he had seen that she cared deeply about other people, and he found being cared for by her more appealing than he should. It wasn't something he was used to.

He tore his gaze away and looked back up at the clouds. He had no right to think these things. Not only was there his imminent betrayal of her, but she was all but promised to an acquaintance of her father's. Not that she knew that yet. The Earl of Borwyn was her father's favoured suitor—and, as his lands were closest to Ogmore's, he was probably going to be successful in winning her hand.

He was reputed to be a handsome devil, with no scars marring his face. Braedan, with no home to call his own, was about as likely to have success with her as the tree stump by his left foot.

Braedan curled his hands into fists, and he must have made some sort of sound because he heard Ellena turn towards him.

'You're awake,' she said.

'Yes,' he said, slowly sitting up. 'Have I been asleep long?'

'Most of the afternoon,' she said, gesturing to the sky. 'I was going to wake you in a bit...' She paused and prodded the fire again, sending sparks into the air around them. 'What are we going to do now?'

He wanted to suggest she come and lie next to him and that they forget all about their families and their obligations as they explored one another's bodies. But after her horrified reaction to that bed in the inn yesterday he knew she would recoil from such a thought.

He cleared his throat. 'First we should sort through the saddle bags we've got and decide what we really need and discard the rest. I didn't pay much attention to what I was grabbing last night.'

His heart dipped as he thought about Stoirm. Stoirm had been with him for years—he'd trained the stallion himself—and now he was lying abandoned among the rotting leaves of the forest floor.

He clenched his teeth. Copsi and his men would pay dearly for that.

'I've already done it,' she said, pointing to a pile of discarded items.

'Oh…' he said, looking at the unnecessary pans he'd saved from Stoirm's side and carried through the night, too desperate to find her to check what he was carrying. 'Have we got anything useful?'

'Yes,' she said briskly. 'I've packed some blankets, some dried foodstuff and a comb.'

He surprised himself by laughing. 'I'm glad you've packed *that*.' He ran his fingers through his hair and pulled out a twig.

She giggled and he glanced up at her, catching her smile of amusement before it faded. Satisfaction purred through him. In the short time he'd known her he'd not seen her laugh. That he'd been the one to make her smile made unfamiliar warmth spread through his body.

But as the light in her eyes died he felt the weight of responsibility settle on his shoulders once more.

She looked at the forest around them. 'Do you even know where we are?' she asked.

'Roughly,' he said, although that was not entirely accurate.

He knew where they *weren't*, and in which direction they needed to go to get back on track, but she didn't need to know that. It was his responsibility to lead, and those following had to have confidence in his actions—even if he sometimes wasn't sure himself.

'We're going to head back the way we came.'

'Are you crazy? We'll walk straight into Copsi and his men.'

Her expression suggested she thought he was a few arrows short of a full quiver. He didn't blame her. They were trying to avoid Copsi, not walk straight into his hands, but they had no other option.

He scratched his beard. 'We need to get back towards

the river. Alternative routes could take us weeks to get back to Ogmore—especially as we now don't have any transport.'

Tears swam in her eyes and she dropped her head as if to hide them from him. He pulled a bag towards him and busied himself with retying the cords. He didn't need to, she'd done a very good job of securing them, but they were going to get very little privacy over the next few days so he'd afford her this little courtesy.

Out of the corner of his eye he saw her swipe at the few tears that had spilled over onto her cheeks. When she spoke her voice was as calm as always.

'I want to return home to Castle Swein.'

He rubbed his eyes; he'd been expecting something like this. He could understand why she wanted to go back. As far as she was aware she'd been safe there, whereas during the last few days her life had been on the line several times. She didn't realise that Copsi was only one of several men plotting to force her into marriage. Her lack of male protection was making her far more vulnerable than she realised.

He wasn't about to enlighten her; he didn't want her any more frightened than she was already. But he couldn't allow her to return. Even if there were no threats to her freedom, his future depended on it.

He needed to get her to her father, who would marry her off to someone who wasn't the crazy madman Copsi. Once she had a husband the threat would disappear and her life could return to normal—albeit not in the castle she wanted, but she would still be in a role she'd been born to play.

'It won't be safe for you there,' he said, getting reluctantly to his feet and pulling the two heaviest packs onto his back. 'Copsi has shown how determined he is to marry you—we know the lengths he will go to. He will want to secure a marriage to you at all costs before you reach your father. Your best option is to get to Ogmore's fortress. No one will get to you through his guards.'

'But I don't want to stay at my father's castle forever. I want to return to Castle Swein at some point. What will happen to Copsi then?'

She pushed herself up from the floor, ignoring his hand outstretched to help her.

'You will need to discuss that with your father,' he said, avoiding eye contact with her.

She looked at him for a long moment while he pretended to take in the surrounding woodland.

'You don't think he'll let me run Castle Swein by myself, do you? Your whole argument for getting me to go to Ogmore to discuss my future with him was a ruse just to get me to leave. I can't believe I fell for it.'

His heart bumped uncomfortably in his chest. What she said was true, but it turned out he didn't want her to think badly of him.

'Ellena, I...'

She held up her hand. 'I've changed my mind. We will go back to the formalities, if you please.'

He sighed. 'Lady Swein, I...'

'I don't want to hear what you have to say. Let us get to my father's lands so that I may speak to him directly. I *will* return to my castle and I *will* run it in a way that I see fit.' She swung the remaining bag onto her shoulder and looked at him down her imperious nose. 'We should get going. It will be dark soon.'

Even though moving on was exactly what he wanted to do, he found it galling that she thought she was the one who could give orders. For half a heartbeat he was tempted to refuse, but he swallowed the protest. Perhaps this expedition would run smoother if she thought she was in charge.

He turned without saying anything and began to make his way through the densely packed trees. Eventually he heard twigs crunching behind him as she followed. Without turning, he could feel her glare directed at his back.

He sighed again. He was used to furious looks being thrown at him. They normally bounced off him without making a dent. But her anger hurt more than he wanted to admit even to himself. His duties as Ogmore's lead warrior made him unpopular with those who thought they could disobey his liege, but Ellena wasn't like the rest. She wasn't afraid of him and she treated him with respect.

As dusk fell so did her ability to move unhindered. Twice she stumbled, but when he reached back to help her she ignored him. In anger, he moved quicker. It wasn't his fault she was in this predicament. He was only following orders, and in delaying leaving her castle she'd given Copsi time to set his traps. Now not only was Eluard—a young man he cared deeply about—gravely injured, he'd also lost his favourite horse.

She was naive if she thought she could survive alone in a man's world.

His fury made his steps even faster, and after a while he could only vaguely hear her moving after him. Then he realised he couldn't hear anything at all. He slowed and turned in her direction.

'Move faster!' he yelled through the trees.

There was no response.

'You'd better be in serious trouble,' he muttered under his breath as he strode back the way he had come, 'or I'm going to make you regret trying to defy me.'

'Sir Leofric.' Her cool voice came from his left.

He turned and saw her just standing there. His blood thundered in his ears. Why had she stopped? They were running for their lives here and she was playing around.

'What is it now?' he ground out.

'I'm stuck,' she said, and this time he heard the fear underneath her calm words.

He looked down at her feet. Sure enough, her boots had disappeared into some boggy mud. He took a step towards her.

'Don't come any closer.'

He froze.

'I don't want you to get stuck too,' she clarified.

He looked down at his feet. They were dangerously close to the sticky substance.

'Pass me your bag,' he said, trying to make his voice sound as calm as hers, even as his heart rate picked up. He couldn't lose her now—and to mud, of all things.

He noticed her fingers trembling as she slipped the bundle from her back. Was her calm voice all for show? He tucked that little titbit away to think about later, when hopefully they would be safe and dry. She threw the pack to him. He caught it and set it down next to his own.

'Don't worry,' he said. 'I'm going to get you out of there.'

She seemed to sink a little even as he spoke and his heartbeat ratcheted up another notch.

'Every time I move I seem to go a little deeper,' she whispered, her fear now coating every word.

'I'm going to set up a crossing,' he said, 'and then I'm going to pull you out. In the meantime, try not to move.'

He laced his voice with a confidence he didn't feel. And it must have worked because she nodded and looked at him expectantly.

He pulled thick logs towards him and laid them across the mud. He tried a few with his weight, and when he was satisfied they could take it he began inching towards her.

'What was that noise?' she asked when he had nearly reached her.

He stopped.

'It sounds like a dog,' she said, almost conversationally, as the faint sound of howling reached them.

He reached over, grabbed her arms and pulled. Nothing happened.

'It is a dog,' she said, still in that strange calm voice. 'Maybe more than one. Doesn't Copsi keep hunting dogs? I think he does. I heard a rumour about what happened to a young boy who accidentally broke Copsi's favourite chair. Have you heard it?'

'Aye,' said Braedan as he bent down and yanked at one of her feet. It came free with a loud squelching noise. He began to work on the second one.

'He gave the boy half a morning to run and then he sent his dogs after him,' she continued.

'I don't think we need to hear this story right now, Ellena.'

Sweat began to coat his brow and he wiped it away before it could drip into his eyes.

'The dogs tore the boy to pieces,' whispered Ellena.

'That's not going to happen to us,' said Braedan, tugging fiercely at Ellena's foot. The thought of one of Copsi's dogs sinking its teeth into Ellena's pale skin was making his actions jerky.

'The dogs are coming closer,' she commented as the sound of braying hounds drew nearer.

Her second foot came free, but her boot remained in the mud. He tugged at it but it wouldn't budge.

'We're going to have to leave your boot there,' he told her.

She nodded and didn't argue.

He grabbed one of the bags and then began to drag her after him.

'What about our things?' she asked as she stumbled behind him.

'They're not as important as getting away. If those dogs do belong to Copsi's hunting pack then he won't be far behind. If they're wild we're in just as much trouble. Either way, it's not good for us.'

He could hear the sound of dogs crashing through the undergrowth as he tugged her after him. She gave a gasp of pain as she tripped over a fallen log but she didn't stop. Soon they were running through the trees, branches whipping them in the face, but he didn't dare stop to check whether she was hurt or not. The only thing that mattered right now was getting her to safety. A few cuts and bruises were nothing in comparison to being caught by the dogs—wild or not.

He didn't tell Ellena, but he'd heard far worse stories about Copsi's hunting dogs than the one she'd told. If they were caught then they would probably die even before Copsi caught up. Now that they were separated from Braedan's men, there was nothing to stop Copsi claiming Ellena had been married to him before she died. All it would take was a few false witnesses and Ellena's land would become Copsi's.

Fear for her life had him running faster. And all the while the sound of the barking dogs came nearer.

He hadn't realised they'd reached a stream until cold water rushed over his feet.

'This is good,' he told her as he splashed forward. 'Hounds cannot smell us through water.'

'Then we'll follow the stream for a bit,' she said, and stepped into the water herself.

He saw her eyes widen as cold water lapped over her ankles but she didn't comment. She was so brave—far braver than many noblemen he'd met, who would have insisted Braedan find another option.

He laced his fingers with hers as they moved slowly downstream. The water soon reached up to his thighs and he could hear her teeth chattering madly. He needed to find a place for them to climb out of the stream and get her warm as soon as possible. He didn't dare do it now; they'd keep going until he could no longer hear the dogs.

He heard her sharp intake of breath as their joined hands skimmed the top of the water. It was getting deeper, and there was no way she would be able to swim with her heavy clothes on. He paused briefly and tilted his head to one side, listening for the sounds of the dogs. When he couldn't hear them he stood and looked around him. A low bank was just visible in the distance. Yanking her behind him, he made his way over to it.

'We'll climb out here,' he said. 'You go first.'

Her movements were becoming more rigid as the cold started to take hold, and in the light of the moon he could see that her lips had turned blue. He helped her clamber onto the bank and she slipped over in the mud, falling into an untidy heap on the ground. He pulled himself onto the bank next to her and stood. She didn't move.

'I'm sorry, Ellena, but we can't stop here. We need to get you warm.'

She made to stand but couldn't, her legs giving way beneath her.

'Come on, Ellena. Don't give up now.' He slipped his arm underneath hers and tried to tug her.

'C-c-can't. H-h-hair caught,' she stuttered.

He swore and reached behind her. Sure enough, her hair was entwined with the bramble bush she had fallen next to.

He leaned over her and tried to pull the strands from the branches.

'C-c-cut it.'

'No, there must be another way,' he said, his cold fingers pulling futilely at the locks he'd so admired and creating lumps of thick, knotted hair.

'Cut,' she said again. 'So cold.'

He pulled out his dagger and with only the briefest of hesitations sliced through the locks, freeing her instantly. She fell into him and he could feel her whole body trembling. He staggered to his feet and threw her over his shoulder.

'I can w-w-walk,' she said to his back.

He didn't respond, and she didn't protest when he didn't put her down. That alarmed him more than anything, and he tore through the forest, looking for a place to shelter.

He eventually came to a tumbledown ruin of a hut. Chunks of the wall were missing, but it was better than nothing. The door had long since rotted away, but most of the roof was still intact.

He set her down inside and she staggered drunkenly into the middle of the room.

'We need to get these wet clothes off you,' he said.

His fingers felt large and clumsy as he undid the ties of her cloak. Eventually he managed to get it off and it hit the floor with a thud. She stood still as he removed the outer layer of her clothing, but her hands came up to stop him as he began to pull at her undergarments.

'Enough,' she said.

He shook his head. 'This is no time to be modest, my lady.'

The fine trembling all over her body nearly broke him. He hadn't seen her look this frightened on the whole trip. Swein's treatment of her must have been far worse than he'd imagined. She wasn't just a woman who didn't like what happened between a man and a woman. She was terrified of it.

It was a shame Swein was already dead, because Braedan wanted to tear the man to pieces with his own bare hands.

But for now he needed to get Ellena warm. He reached up to cup her cheek with his hand. Her skin was deathly cold. 'I promise that you are safe with me. We must get you dry.'

She didn't push his hand away, but she made no move to undress any further. His foot nudged the one bag they had left and he reached down to open it.

'Here,' he said, pulling out a blanket. 'Wrap this around you and then take your undergarments off.'

He turned away and studied the hut while she complied.

In a corner of the room he saw the remnants of an old fire. He stepped outside for a moment and found some kindling to place within the stone circle that had encompassed it. Back in the hut, he found her tightly wrapped within the blanket, her undergarments in a pile on the floor.

Her large eyes were wide and unseeing. Her hair hung in clumps that stopped just above her shoulders. Thick streaks of dirt marred her face. But it was her vacant gaze that unsettled him the most. He was so used to seeing her eyes reveal every fiery emotion she experienced that their blank expression was like a little death.

He gently guided her to a space near the fire as he set to lighting it.

'You need to change out of your clothes too,' she said softly as the fire crackled to life.

He was so pleased to hear her talk that his bones momentarily turned to liquid, and he didn't trust himself to speak without his voice breaking a little. Instead he nodded and headed over to the pack at the back of the room.

He found another couple of blankets and draped one over her shoulders before stripping off his own wet clothes. He tied a blanket around his waist and then sorted through the damp clothes they'd both discarded, hanging them up to dry on the low, damaged wall of the hut.

When he could avoid it no longer, he joined her by the fire. 'Here,' he said, handing her an oatcake.

She took it, but only held it in her hands.

'You must eat,' he said.

She took a small bite and chewed listlessly.

Fear spiked his chest. This defeated woman who sat huddled on the floor was not the spirited one who argued with him and set his nerves on edge. She was not the person who always wanted to know where her next meal was coming from. The Ellena he knew would never obey one of his orders, but this must be the third one she'd accepted without any argument at all.

'Would you like to sleep, my lady?' he asked gently.

She shook her head. 'I don't think I could.'

'Try. It'll make you feel better.'

She finally met his eyes. 'I'm too cold.'

He reached across and touched the skin of her forehead. She felt like ice. He quickly reached a decision and acted on it before he could change his mind.

He pulled the saddlebag towards them and gently pushed her head down onto it until she was lying on the floor. Then he undid his blanket and lay down behind her. Covering both their bodies, he pulled her close towards him.

He could feel the rigid set of her shoulders through the two layers of fabric that separated them. He'd already assured her that he wouldn't hurt her, so he kept still and hoped that his actions would speak louder than any words he could say.

Gradually, over the space of a thousand heartbeats, he felt her muscles relax and her breathing grow heavier as she drifted into sleep. Gently, so as not to disturb her, he reached up and touched the skin on her forehead again. She was no longer icicle-cold, but she was a long way from being warm.

He lay back down behind her and tugged her closer.

All his instincts were roaring at him to remove the blankets between them and press their flesh together. It would warm her faster—of course it would. But while he lay there, fighting his impulse, he admitted to himself that her warmth was not the only thing at the forefront of his mind.

He wanted to feel her skin against his more than he'd ever wanted anything else.

He wanted to know if her skin was as soft as it looked.

He wanted to slide his hands over every inch of her perfect body and for her to welcome his touch.

But she trusted him so he didn't move.

Chapter Seven

Ellena woke to the strangest feeling. For a moment she didn't recognise it—and then it came to her. She felt *safe*.

She couldn't remember ever feeling the sensation before. Perhaps she had when she was a child, before she'd realised she had to move away from her family to marry, but she couldn't remember.

Before Lord Swein's death she'd been terrified of the things he'd done to her body and her soul. And afterwards she'd been frightened that her hard-won sanctuary would be taken away from her. But right now, in this moment, she was protected and secure. And it was all down to Braedan.

His arm—the arm that had provided her with so much warmth last night, when she'd been so cold she had thought she might not live to see daybreak—was wrapped firmly around her waist. Her fingers wanted to trace the corded muscles she could see there, to discover whether they were as unyielding as they looked. She could feel his body the whole length of hers, and her skin hummed at the contact, even though there were two blankets between them.

His gentle snores sounded in her ear and she smiled at the sound. She wanted to turn and watch him, as she had when he'd slept yesterday. He looked innocent and young when he was asleep, instead of like the hardened warrior he was.

She breathed out slowly. It would be better if she could regain the anger she'd felt when she'd realised he'd tricked her into leaving her castle. She still couldn't believe she'd fallen for his false insistence that it was best for her to return to her father's lands to negotiate with him. As if her father would listen to *her*. She was only a woman, and a woman's role was to be useful and make good alliances. But Braedan had been so convincing. And he'd seen how well Castle Swein was being run, and he'd known that was all down to her. So she'd believed him.

Yesterday she'd been so angry with Braedan—but also with herself, for being so easily persuaded. As they'd traipsed through that endless forest she'd plotted to slip away from him when he next slept.

How naive that sounded now. Their flight through the woods had been so utterly full of terror that she couldn't imagine being on her own again. If it hadn't been for Braedan she would have died. There was no doubt in her mind about that. She hadn't even been able to get herself out of the mud, let alone run away from those dogs or warm herself after their dip in the water.

She shifted, and his arm tightened around her before relaxing again. She sighed. Propriety demanded that she roll away from him and dress before he woke, but she couldn't bring herself to do it. He was nothing like Lord Swein. He'd considered her safety and comfort before his own, and the feel of him against her didn't repel her like it should. In fact it was quite the opposite. She longed to stay like this, cocooned in the safety of his arms.

She burrowed further under the covers and snuggled closer to the warmth of his body.

She knew the moment he awoke. His breathing changed and the muscles in his arm tightened again. She waited for him to move away from her but he didn't. She became aware of a hard length pressing into her back, but still he didn't move. She didn't either.

He'd promised not to hurt her and she believed him. He was not like Lord Swein, who had thought only of his pleasure and given no regard to the pain he had deliberately inflicted on her.

She wanted to know what Braedan was thinking.

Slowly...achingly slowly...she turned in his arms, careful not to dislodge the arm that was around her.

His eyes were open and he was watching her as she rested her head on the makeshift pillow next to his. His breath whispered across her skin and the little hairs on the back of her neck stood to attention in response.

She reached up and brushed a strand of hair away from his face, her fingers skimming his beard as she did so. His sharp intake of breath surprised her and she snatched her hand away, scared that she had hurt him in some way.

When he lay unmoving and uncomplaining she brought her hand back to his face. She gently rubbed away some of the dirt that had gathered beneath his eye.

The corner of his mouth tilted upwards in a slight smile and the fine lines around his eyes crinkled.

His own hand slowly moved up her spine to touch the edges of her newly shortened hair. Her scalp tingled and she closed her eyes. No one had ever touched her so gently or so reverently.

His fingers brushed her jawline and came to rest lightly on her lips. Barely moving, she placed the softest of kisses on the very tips. His hand moved back to her hair and he lightly pulled her towards him.

At first his kiss was soft and gentle, barely a press of lips.

It wasn't enough.

She moved closer towards him and felt his grunt of surprise against her mouth. Then he tilted his head and deepened the kiss.

Her skin was sensitised, and she felt the brush of the rough fabric against her breasts as he crushed her to him, his tongue sliding into her mouth.

She gasped at the invasion. No one had ever done such a thing to her before. But instead of protesting she allowed him to continue, welcoming his touch.

Within the space of a heartbeat her whole body ignited, her nerve endings coming alive all at once. She swept her fingers into his hair and pulled him closer still. He responded by rolling her onto her back and leaning above her. Then he broke away and ran his lips along the curve of her jaw and down into the hollow of her neck.

The sound of their heavy breathing filled the air. The delicious weight of him pressed her down as he returned his attention to her lips…

Then he was gone.

Her eyes snapped open as the cold rushed over her body in the absence of his warmth.

'I'm sorry, my lady. I don't know what came over me,' he growled.

Without looking at her, he swept up his clothes and strode out of their makeshift camp.

Humiliation washed over her. He'd apologised, but it had been *she* who had started it. It was she who had touched his face and pulled him close.

Only yesterday she'd been frightened of him trying to take advantage of her, but she was no better than all those lords who thought they could have any woman they wanted and who treated their female servants as if they were playthings. True, she hadn't hurt him. But, really, was she any better than her late husband, who had taken whatever he wanted from women whether they were willing or not? She should never have touched him.

She slowly pulled herself to her feet. Her legs were weak and the skin on her unbooted foot throbbed as she made her way over to her clothes. The garments were dry, but stiff with mud as she pulled them on.

When she was fully covered she fetched a water skin and splashed a little liquid onto the sole of her foot, to wash the worst of the dirt off. She sat down to examine it. It was scratched, and bleeding in several places, but nothing was too deep or serious-looking.

She'd need something to cover it if she was going to walk today. She certainly wasn't going to let Braedan carry her again.

She heard the stomp of Braedan's footfalls returning to the hut and kept her eyes on her wounds. She knew she'd have to make eye contact with him at some point, but it was too soon after their encounter to do so now.

'Here,' he said, thrusting an odd-shaped piece of bark into her eyeline. 'I thought you could use this as a boot until we reach the next town.'

His fingers brushed hers as she took it and a bolt of

awareness jolted down her arm. He flexed his fingers, as if he'd felt something strange too.

'Thank you,' she murmured.

He stood in front of her as she slipped the bark over her foot. It was surprisingly soft, and she wiggled her toes experimentally. The bark immediately slipped off.

He cleared his throat and knelt beside her. 'Tell me if this hurts,' he said, and he took a bit of twine and gently wrapped it around her foot, securing the bark to her.

He didn't look at her as he worked and she felt a fresh wave of humiliation as heat crept up her neck and washed across her face. She'd offended him by her actions and made things awkward between them.

He finished and then cleared his throat again. 'About this morning…' he said, still keeping his eyes on her odd shoe. 'I'm sorry about my actions. It won't happen again.'

She nodded, and although he wasn't looking at her he seemed to take her silence as enough of a response.

'Are you ready to go?' he asked abruptly.

'Yes,' she croaked.

'Good.'

He swept up the blankets and stuffed them into his bag while she stood with her hands clasped in front of her. Now they were left with only one piece of luggage between them there was nothing for Ellena to carry, and she had nothing to add to it.

She felt oddly redundant with nothing to do.

Her stomach growled. 'Do we have any food left?' she asked.

'A couple of oatcakes,' he said. 'Can you manage without having one now? I don't know how far we are away from a town.'

'I can manage,' she said.

Her stomach growled again at the lie, but she refused to show any weakness.

'Do you have any idea where we are?' she asked as they stepped outside the hut.

She squinted in the morning sun as her eyes adjusted to the sudden brightness. The air was warmer than yesterday, and she could hear birds singing high up in the trees ahead. It seemed so tranquil, compared to yesterday's nightmare.

She turned when he didn't answer and their eyes met for the first time since that kiss. As soon as their eyes locked her heart sped up, until it was beating painfully fast. She quickly dropped her gaze and waited for him to speak, keeping her eyes on a busy network of ants scurrying about to the right of his foot.

'I…um… I'm not sure exactly,' he admitted, for the first time ever sounding unsure.

She nodded. She hadn't really expected him to know, but she still felt a thud of disappointment.

'We want to be heading east—which is that way,' he said, pointing away from the hut and in the opposite direction from where they'd come yesterday.

'How do you know?' she asked.

'Ogmore is east of Swein, and as the sun rises in the east that's the way we should head,' he said, nodding towards the orb of light she could just make out through the leaves above them.

That made sense, as they'd been running in the opposite direction for most of the last two days.

'Right…' she said. 'Well, you lead the way and I'll follow.'

She didn't want his hulking presence behind her for

the rest of the day. It was hard enough to concentrate when he was standing in front of her.

He nodded and strode past her while she kept her eyes fixed on the busy ants. When he was far enough away that conversation wouldn't be required she followed him.

They walked until the sun passed overhead and began to carry on its journey behind them. Ellena's bark boot had remained in place, but the cuts were making themselves known with every footstep and the growling in her stomach was becoming painful.

Up ahead of her Braedan finally stopped, and she limped to catch up with him.

'We've reached the edge of the forest,' he told her as she stopped next to him. 'And I think there's a settlement down there.'

He pointed downhill, to where Ellena could just see a wisp of smoke curling over the horizon.

'It could be Copsi and his men camping,' she said.

He nodded, keeping his eyes on the distant smoke. 'Which is why we'll stay here until nightfall and then I'll go and check it out. If it's a settlement I'll get us a room at an inn and come back and get you.'

'And if it's Copsi?'

'I will come back and get you and we will retreat back into the forest.'

Her stomach let out a loud rumble in protest at this idea.

He smiled slightly and dived into his pack, retrieving two oatcakes. He handed them both to her.

She bit into one of the biscuits and greedily finished it in three mouthfuls.

'What about you?' she asked, when she realised he hadn't got any for himself.

'Don't worry about me. I'll get something when we get to a town.'

'You should eat *now*,' she protested.

He shook his head. 'I'm fine.'

She looked at the oatcake in her hand. She wanted to eat it so badly she had to clench her hand to stop herself shoving it into her mouth, but something wasn't right...

'Is this all we have?' she asked.

He kept his gaze away from hers as he stared intensely towards the horizon.

'It *is* the last oatcake,' he said eventually. 'But I am used to being on campaign and not eating for protracted periods. I don't need anything now.'

Yet another act of kindness from The Beast. He wasn't at all like his reputation, which painted him as a cold-hearted bastard. Her heart twisted in remorse at the way she'd treated him. He was a better man than most, and even though he'd manipulated her into leaving her home he'd only been doing her father's bidding. She couldn't hold that against him. His whole existence relied on serving the Earl of Ogmore.

'Please,' she said gently. 'Take it.'

For a long moment he ignored her outstretched hand. She was about to stamp her foot and insist when he turned and slowly took the dry biscuit from her hand.

'Thank you,' he said, and then he turned his back on her once more.

As daylight faded and the silence between them stretched on, Ellena's resolve quickened. She would *not* be left cowering in the shelter of the trees while he risked his life yet again.

When darkness finally fell he stood and brushed dirt from his tunic. 'I will be back as quickly as I can,' he told her.

'I'm coming with you,' she said, and stood and joined him at the edge of the forest.

'No, you are not.'

'I don't see how you can stop me.'

'I can tie you to that tree,' he ground out.

'What with? I know there is no rope in that bag.'

He growled.

'You can growl all you like but you don't scare me,' she said defiantly, crossing her arms and glaring up at him.

'And if I appeal to your common sense?' he asked, the set of his shoulders rigid and unrelenting.

'It isn't common sense to leave me here alone. What if that is a settlement down there and Copsi's men find me alone in the woods? I won't be able to fight them.'

That wasn't the only reason she didn't want to be left alone. She doubted Copsi's men would find her here. It was so dark that she could easily blend into the trees. Although if he had his dogs with him… She shuddered. It didn't bear thinking about what would happen to her then.

The other reason sending her from the safety of the trees was the knowledge that she couldn't stand the thought of something happening to him and her not knowing. She needed to know that he was safe.

'I will take you with me,' he bit out, 'if, and only if, you promise that you will obey my orders. If I tell you to run you must go, without stopping to argue with me.'

She nodded.

'I want to hear you promise,' he insisted.

'I promise that I will obey any commands you give me.'

His shoulders relaxed a little and he turned to leave.

'This promise only extends until we are safe,' she clarified. 'After that I will use my own common sense.'

'I'd be surprised if you have any,' she heard him mutter as he strode away from her.

'I heard that,' she said to his back.

'Good.'

'Well…' She stopped and folded her arms across her chest but he kept going. After he'd gone about ten steps she hurried after him. She was not about to be left out in the open.

As they neared the spot where the smoke appeared to be coming from it became obvious that it *was* a small settlement they had spotted. As they slowly passed a row of densely packed houses Ellena could smell the scent of cooking meat. It took everything she had not to follow the smell into one of the homely dwellings.

The sound of laughter and deep voices engaged in conversation greeted them as they came across a small inn in the centre of the settlement. Braedan stopped outside and watched the doorway.

'What are we waiting for?' whispered Ellena. 'I'm so hungry I might start eating *you* if we don't move soon.'

'I doubt I'd taste very nice,' said Braedan, his lips twitching slightly.

An unbidden image of licking the bare skin of his neck flickered across her mind and she quickly stepped away from him. Where had *that* come from?

'I'm wondering how we can find out who's in there,' Braedan continued. 'We don't want to deliver ourselves to Copsi and his men. Come.'

'Where are we going?' Ellena protested as they moved away from the door of the inn. She'd been so close to getting food, and now she felt as if it was being torn away from her. Her stomach rumbled painfully.

'We're going to talk to the stable lads. They always know what's going on.'

They headed to the back of the inn and found the stables. Braedan told her to wait in the shadows, and for once she didn't argue. She stepped back and watched, her heart pounding, as if she expected Copsi to emerge at any minute.

'It's all right,' said Braedan appearing at her elbow. 'It's only locals inside.'

She sagged against the wall. She'd been so prepared to start running again that her energy had suddenly failed her completely.

Braedan grabbed her elbow and she allowed him to propel her to the back door. 'Why aren't we going in the front?' she asked as they neared the inn.

'I don't want the men inside to get a look at you,' he said, glancing down at her briefly.

He ushered her into a narrow hallway and bade her wait once again. She was already getting tired of following his orders so blindly, but she had promised so she bit her tongue and leaned against the wall of the inn.

A young maid was following Braedan when he returned. The girl gasped when she caught sight of Ellena and she felt heat spread across her cheeks. She wasn't wearing her veil, and for the first time since she'd given it to Aldith she felt naked—despite the fact that she was fully dressed…albeit very shabbily.

Floorboards creaked below them as they made their way to the first floor. A tiny landing led to four doors and the maid opened the first one on the left.

'Thank you,' said Braedan, slipping the girl a silver coin. 'Bring that water I ordered quickly, please.'

The girl nodded, and after another horrified glance at Ellena she scurried off.

'What was that about?' asked Ellena, when Braedan had closed the door.

Braedan dropped the pack to the floor and pulled off his chain mail. Ellena watched the play of muscle as his arms stretched and bent and then, realising what she was doing, she turned away.

'I told the landlord that we were attacked by highwaymen, but I'm not sure I was believed.'

Ellena gasped. 'How can they possibly know who we really are? Have Copsi and his men already come here looking for me? We should go.'

She made to move to the door, but Braedan blocked her way.

'That's not why they don't believe me,' he said.

'Then what is it?'

He looked at the ceiling, and then at the floor, 'I don't think,' he said slowly, 'that you would pass as a lady right now.'

'What do you mean?'

His gaze flickered down the length of her body before returning to the ceiling. 'You look a little...' he waved his hand around for a moment '...dishevelled.'

She glanced down at her clothes. Before she could respond there was a knock at the door. Braedan went to open it and a young man strode through carrying a large pail of steaming water. Behind him scurried the maid, with a round basin.

The young man openly gawped at her, his gaze raking her whole body and reminding her of Lord Swein and his unwelcome attentions. She stepped back and folded her arms over her chest.

The young man grinned and winked at her as he deposited the water near her feet. The basin clattered to the floor as the maid dumped it and rushed back to the door. The young man sauntered after her.

'Thank you,' said Braedan to the maid as she scuttled out. Just as the young man reached the doorway Braedan reached out and gripped his arm. 'Next time you see my lady you will treat her with respect. Do you understand?'

Although Braedan's grip didn't tighten, there was enough hardness in his voice and ferocity in his eyes to make the young man visibly quail. He nodded quickly, then hurried out to join the maid.

'I thought you might like to clean yourself,' said Braedan as he closed the door behind them and gestured to the water.

Ellena didn't move.

'They think I'm a… They think…' said Ellena. 'They think I'm a woman who sells her favours.'

'I'm sure they don't any more,' said Braedan, crossing the room and pulling the room's only chair underneath the window.

He swivelled the chair around and sat down with his back to her. He obviously wasn't going to leave while she washed, but she no longer cared. She didn't even care that the serving boy thought she was a prostitute. The desire to be clean overwhelmed everything else.

She dipped the basin into the water and filled it, setting it on the little table when it was full. No spices had been added to sweeten it, but it was clear and clean and it was heavenly to be so close to such warmth.

She leaned over and caught sight of her reflection.

No wonder the two young people had thought she was a lady of the night. Her short hair hung in limp straggles around her face and it looked as if it had never been clean. A quick glance down at her dress confirmed that it was torn and grubby.

She must have made some sound of distress, because Braedan muttered, 'Don't worry…it will grow again.'

'I'm not upset about losing my hair,' she said. 'It's better to lose that than my life. And my head feels lighter without it.'

She turned her head from side to side, revelling in how easy it was without the weight of the curls she'd carried around with her for years.

'It looks pretty,' said Braedan gruffly.

She turned to look at him. Although he was still turned away from her she could see the tips of his ears turning a burning-hot red. She smiled. It was clear that The Beast was not used to giving compliments. A little bubble of joy floated through her. It had been years since anyone had called her pretty, and then it had only been her mother who'd said it in the first place. She was renowned for being the Earl of Ogmore's plain daughter.

As she splashed water onto her face and neck she wondered if Braedan was married, or promised to someone. In all the talk about her father's most fearsome warrior there had never been any mention of a woman, but perhaps that was why he had stopped kissing her this morning.

She stumbled and knocked into the table.

He turned sharply to look at her and she shrugged her shoulders. 'I'm tired,' she said.

He nodded and turned back without asking any questions.

She splashed more water on her face and closed her eyes. Just the memory of that kiss had caused her legs to go from underneath her. What would it be like if he did it again? Not that she wanted him to, of course. He was a wild warrior, with a horrible reputation, and she'd had a bad experience with a man whom everyone had thought was good. She wouldn't let the fact that her body seemed to enjoy his attention cloud her judgement. He was still a man—even if he was an honourable one.

She was carefully washing her damaged foot when another knock sounded on the door.

'This should be our food,' said Braedan, standing and letting the person in.

It was a different maid this time, and thankfully she was carrying dinner. Ellena had to force herself to stand very still with her hands by her sides as the maid carried the steaming bowls past her and laid the food on the table. Not a word was spoken until the woman had left the room.

As soon as Braedan closed the door Ellena fell on the food. She tore a large chunk of bread and dipped it into the wholesome-looking stew. It could taste dreadful for all she cared, just as long as she ate.

Braedan chuckled as he joined her. 'I'm not sure anyone would believe that you were the Earl of Ogmore's only daughter if they could see you now.'

She frowned at him over a large mouthful of bread, but her heart wasn't really in it to get truly annoyed. It didn't matter what anyone thought of her. She was getting food into her desperately empty belly.

Next to her, Braedan attacked his food too.

With the last of the hunger pains dying away she stopped shovelling food into her mouth and paused for a breath.

'Are you feeling better?' Braedan asked.

Ellena didn't like the way the laughter in his eyes was making her feel. It called to something deep inside her which made her want to make him laugh again, just to see his expression.

'Yes, I'm feeling sane now,' she said, stepping away from the table and the proximity of him.

'Good,' he said. 'We'll get some sleep and then to-morrow we'll buy more supplies before heading off again.'

'All right,' she agreed. 'I'll need some new boots, ribbons to tie my hair into a braid, and a needle and thread to repair the damage to my dress.'

'I've already asked the landlord to acquire those for you before we leave.'

She nodded. He really did think of everything.

'Get some rest.' He nodded to the bed.

'What about you?'

'I'm going to head down to the taproom and see if I can find out more about where we are in relation to your father's lands, and whether Copsi and his men have been spotted anywhere near here.'

'Will you come back?' she asked. She wasn't sure whether she wanted him to answer yes or no.

'I will, but I may be some time. It would be best if you got some sleep while I'm gone. I'll lock you in.'

He strode over to the doorway and stopped when his hand was on the doorknob.

'I'll sleep on the floor,' he said.

Ellena paused for a moment. She was about to say that he could join her on the bed—she trusted him, and she would tell him he could trust her too—but he opened the door and was gone before she could get the words out.

Chapter Eight

Only a handful of the hardier guests were left in the smoky taproom by the time Braedan reached it. He ordered himself an ale and sat down at a table in a dark corner by himself.

He'd lied to Ellena. He already knew where they were and he'd made all the enquiries about Copsi that he intended to. To ask any more would invite curiosity, and he wanted to pass unnoticed through this quiet little town.

He'd had to get out of the room because he didn't think he had the strength of will to stay standing when she climbed into bed. It had been bad enough watching her sleep the first few times he'd done it, but now, knowing what it felt like to hold her in his arms while she slept, it would be unbearable.

He knocked back half of his drink without even tasting it.

He closed his eyes as yet another image of Ellena's face so close to his flitted across his mind. This morning already felt like a dream. When he'd woken and realised she was awake, and not struggling to get away from his arms, it had felt like a miracle. Then, when she'd turned and looked at him, with interest rather than fear, he'd almost forgotten how to breathe.

He'd thought that at any minute she would pull away from him, but she had seemed as content to look at him as he'd been to stare at her. When her soft fingers had touched his face he'd been lost. Kissing her had seemed the most natural thing in the world. And when she'd responded passionately he'd momentarily forgotten who he was.

Just as he'd been about to tear away the blankets that separated them his conscience had woken up and all but slapped him in the face.

She was his liege's daughter. The woman he'd sworn to protect and return to Ogmore unharmed. She was the King's niece—not some random woman he could tumble in a rundown hut. She was also the woman whose castle he was planning to take. She wasn't going to forgive him for that, but if he'd taken advantage of her as well…

He'd forced himself to pull away and put as much distance between them as he could.

But he knew that to his dying day he would remember the feel of her mouth beneath his.

He knocked back the rest of his drink and went to order a second.

'Where are you and your wife heading?' asked the barmaid as she poured his ale.

'Ogmore,' he said. There was no point pretending otherwise. He'd asked for directions there earlier.

Ogmore was a huge town, and most of the surrounding area traded there. He'd banked on this small settlement being a natural stopping point for people heading there and he'd been right. Many of the other guests staying here were bound in that direction too.

'Are you from there, then?' she asked as she placed his drink in front of him.

He nodded as he rummaged in his clothes for some money.

'Have you ever seen The Beast?' she asked, her eyes wide with curiosity.

He froze in the act of counting out his coins. He knew people called him that. Hell, he'd been called that to his face more than once. But it still got to him.

He'd not set out in life to become a terrifying monster of legend. He'd done his knight's training because it had been the right thing to do. He'd always believed he would inherit his father's lands, and what had really interested him was the management of them. He'd wanted to build on what his father had and make it into a rich and profitable homestead, so that he could arrange good marriages for his sisters and his own children.

His father had destroyed any chance of that happening. But if he was successful in this mission he might get back some of that dream.

Aware that the barmaid was waiting for an answer, he nodded and said, 'Occasionally.'

This wasn't technically a lie. He did sometimes catch a glimpse of his reflection, but it wasn't something he tried to do. The reaction of his own mother, not to mention strangers, who cowered in horror when seeing his face, didn't encourage him to look too closely.

'Is he as fearsome as the rumours?' she asked as he handed over his coins.

'Worse,' said Braedan, snatching up his beer and taking it to his corner of the room.

He wasn't in the mood for conversation.

He sipped his second drink much more slowly than

his first. He was tempted to go for a third when it was finished, but he managed to stop himself. Ogmore had been generous with his allowance for this trip, and Braedan had some money of his own, but he didn't know how much longer they were going to be on the road and he needed to conserve what they had.

Reluctantly he stood and slowly climbed the stairs to their room. He hoped Ellena was sleeping—and then he hoped that she was awake and waiting for him to come back. Even if they argued it would mean interacting with her, which was something he'd never do again once this trip was over.

He turned the doorknob slowly and stepped inside as quietly as he could. Her back was turned to him and she was breathing slowly and evenly, giving every indication that she was deeply asleep. But something inside him doubted it, and he was half tempted to speak to her just to test whether she would respond.

On the table she'd placed some blankets and a pillow. He took them and lay down on the floor at the bottom of the bed. He heard her shifting around and he smiled to himself. She wasn't asleep, then.

He closed his eyes and willed his muscles to relax on the hard floor. The next few days would be long and difficult and he needed as much rest as possible.

Ellena awoke to the soft sound of snoring again. It had taken her an age to fall asleep after Braedan had returned to the room. She'd spent so long trying to pluck up the courage to tell him he could join her in the bed without it sounding like a proposition that she'd heard him fall into sleep before she'd even got the words out. She'd hoped that would help her fall asleep herself, but she'd spent an agonisingly long time fighting the urge to get up and watch him.

She didn't know where these strange urges were coming from. She'd been convinced that Lord Swein had killed stone-dead any romantic notions she'd had as a green girl, but now they seemed to be resurfacing—and towards the most inappropriate man in the whole kingdom.

This was a man who made his living out of violence—the one thing that terrified her more than anything. Just because he was being kind to her now, it didn't mean he always would be. She would never be able to defend herself against a man as strong as him. She should be cowering from him, not longing to touch the skin of his face.

She pushed the covers back and slowly slipped from the bed.

The water from last night was covered in a layer of grime. She scooped off some small twigs and leaves and dropped them onto the table. The water underneath wasn't much better, with mud settled on the bottom of the basin, but she splashed some on her face anyway. She went through the one remaining pack and was delighted when she pulled out the comb. She took it back to the bed with her and began to systematically work through the tangles of her much-shortened hair.

Braedan sat up just as she was experimenting with arranging the strands into a short braid. He blinked sleepily at her, and she couldn't help the giggle that escaped. He looked like a startled owl.

He smiled sleepily back and then rubbed his eyes.

'Well, that's a first,' he said, his voice rough with sleep.

'What is?'

'We made it through a whole day and night without a catastrophe.'

She laughed again. He was right. She felt a lot better for having spent a whole day without running for her life and a night of complete rest.

'Thank you for the pillow,' he said.

'I could hardly let you sleep on the floor with nothing.'

'You'd be surprised,' he muttered.

'What do you mean?'

'I've travelled with many a lord and lady who have treated me no better than a dog,' he said bitterly.

She jumped down from the bed and padded over to the table again. 'But you were born a nobleman, weren't you?'

'I was. But after my father…' He shrugged. 'It doesn't matter. I am not in this line of work to make friends.'

A smile briefly touched his lips but didn't reach his eyes. Her heart ached for him as he stood and began to sort through their belongings again, laying out their meagre possessions on the bed. How humiliating it must be to serve people who had once been below him in the pecking order. No wonder it annoyed him when she tried to give orders. She would try to phrase her demands as suggestions in future, and see whether that made him more amenable.

'I'm going to see if your new boots have arrived,' he said. 'If they have we'll head to the market and buy some provisions, and then we'd best set off.'

'Did you find out how far away we are from my father's castle?'

He nodded as he placed the last of the items back in the saddle bag. 'We're about a week's walk away.'

'A week!' she exclaimed. 'But we've already been travelling for days.'

He nodded and put the pack on the floor. 'I'm afraid so, yes. We've gone a long distance out of our way, trying to get away from Copsi and his men. I'll go and see about those boots. You'll need them.'

She sat down on the only chair in the room. A whole week of walking stretched ahead of her. She'd be totally ruined by the time she got back to the castle. There was no way anyone would believe that nothing had taken place between her and Braedan. She'd be forced to marry him.

She closed her eyes tightly. She didn't want to admit, even to herself, that the idea didn't fill her with as much horror as it should have done. She'd sworn to herself she'd never marry again and, as powerful as Braedan's kisses were, she wasn't about to break that vow.

'Do you want the good news or the bad news?' asked Braedan, returning to the room carrying a pair of ladies' boots and a large empty satchel.

'The bad first, please.'

'The bad news is that there is no time for us to go shopping for food.'

'Oh?' She puffed out a breath. 'Why not?'

'Well, the good news is that one of the other rooms has been taken by a family travelling in the direction of Ogmore, and they've offered us room on their cart for a very small fee. They have a spare horse for me to use. It won't be comfortable, but it will help us to disguise ourselves and it will save time. They want to leave right now.'

Ellena gasped. 'How many days will that shave off our journey?'

'It should halve the time.' He grinned and Ellena resisted the urge to fling her arms around him.

This was fabulous news.

He bent and started to push his chain mail into the empty satchel.

'Perhaps they will have some food they are willing to share,' she suggested.

He laughed out loud. 'You and your stomach.'

'What do you mean by that?' She was too pleased to be cross that he was making fun of her—and, really, what was so funny about wanting to know where your next meal was coming from?

'Only that you appear to be ruled by your appetite.'

He was still smiling gently at her, so she didn't think he was criticising.

'I just like to know when I'm next going to eat,' she said, remembering a time when she hadn't always known. It had been one of Lord Swein's crueller mental punishments. It hadn't hurt as much as his physical ones, but it had still frightened her to know that he had so much control over her life.

One particular instance stood out in her mind.

Her bleeding had been late starting one month. It hadn't been something she'd been able to hide from Swein—he had wanted daily updates from her and had paid a maid handsomely to spy on her. He'd been so sure that this time she had finally fallen pregnant and he'd actually treated her to her favourite meal. She'd hardly been able to eat because she'd been so full of dread and hope in equal measure.

When her bleeding had started a few days later his anger had been ferocious. She could barely remember the beating he'd given her, but she did recall waking up alone on her bedchamber floor, the door locked to prevent her from leaving. He'd left her for days without food, and her only water had come from the washbowl that had been left in her room.

She'd truly believed she would die and she'd almost welcomed it. Anything would have been better than the life she was living. But it had turned out that Lord Swein wasn't done with her. After that his attempts to get her with child had become increasingly unpleasant, until he'd fallen too ill to attempt it any more.

'I'm sorry,' Braedan said, his smile dying. 'I didn't mean to offend you.'

'You haven't,' she said, wishing she'd been able to laugh the moment off. She'd been enjoying his more relaxed demeanour around her after the tense day yesterday. 'Shall we go?' she asked, before the mood could deteriorate even further.

She followed him out of the room and down into the courtyard.

'By the way,' he said as they emerged into the sunlight, 'I've packed away my chain mail because we're now Mr and Mrs Carpenter. We're travelling from our home in Nerdydd to visit your mother, because your father has just died and I'm taking over his business.'

'Do we have any children?' she asked, her voice cracking slightly.

He glanced down at her. For a moment their gazes locked and the shared knowledge of their kiss surged between them.

'No,' he said. 'No children.'

A babbling family emerged from the inn behind them and the moment was broken.

'Ah, Mr Carpenter,' said a jovial man who was nearly

as round as he was tall. 'Is this beautiful young lady your wife?'

'Yes, this is Mrs Carpenter. This is Mr Webb, my dear.'

Ellena was welcomed into the family and she climbed up into the cart, settling into a space amongst the family's luggage, along with Mrs Webb, who was either heavily pregnant or just as round as her husband, and their four young children. Braedan climbed onto one of the horses, next to Mr Webb.

The morning passed quickly as the children kept Ellena entertained by involving her in their games. One day her maid and dear friend Bronwen would have children, and she would be a doting aunt to them because she would never have any of her own.

When the children eventually fell asleep Mrs Webb kept up a steady stream of conversation, obviously pleased to have an adult to talk to for a change. She didn't ask any questions, and Ellena was content to let her animated conversation wash over her. It made a relaxing change from being on high alert all the time.

Their progress was slow and uncomfortable, but they weren't fighting for their lives and she was thrilled when they stopped for an extensive lunch at an inn. By the time they'd arrived at their evening destination she'd almost forgotten she and Braedan were on the run.

The situation only came crashing back to her when once again she realised that she and Braedan would have only the one room between them.

Despite her protesting that it was her turn to sleep on the floor, he insisted that she take the bed before he left for the taproom again. She meant to stay awake and argue with him when he returned, but she fell asleep as soon as her head hit the pillow.

The next day was almost an exact repeat of the day before, and by the time she crawled into bed once more that night Ellena was almost relaxed.

On their third and last day with the family, Mrs Webb finally showed some interest in Ellena and Braedan.

'How long have you and Mr Carpenter been married?' she asked.

'A little over a year,' said Ellena, having been briefed by Braedan beforehand.

'Are you expecting yet?'

'Not yet,' said Ellena, running her hand over her flat, barren stomach.

Her look of anguish must have been apparent, because Mrs Webb's face contorted in sympathy and she said, 'Oh, don't worry about that, pet. It took me three years to fall with Rulf, there. Now I'm pregnant nearly all the time. Peter can't get enough of me!'

Mrs Webb threw her head back and laughed.

Ellena's heart stopped. It had taken the Webbs three years to conceive and they now had four children, with another one on the way. Could it be that she *wasn't* barren? Could it possibly be that she might one day have four children of her own? But, no, she mustn't go down that route. To have children she would need to remarry and engage in that awful act again. It was not going to happen.

The memory of Braedan's hand in her hair as he pulled her towards him flashed through her mind and made her face heat.

'Ah, look at your face,' crowed Mrs Webb. 'It's obvious what you're thinking about and I don't blame you. With that strapping husband of yours *I* wouldn't be able to think of anything else either.'

She waggled her eyebrows at Ellena and Ellena couldn't help but smile.

'You must tell me,' she continued. 'Is he that big all over?'

Braedan took that unfortunate moment to ride up alongside the cart, and Mrs Webb let out one of her wild cackles.

'In case you're wondering,' she screeched at Braedan, 'yes, we *are* talking about what you think we're talking about.'

Pleased with herself, Mrs Webb burst into fresh peals of laughter.

Mortified, Ellena didn't know where to look. She settled on Braedan's chin as Mrs Webb carried on laughing, evidently finding Ellena's embarrassment hilarious.

Braedan cleared his throat and Ellena felt her own lips twitch slightly; she'd noticed he did that when there was a slightly uncomfortable moment between them.

'We're coming up to the point where we shall leave you, Mrs Webb,' said Braedan, and then he abruptly spurred his horse on.

'Oh, my,' said Mrs Webb. 'I do enjoy it when these big men get all flustered. But I am sad we are parting already, my dear. What am I going to do without you?'

The children were equally disappointed, and they clung to her in their last moments together. But at a crossroads in the middle of nowhere Ellena clambered down from the cart, hugging everyone as she did so. She promised them all that she and Braedan would visit them at their home during the following summer, even though she knew that was impossible.

'What now?' she asked as the carriage trundled

slowly away, the children waving madly until they disappeared from sight.

'We start walking.'

'We'll find somewhere to get some food, though, won't we?'

He grinned down at her.

'Surely you're hungry too?' she protested as they started to walk.

He laughed, and her heart thrummed at the boyish sound. He was serious so often that surely it would do him good to laugh more.

'We've got the provisions I picked up at our last stop,' he said, amusement running through his voice.

'Yes, but we'll want decent food too.'

'We will eat at an inn this evening—but we must be careful and stop less in towns, because we don't want to run into Copsi and his men. We'll be more conspicuous now that we're travelling alone.'

'Surely he's lost our trail?' protested Ellena.

They'd seen and heard no trace of Copsi or any of his men since that night in the forest.

'I wouldn't count on it,' said Braedan, his voice sounding serious all of a sudden. 'The closer we get to Ogmore, the wider his nets are bound to be. We're only two or three days away now, so his traps will be wide and varied. Don't forget he is determined to marry you.'

'I don't see what he's hoping to get out of the alliance,' said Ellena grumpily.

'Don't you?' said Braedan, slanting his gaze down to her.

'It's not as if my father will accept Copsi's claim to Swein's land. He'll fight Copsi for it and probably win. Then Copsi will be left with a wife he doesn't want.'

Braedan took another few steps before saying, 'I think you are underestimating your worth to your father. He would fight to keep you too.'

Ellena snorted. 'I am useful to my father only as a negotiating tool. I'm worth about as much to him as maybe a chest of gold, or something equally likely to find favour with a high-ranking lord.'

Braedan scratched his beard. 'I have heard your father speak about you many times. He is proud of you… and I can understand why.'

'Oh?' she said, quickly losing interest in her father. She wanted to know what Braedan thought of her, because up until this moment she'd been convinced he thought of her as an irritating burden.

Braedan smirked. 'You don't need me to dish out compliments. I bet you hear them all the time.'

She kicked a stone and watched it skitter along the road in front of them. 'I can't remember ever hearing a compliment about myself,' she said quietly.

She heard Braedan huff out a breath and she thought he wasn't going to say anything further. Then he surprised her.

'You're kind, resilient, hard-working…tough when you need to be and soft when it's appropriate—like when you were playing with those children.' He ran his fingers through his hair and added, 'Any man would be proud to have you as his daughter.'

He picked up his pace a little and she had to scurry along to keep up with him. She pondered his words as his long legs ate up the countryside with ease. His description of her hadn't been mere empty praise. He'd picked up on traits about her that she was sure no one else had noticed, but about which she was most proud.

'You're kind too,' she said, when they'd walked so far she could no longer see the crossroads they'd left behind.

He gave a bark of laughter. 'No one has ever called me *kind*. I'm The Beast, remember.'

She stopped in shock. 'You know people call you that?'

'Yes,' he said, without breaking his stride.

'Do you mind?' she asked, catching up with him quickly.

'Mind? No, it's appropriate, isn't it?' He gestured to his face.

'What do you mean?'

'The scars on my face make me look like a hideous beast. I'm told that parents warn their children to go to bed when they're told, just in case The Beast comes and gets them. I'm the stuff of nightmares.' He smiled without humour.

Ellena stumbled on a stone and he grabbed her to stop her falling to the ground. His hand was warm through the layers of her clothes. She felt a pang that could only be disappointment when he let go.

'I don't think it's your face that's given you the name,' she said, when they were walking again. 'I think it's your reputation as a fearsome warrior.'

'Ah, but you're being kind again. There are men equally as fierce as me, but without hideous scarring like mine. They all have heroic names, like "The Spear Lord", or something just as ridiculous.'

She giggled. 'The Beast sounds better. It's a lot fiercer. No one would quake in their boots if they thought The Spear Lord was laying siege to their castle. But, honestly, your scars aren't hideous or scary.'

She didn't know why, but she thought it was important that he know this.

'My own mother can't bear to look at my face any more,' he said, keeping his gaze fixed on the road ahead of them.

Was it her imagination or was he walking even faster than before?

'Perhaps she feels guilty?' suggested Ellena as her legs moved quickly to keep up with him.

'Guilty?'

'Yes. She didn't stop your father when he made those silly decisions. If she had then you would still have a castle and lands to run and you wouldn't have to fight for your living. I expect she feels terrible. I wouldn't give your face another thought—you're an attractive man and your scars don't take that away from you.'

He stopped so quickly that she crashed into him. He turned and caught her against his chest to stop her from falling. She stepped back slightly before she could enjoy leaning against his solid body too much. He let her move away, but he still held on to her arms.

She was so close she could see his pulse beating at the base of his neck and a few red hairs scattered through his beard. Slowly she raised her eyes to meet his. She couldn't read the expression on his face. For a long moment she thought he was going to kiss her again, and she couldn't tell if she wanted him to or not. She didn't pull away.

Without warning, he let go of her and strode off. 'Come on,' he called over his shoulder. 'We don't want to miss our evening meal, do we?'

They didn't speak for the rest of the afternoon.

Another taproom and another lonely ale. Braedan scrubbed his face and then dropped his hands to his knees. He should be thinking about this mission and keeping watch for any sign of Copsi and his men, but he wasn't.

She thought he was kind and she thought he was attractive. Marriages were often formed on less than that. He dropped his face into his hands again. He must not think like this.

He straightened and again began to tick off the reasons why he should not: she was the Earl of Ogmore's daughter, the King's niece and the woman he was about to betray. He would never be able to marry her.

But, his mind tormented him, *you could marry her tomorrow.*

There would be nothing Ogmore could do about it, short of having him killed—which would be a distinct possibility but might be worth it. Death would be a reasonable price to pay for the few days of bliss he was sure he would experience if Ellena became his wife.

He hung his head. He wasn't good enough for Ellena and he knew it. The fact that he wanted to be, more than anything, alarmed him.

The sooner this mission was over the better. She would be married and he would be living in Castle Swein. Their paths would never cross again.

He rubbed his chest where an unpleasant ache had started up and downed his tankard. It was time to get another drink.

Much later he stood up and realised he'd had too much ale when the room swayed alarmingly. *Damn it.* She was messing with his mind. He never became drunk—not even when he was off duty. There was always potential danger lurking and he needed to have his wits about him.

He stumbled up the stairs to their room. He wished he'd rented two but the possibility of something happening to her during the night was so high he wanted to be with her.

He snorted. As if that was the only reason he wanted to be in the same room as her! He might as well be honest with himself, even if he wasn't being so with her. The truth was he hated being parted from her. When they weren't together she was all he could think about. He worried about whether she was safe or whether she had enough to eat.

Those three days when he'd been forced to ride behind the cart had been torturous. He'd missed watching the many varied expressions that crossed her face and he'd longed for a conversation with her—even one in which she was trying to give him orders—just so he could see the emotions shining out of her eyes. He was pathetic.

He paused outside the bedroom door and took a deep breath. He might have had too much to drink but he mustn't act out of character. She must never know how deeply he cared for her.

He groaned as he entered the room. For the last two nights she'd been insisting that he take his turn sleeping on the bed. He should have known something was up when she hadn't protested this evening. She was curled up in a makeshift nest of covers and pillows in a corner of the room. The bed lay temptingly free.

He crept over to her. She looked so young and vulnerable in her sleep. Gone was the stubborn lady who gave orders throughout the day, to be replaced by a soft woman who had curves in all the right places. He'd got used to her short hair now, and although he'd admired the long, luxurious locks he had to admit he enjoyed being able to see more of her now the hair was gone.

Even though the room was dark he could see her long, graceful neck and the way her lips were parted as she breathed softly in and out.

He bent down and scooped her up. He was taking so much from her. He was damned if he was going to take her bed as well.

Ellena awoke to find she was airborne. She should have known Braedan wouldn't let her lie on the floor, but she'd hoped he would see sense.

'What are you doing?' she asked. 'Put me back at once.'

'No, you must sleep on the bed,' was his stubborn reply.

She smelt the sweet smell of ale on his breath and wrapped her arms around his neck as he stumbled over one of the satchels lying on the floor.

'Sorry,' he muttered.

'Are you drunk?'

'No,' he said as he arrived at the bed. 'I'm never drunk.'

He dumped her on the bed, but she held onto his neck and he fell down next to her.

She scrambled to the edge and slipped off. 'You're on it now,' she said. 'Stay there.'

'No.' He reached up and pulled her back. 'The bed is yours.'

For a moment she wrestled with his arm, trying to break free of his hold, but although he didn't hurt her, she realised she was not going to get out of his iron grip.

'Stop squirming,' he muttered, clearly irritated by her efforts.

She gave up and collapsed back on the bed. She was

breathing heavily, whereas he sounded no different from normal. He kept his arm locked around her, holding her in place.

'Why are you so stubborn?' she asked, kicking the bed in frustration.

'Hah—it is not me who is stubborn. It is you.'

As his breath whispered over her skin she smelt ale again. She'd never noticed drink affect him before, but maybe he had drunk more tonight. Since that morning in the hut he'd kept his physical distance from her, but now she was cocooned in his arm and he wasn't moving away.

There was no pain in the way he held her; instead there was a strange sense of security that would have felt almost peaceful if it hadn't been for the frisson of desire sweeping through her. Lord Swein had been particularly vicious when he was drunk, but for some reason she wasn't afraid of Braedan. He'd only ever tried to protect her, and she trusted him to do the same even now.

She turned slightly, so that she could look at him. 'If I promise not to touch you again will you share the bed with me?' she asked.

'Why would I want you to promise such a thing?' he asked, sounding very shocked.

'The other morning…in the hut… I took advantage of you. You were angry with me for doing so but I promise it won't happen again.'

He looked at her for a long moment, and then he threw back his head and laughed and laughed.

She'd never seen him so amused, but as he was laughing at her she didn't really enjoy the sight.

'Oh, sweet, lovely Ellena—you didn't take advantage of me. I was very, very willing to kiss you, and I would so again in a heartbeat if I thought it was a good idea. But it isn't. It's a terrible idea...truly terrible.'

Her heart started to race. He wanted to kiss her and he was pulling her towards him. Perhaps he would do so, despite his ominous words. Maybe he would even take it further. Perhaps the whole thing wouldn't be so horrible if it was with someone as considerate as Braedan. Mrs Webb certainly seemed to enjoy her marital bed.

She held her breath as Braedan curled his large body around hers.

'Ah, Ellena,' he whispered. 'I wish I was good enough for you... I really do.'

She waited for his lips to meet hers, but was greeted with the soft sound of his snores.

'Braedan?' she whispered. 'Braedan...'

But she didn't get any response. He was already asleep.

Chapter Nine

A shard of light broke through the shutters and hit Ellena square in the face. She squeezed her eyes tightly as
she woke, wishing the morning would go away and leave
her alone. She was so tired. She rolled over, away from
the bothersome light, and hit something solid.

Her eyes snapped open.

She was in bed with Braedan.

She stared at his chest for a long moment and then
slowly, ever so slowly, looked up and met his gaze.

His eyes were wide and he was staring at her un-
comprehendingly. He looked even more owl-like than
he normally did when he woke.

Her lips twitched. 'Do you have a sore head?' she
whispered.

He touched his skull. 'No. Why? Have I been knocked
out?'

She smiled. 'You drank a bit too much ale, I think.'

'Oh.' He paused. 'I didn't…?' He stopped and looked
the length of her. When he saw she was fully dressed he
sagged into the bed. 'I didn't do anything inappropriate, did I?' he asked.

His look of bashful remorse made her want to wrap her arms around him.

'No,' she said. 'You didn't do anything. We argued about who was going to sleep on the bed and then compromised by both sleeping here. It was fine.'

He brought his hand up to his face and rubbed his eyes. 'Good,' he said. 'And I'm sorry I had too much ale. I've not done that since I was a young lad.'

She slipped out of bed, 'I'll fetch you a drink of water. I'm sure you're feeling thirsty.'

'How do you know?' he asked, pulling himself up into a sitting position. 'You don't strike me as someone who drinks too much.'

She smiled as she pulled on her boots. 'I've never been drunk but Lord Swein was—frequently. In the mornings he always had a raging thirst.'

'I wouldn't describe my thirst as "raging", but... I would be grateful for a drink, thank you.'

'Ellena?' he said when she reached the bedroom door.

She paused.

'Be careful.'

She nodded and let herself out onto the landing, closing the door softly behind her. When she was alone she took a deep breath and let it out slowly.

Things were getting complicated with Braedan. He didn't seem to remember what he'd said to her last night, when he'd all but told her he had feelings for her. But even if he remembered, what exactly did she feel for him?

She twirled his large signet ring around on her finger. It had been there since he'd given it to her on that first day they had begun to run for their lives. She was used to its heavy weight now and didn't relish the idea of taking it off.

She began slowly to climb down the stairs. In the end it didn't matter if they cared about each other more than they should. If her father wouldn't let her run Castle Swein by herself then he was unlikely to let her marry someone of her own choosing.

She pushed the thought out of her mind—she was getting carried away. Braedan had said he wanted to kiss her, but that was very different from wanting to spend the rest of his life with her. Besides, she never wanted to marry again, did she? Being in close proximity with Braedan was messing with her mind. She needed some time alone, to get things back into perspective. She was going to be in charge of her own destiny from now on.

Ellena paused at the bottom of the stairs. The inn was so quiet she could hear her own breathing in the stillness. Most of the inhabitants must still be abed, and she knew that Braedan would want to get going before most of them were awake. Everyone had got a good look at them yesterday, so he'd not want any of them to know where they were headed this morning.

She made her way down the narrow corridor and went to push open the door to the taproom. Something about the voice she heard through the thick wood made her stop.

'It's a delicate situation,' said the voice, which sounded hauntingly familiar. 'So I hope I can rely on your discretion?'

She heard a murmur of agreement.

'I'm looking for my wife,' the person continued. 'She's run away with a man and I believe they are posing as a married couple. I don't blame my wife, so you mustn't worry that you'd be getting her into trouble. But the man she's with is very dangerous and manipulative, and although I'm sure he's promised her all sorts of things I know he's only after my money. I'm afraid he'll hurt her to get it.'

Goosebumps broke out over the back of Ellena's neck as a creeping sense of dread washed over her.

'There are several married couples staying here at the moment,' she heard the innkeeper respond. 'Perhaps you could describe your wife?'

'It would be easier to describe the man. You see, he is very distinctive in that he has several facial scars. One thick one that cuts…'

Ellena had heard enough. She spun on her heel and raced back up to the room.

She barged in without knocking and found Braedan with his top half bare as he rinsed himself in the basin of water.

'Urgh…' she grunted, momentarily robbed of speech.

The muscles of his chest rippled as he pulled on some clothes, covering himself. Even in the direness of their situation she was disappointed.

'What's the matter?' he demanded.

'Man. Downstairs. Think Copsi. Must run,' she managed to get out as she rushed over to the sideboard and began to throw a few things into one of the bags.

He took two steps towards her. 'Say that again—slowly.'

She took a deep breath and said, quickly but more coherently, 'I went downstairs and heard a man speaking to the innkeeper. The voice sounded familiar. I'm not sure, but I think it might have been Copsi.'

She carried on moving about the room, checking that she'd not missed anything to add to the pack.

'He said he was looking for his wife and the man she'd run away with. When he described the man he said that he was distinctive because he had certain scars on his face. The voice sounded familiar. I didn't wait to hear more.'

'Right,' said Braedan, taking the bag from her and picking up the other one from the floor. 'Let's go.'

They hurried out of the room, with Braedan in the lead. He stopped abruptly at the top of the stairs and Ellena only just managed not to smack into the back of him.

'Someone's coming,' he whispered.

He turned and gently pushed her along the landing. Instead of going into their room he opened one several doors along and gestured for her to go in.

'How did you know there was no one in here?' she asked quietly as they stepped inside.

Braedan strode over to the window. 'I always check who's staying where at every inn we stop at.'

Ellena pressed her ear to the door as Braedan unlatched the shutters covering the window. She heard two sets of footsteps walking along the landing.

'Oh,' she heard the innkeeper say. 'They must have left already.'

She heard Copsi speak. 'I'd like to look in the other rooms, in case they're hiding. You don't know how dangerous this man is—he could have hurt someone by now.'

'I don't think going into other guests' rooms is appropriate,' said the innkeeper.

Some coins must have changed hands, because after

a brief silence the innkeeper said, 'Ah, well, I'm sure everyone will understand.'

'Ellena!' whispered Braedan.

She hurried over to the window. 'They're about to start searching the rooms,' she told him.

'Then we'd better hurry.'

He flung a leg out through the small space and she peered below. Their bags lay on the ground, which seemed to be an awfully long way down.

'Braedan,' she whispered. 'I don't think I can do this.'

He took her face in his hands. 'I know that you can.'

She closed her eyes and felt tears start to form and then spill onto her face. She felt him brush them away with his thumbs and then, very lightly, she felt his lips brush against hers.

'Come on,' he said softly. 'I'll show you what to do— and don't worry. I will catch you.'

She watched as he swung both his legs out of the window and then turned to hold onto the windowsill and lower himself to the ground. He jumped the rest of the way down and landed easily.

Her whole body began to shake as she slipped her feet over the edge of the window frame. Her breathing began to come in short, sharp gasps as she lowered herself over the edge. She clung to the window ledge and sweat broke out across her hands.

'It's all right—you can let go,' came Braedan's reassuring voice from below.

'I can't...' she whimpered.

'Yes, you can. Please hurry. I promise I will catch you. Trust me.'

She held her breath, scrunched her eyes shut and unclenched her fingers.

She briefly felt the wind rush past her cheeks before she landed in Braedan's arms with a thud. He quickly set her on her feet, keeping her within his arms.

'I'm sorry we don't have time for you to regain your equilibrium,' he said into her hair. 'But we must go before Copsi finds us.'

She nodded against his chest and after a few moments he let her go. But instead of going to the front of the inn, as she'd anticipated, he headed towards the stables.

'Where are we going?' she asked in a loud whisper.

'Copsi has probably brought his horse with him. I think we should slow him down while speeding ourselves up, don't you?'

'We're going to take his horse? But then won't he know that the couple was definitely us?'

'I think our disguise is well and truly ruined already,' said Braedan, entering the stables. 'Next time we stop anywhere I'll have to hide my face.'

There was only one horse in the stables. It was a dark-haired stallion with white markings and an impressive saddle.

'This is Copsi's,' said Braedan, opening the stall door and gently rubbing the horse's nose. 'I recognise him from various run-ins we've had. He's an impressive animal.'

Braedan whispered sweet nothings into the horse's ear as he led him from the stables and out towards the main thoroughfare of the town. Before they reached the road Braedan climbed into the saddle and pulled Ellena up after him.

'Copsi is bound to have men waiting outside,' said Braedan. 'So although in an ideal world we would sneak out of here unnoticed, we're actually going to race as fast as we can. We'll make a scene, but that can't be helped.'

'That tactic didn't work out so well for us back at the bridge,' she said, feeling her heart start to hammer so hard against her ribcage she half expected it to leap out.

'We got out of there alive, didn't we?' said Braedan. 'I think we can rate that as a success.'

Ellena knew how much he missed Stoirm; he seemed to have an affinity with horses. She guessed that Braedan was trying to distract her from her worry rather than truly believe they would make it unscathed.

Without giving her further time to prevaricate, he kicked Copsi's horse into action and pelted onto the street. They were already going at a gallop by the time they raced past the inn's entrance.

Ellena heard Copsi yelling, 'Stop them!' as the wind flew past their faces and the speed pushed her further back into Braedan's lap.

They were out of the market town and heading into open countryside when she heard the sound of many hoof beats following them. Braedan's heavy breathing sounded in her ears. She thought he gave a grunt of pain, but he didn't slow the horse.

'You can't run forever,' screeched Copsi over the loudness of the rushing wind. 'I will catch her and she will be mine.'

Still Braedan didn't slow.

Ellena could tell he was aiming for the woodland. She wanted to tell him to go a different way. The thought of being amongst claustrophobic trees again made her breath come in short, frightened puffs, but she couldn't see where else they could hide.

He thundered into the shelter of the trees and slowed the horse down.

'Is the horse hit?' she asked as she tried to twist around and take a look.

'No,' he said, holding her in position. 'I just need to get my bearings and then we'll be off again.'

She waited in silence as she felt him shift in the saddle. Then they were off again, leaping over fallen logs and narrowly avoiding colliding with low-hanging branches.

By the time they slowed the morning was well over and they hadn't heard the sounds of anyone following them for a long time.

'Do you think we're safe?' she asked.

'For now,' he said. 'But I think we should avoid stopping in towns from now on.'

Ellena sagged in her seat but didn't comment. Now that they had a horse it should only take a day or two before they reached the sanctuary of her father's castle, where they would be safe from Copsi. But then a whole new set of trials would begin.

They let the horse walk slowly for a little while longer, but it soon became apparent that the animal was exhausted.

'We should make camp,' said Ellena when they came to a small clearing.

'Mmm...' said Braedan.

'Are you all right?' said Ellena, suddenly realising that Braedan was leaning on her more than she was leaning on him.

'I've been hit,' he said.

'What?' she twisted round in the saddle.

Braedan's face was pale, and sweat coated his forehead, but he wasn't bleeding from his skull, so Ellena looked down.

'Oh, no!' she gasped when she spotted an arrow protruding from his arm. 'Why didn't you say something earlier?'

'We needed to get away. Besides, I think it is only a flesh wound. It'll be fine once we get it out.'

'Only a flesh wound! There's an *arrow*! In your *arm*!'

He didn't seem to grasp the gravity of the situation.

'I've had worse,' he murmured.

'I'm sure you have—but not when you were with someone who doesn't have the first clue how to deal with injuries.'

He smiled wanly. 'It's not like you're going to have to cut off my arm. I'll tell you what to do. It'll be fine. We should get off the horse first, though.'

He swung his leg over and dropped to the ground. He tried to hide it but she saw the wince of pain he gave as he planted his feet on the ground. Stupid, stubborn man.

He held up a hand to help her dismount, but she ignored it and dropped inelegantly to the ground without touching him.

'Right—what do you want me to do?' she asked, keeping her eyes away from the arrow. It made her feel queasy just thinking about it.

'Let's have a look through Copsi's saddle bags and see if we can find anything that will help make a shelter,' said Braedan.

'But what about your arm?' she argued.

She didn't want to wait too long before she dealt with it. She might lose her nerve.

'A shelter is the priority. I may not be able to do anything once you've taken the arrow out.'

She busied herself on the other side of the horse, so that Braedan couldn't see her face. She didn't know how he was being so calm about the situation. She wanted to cry, but whether that was because he was hurt or because she had to deal with it she wasn't sure.

Tears pricked her eyes and she brushed them away angrily. She didn't want to care for Braedan at all, but he was making it very difficult. She'd found herself wondering today how she was going to do without him when she returned to Castle Swein. She might never see him again, and instead of feeling relieved by the thought her heart felt as if it would shatter.

'I've found something,' called Braedan, jerking her back to their current predicament. 'Come and help me pull it out.'

She found him trying to pull a large, folded piece of cloth from a saddle bag, only using one hand.

'Here—let me,' she said, taking it from him. 'What do you think it is?'

'It's some kind of shelter. Did you find anything?'

'Only some food and a few blankets,' she said.

'Ah, you'll be all right, then,' he grinned at her.

'Are you in any pain at all?' she demanded, feeling a flicker of annoyance running through her.

Why wasn't he taking the situation seriously? He was hurt, and because of that they were in more danger than they had been at any point before. Besides that, she didn't feel like making jokes; she was going to have to deal with the blood and the gore, after all.

If it had been her arm with an arrow poking out of it she'd be passed out on the floor from the shock.

'It does hurt—but as I said, I've had worse. Now, come on, let's get this sorted.'

Braedan took the material back from her and tried to shake it out by himself, but with only one arm all he succeeded in doing was creating a tangled heap of cloth. Ellena took it off him and shook it out herself, giving him one corner when it was smooth.

'Now what?' she asked when they stood with the sheet stretched out between the two of them.

'If we drape it over these two trees it should form a rudimentary shelter.'

'Hmm…' she murmured, unconvinced.

She heard him muttering curses as they wrestled with the covering. The end result did not look good. The cloth sagged in the middle and draped across the forest floor at the edges. She lifted a corner and wriggled underneath. There were no gaping holes that she could see and, although small, the space would allow them both to lie down. It was better than nothing, but not by much.

She wriggled back out and found Braedan sorting through firewood. She rifled through all the saddle bags they had, trying to find all the blankets she could.

'I'll get a fire going. And then, if you'd be so good as to remove the arrow, I'd appreciate it,' said Braedan conversationally.

Ellena stopped in the act of sorting out the bedding. 'Oh, yes, of course. I'll just pop the arrow out and then we'll have some dinner, shall we?'

Braedan laughed, the corners of his eyes crinkling in amusement. 'It'll be—'

'If you say "it'll be fine" again, I'm walking out of this camp and leaving you to deal with the arrow by yourself.'

Braedan smiled tightly and lowered himself down onto a boulder. 'I found some material you can use for bandages and put it over there.' He gestured to a pile of white cloths with his good arm. 'So let's get this over with so that you can stop worrying about it.'

'It's you who should be worrying,' she said, stepping tentatively towards him. 'I've never done anything like this before.'

He pulled one of his knives free from its sheath and handed it to her, handle first.

'You need to saw off as much of the wood from the shaft as you can—preferably all of it, although I know that will be difficult. Then push the arrowhead and whatever's left of the shaft through the flesh. Don't try and pull it out the way it went in as that will cause more damage.'

Ellena took the knife from him and stared at the wound. The arrow wasn't very deep, but no matter how she did this it was going to hurt him. She took a deep breath; if he was making a show of being brave then she would try too.

'Oh,' he said, as she brought the knife to the wood. 'And if you could do this without shaking I'd appreciate it.'

'I'm sure you would,' she said. 'But I can't guarantee anything.'

He barked out a laugh.

She grasped the shaft and began to saw.

No sound passed his lips but his jaw tightened with every action she made and sweat began to bead across his brow. Neither of them spoke until the shaft was completely cut in two.

'Would you like a rest?' she asked as she dropped the broken wood to the floor.

'No. Just do it.'

For a few short moments she just stared at the metal arrowhead. She'd done a reasonable job of cutting away the wood, but some of it still stood out and the rest of the arrow was beneath his skin. She didn't think she could push it out. The thought of hurting him further made her guts twist.

'Please, Ellena,' he whispered.

He turned slightly and looked up at her. His eyes were wide and pleading. It was not a look she'd seen on him before and she doubted anyone else ever had. He always looked so in command, in control of himself.

She studied his expression for a long moment and then nodded. She could do this. If he could endure the pain, then she could cope with helping him.

She swallowed and slowly pushed. His whole body went rigid and his jaw clenched tightly.

'Faster, please,' he ground out.

She gave the arrowhead a much firmer push and it came free from his body with a sickening sound.

He roared in agony and let out a string of swear words.

'I'm sorry… I'm sorry…' she said, over and over again, as he buried his head in his knees and rocked back and forth.

She didn't realise she was crying until he took her in his good arm and held her to his side. Kneeling on the ground before him, she sobbed and sobbed, with her arms wrapped around his waist and her face buried in the warmth of his neck.

He murmured comforting words until the tears slowed and eventually subsided completely.

'I'm so sorry,' she said again, against his skin.

'You have nothing to be sorry for.'

'I do. I'm crying all over you and you're the one who's hurt.'

He laughed and slowly released her.

'Oh, my goodness—that's a lot of blood,' she said as she caught sight of the fresh wound.

'You've gone very pale. Would you like to sit down?' he asked, a hint of laughter in his voice.

'No. Let me bind you up.'

She did very much want to sit down, but she pushed her own feelings to one side. She needed to be strong for him, and going weak at the sight of someone else's blood was pathetic and unlike her. She hadn't felt faint when she'd dealt with Eluard's wounds. It was something about Braedan being harmed which was upsetting her.

She took a deep breath and then tightly bound the wound with clean strips of linen. He winced several times, but didn't say anything. Behind his back she gagged several times as blood oozed over the bandages, coating her hands in sticky liquid.

'Do you mind if I lie down for a bit?' he asked when she'd finished.

'Of course not,' she said. 'I'll heat up some of that potage and then we can eat.'

He nodded, but didn't comment, so she set to warming up the food as best she could. It wasn't easy—they only had a small pot—but she managed to heat enough to almost fill two bowls.

She entered the shelter to find him lying on his back with his good arm flung across his eyes. He wasn't snoring softly, so she assumed he was still awake.

'The food's ready,' she whispered, just in case he wasn't.

He rolled into a sitting position. He looked pale, and there were dark shadows under his eyes.

'Do you need help eating?' she asked.

She didn't think he would accept. He was proud, after all. But it would be worse to sit still and let him try and fail to get food into his mouth.

He paused. 'No, thank you,' he said eventually.

She settled the bowl on the floor next to his good arm, and then sat on the blankets she'd put out for herself.

'Should I keep watch during the night?' she asked, as they slurped their way through the tasteless broth.

'No, we might as well both try and get some sleep. If Copsi and his men come across us now there's not a great deal we can do about it anyway.'

She shuddered and put her bowl down.

'Sorry, I didn't mean to upset you.'

'You didn't.'

He put his bowl down too. It looked as if neither of them was particularly hungry.

'Shall we try and get some sleep, then?' she asked.

'Mmm…' He rolled back onto the blankets and closed his eyes.

She lay down and tried to get comfortable. It was almost impossible. The blankets created only a small barrier between her and the unforgiving, lumpy ground beneath. The cold seeped through the thin layers, stealing into her bones and making her shiver. She pulled her cloak tighter around her but it didn't help.

If she was uncomfortable then Braedan must be in agony.

'Would you like some more covers?' she asked quietly.

Braedan took so long to answer she thought he might have done the impossible and fallen asleep.

'You never cease to surprise, Lady Swein,' he said eventually.

'In what way?' she asked sharply.

He let out a long breath and turned to look at her, rolling onto his good arm as he did so.

'I thought you were going to be like all the spoilt grand ladies I have met over the years—the ones who always think about themselves first and who are selfish and demanding. You are not like that at all.'

She turned on her side so that she was facing him. The black shadows under his eyes were stark, but there was something soft and warm in his expression. Something she'd not seen before, and it made her heart skip a beat.

'I thought you would be a lot more thuggish than you are in real life,' she told him.

He laughed. 'I am *very* thuggish. It's what my whole reputation is based on.'

For a long while they lay looking at one another. She wondered why he didn't turn away, but knew she was trapped in his warm gaze. She didn't know what was happening to her, or what it might mean, but here, right now, in a makeshift shelter, lying on lumpy ground, on the run for her life and fighting for her freedom, she felt content.

Chapter Ten

At some point she must have drifted off to sleep, because Ellena was awoken by pained grunting. It was very dark in the shelter, but as her eyes adjusted she could just make out Braedan. He seemed to be thrashing about in his sleep, in the midst of a horrifying nightmare.

He rolled onto his bad side and awoke with a hiss of pain.

'Are you all right?' she asked pointlessly.

Of course he wasn't. He was probably in agony—both physically and, by the sounds of things, mentally as well.

'No,' he ground out. 'I feel…awful.'

She reached out and touched his forehead. She was relieved to find that he didn't have a temperature. She had no idea how to deal with a fever in these primitive conditions. His skin was worryingly cold to the touch, though, and her own toes were feeling decidedly numb.

Without thinking about it too much, she rolled over to him, bringing her blankets with her. She flung them over him and then curled her arm around his waist as she nestled closer.

For a long moment he lay unmoving next to her, and

then slowly his good arm closed around her, cocooning her in a warm circle.

'I thought we could keep each other warm,' she whispered. 'Don't do anything that makes you feel uncomfortable.'

She didn't stress whether it would be physical discomfort or something else that her touch would bring. She knew better than anyone how horrific it was to feel an unwelcome touch.

'It feels better now,' was all he said.

He shifted slightly and it felt like the most natural thing in the world to lay her head on his chest. Beneath her his torso rose and fell steadily, and she listened to the reassuring thump of his heart.

After a while his hand stole into her hair and he began slowly to stroke the strands. As a child she had loved it whenever her mother had brushed her hair, but it had been years since she had been touched so gently. The movement was causing little shivers to run down her spine. She wondered if she could persuade Braedan to come back with her to Castle Swein with the express intention of lying with her just like this at the end of every day.

'Tell me about your life at Castle Swein,' said Braedan into the darkness.

'What do you want to know?'

'How is it that you are running things? Don't take offence,' said Braedan as she stiffened. 'I'm only asking because it is unusual.'

'It probably isn't that unusual,' she said tartly. 'I'm sure a lot of women run estates while their men take the credit.'

'Is that what happened in your case?'

Ellena scratched her nose and thought about how to answer. She could tell him the truth, or she could give him the version she'd shown to the rest of the world. For some reason she found she wanted to tell him everything. They had been through so much, and she'd had to trust him with her life time and time again. He'd never failed her or let her down. If he knew how hard she had worked perhaps he would put in a good word with her father. The Earl might not listen to her, but his most trusted warrior might be different.

'Lord Swein was a very different man from the personality he presented to my family. I knew he was a lot older than me before we married, but he seemed like a kind and considerate man. He wasn't.'

Braedan didn't comment. He continued to stroke her hair.

She brought her hand to his chest and followed the stitching on his tunic with her fingertips. She felt him suck in a breath as her hand dipped lower. She wanted to keep going, but instead brought her fingers back to his shoulder, where she rested her hand gently against his strong muscles so as not to disturb his bandages.

'I wasn't long into my marriage before I realised that Swein was lazy and cruel. The estate was in a terrible state. The castle itself was dirty and cold, and the people living there weren't being fed enough. He wouldn't invest in the fields around us and he taxed the villagers mercilessly. Many of them were living in abject poverty.'

She took a deep breath.

'I don't think he was very clever. He listened to some terrible advice when he was younger and lost a lot of money. He was very bitter about it, and took it out on everyone around him.'

'Did he hurt you?'

She paused. 'Yes.'

Braedan's arm stilled for a moment. She gently nudged his hand and he began to tease her hair once more.

'About four years into our marriage he became very sick and kept to his bed. His steward died not long after, and instead of engaging someone to take over I decided to save the money and do it myself. Within six months I'd turned the fortunes of the castle around. It took my husband four more long years to die, but fortunately for me, and for the rest of the castle's inhabitants, he was too ill to get out of bed and he never knew what I'd done.'

His fingers dropped to her neck and he began to gently massage the muscles there. Her whole body became boneless and she instinctively arched against his side.

'I didn't… I wanted children so I let him…' She cringed against Braedan, who tightened his arm around her. 'I let him do unimaginable things. When I didn't please him he would lock me in my room for days without food. Then he would start again. In the end it was all for nothing. I am barren anyway.'

Braedan's hands stilled and tears gathered at the corners of her eyes. She'd repulsed him with her talk about the marriage bed. She wondered how long she could stay in the comfort of his arms before it became awkward. She knew she should move if she'd made him uncomfortable, but she really didn't want to.

He cleared his throat. 'Did Swein have any other children?'

'What?' she asked, surprised by the question. She really hadn't thought that was how he would respond. 'No. His first wife wasn't blessed with them either.'

Braedan resumed massaging her neck and she gradually relaxed against him again.

'I know this is not a popular opinion,' said Braedan, 'but is it possible that it was Swein who couldn't have children and not you?'

She raised her head slightly to look at him. 'But that goes against...'

'I know.'

Braedan's hand stole back into her hair and she bit back a contented purr.

'Did Swein have other women?' he asked.

Ellena laid her head on Braedan's chest again. 'Yes,' she said quietly.

She'd known of at least two. He hadn't tried to hide it. At first it had been a source of pain, and then it had become a guilty relief. If he was bestowing his attentions elsewhere then he'd left her alone for a little while.

'Did they have any children?'

'No...'

Braedan didn't say anything further.

Hope unfurled within her. Hope that she'd buried so deeply she'd denied it even to herself. And then she shuddered.

'I don't think I will have children. Lord Swein put me off...' she waved her hand around '...you know.'

Braedan stilled and she tilted her head to look up at him.

'I am not like other men. I don't take any woman who offers herself to me. But I do have...' his gaze flickered to the roof of their shelter and then back to her '...some experience. Enough to know that it can, and should, be pleasurable to both people involved.'

She licked her lips and his gaze dropped to her mouth.

'When I kissed you, you seemed to like it,' he said into the darkness.

Heat washed over her face and she was glad there was no light in the shelter so that he wouldn't see. She returned her gaze to his chest so he couldn't see the look in her eyes.

'I did,' she whispered.

'So if you can enjoy that, then there is hope for you yet.'

'Lord Swein never kissed me, so he hadn't spoilt that for me.'

She felt him jolt in surprise beneath her.

'That was your first kiss?' he exclaimed.

'Yes.'

Braedan groaned and ran his fingers through his hair.

'Is that a problem?' she asked, confused by his re-action.

'Your first kiss should not have been on the floor of a broken-down hut. You deserve better.'

Ellena didn't know what to say. 'I didn't think you enjoyed it,' she whispered eventually.

He reached down and gently touched her cheek so that she tilted her face to his. 'What gave you that idea?'

'You ran away.'

He sighed softly. 'That wasn't because I didn't enjoy it. It was because I enjoyed it more than I should. It was absolutely the wrong thing for me to do. Much as it is now.'

He leant down and gently pressed his lips to hers.

She felt as if she had been waiting for this for days. His touch was like the warmth of a fire on freezing skin.

She stretched upwards and pressed her mouth firmly against his. The effect was instantaneous.

He deepened the kiss, sweeping his tongue into her mouth while his hand roamed down her back to the gentle curve at the base of her spine.

Soft moans filled the tent, and it was a while before she realised the noise was coming from her.

Her hands itched to explore his body, and when he moved his lips down her neck she felt emboldened. She ran her fingers along his jaw and then followed the length of his neck to the edge of his collarbone. Running her fingers underneath the material of his tunic, she felt the soft hair of his chest and the hard muscles underneath.

When his hand wrapped around her ankle she realised she had thrown her leg over his body. The feel of his skin against hers was breathtaking. Slowly, achingly slowly, his hand travelled up her leg, along her calf and to the back of her knee, his fingers leaving a trail of sensitised skin in their wake. Far from being repelled by his touch, she found that she wanted more. She longed to feel the whole of his body pressed against hers.

Mindful of his injury, she tugged at the top of his tunic, revealing more of his broad chest as she did so. He gasped as her hand played across his skin, and she thrilled at the knowledge that she was affecting him as much as he was her.

His hand passed over her thigh and she found herself tugging on the edge of her dress to make it easier for him. She thought he was going to touch her in the place where she ached most for him but he didn't. Instead he pulled his mouth away from hers.

Heavy breathing filled the air.

'We must stop,' he said, his voice gravelly and warm.

'Yes,' she agreed, trying to get her breathing back under control.

Stopping was the last thing she wanted to do. She wanted Braedan's body to banish all the bad times her own body had been through. Not once in all the time she had been married had she ever felt as she had over the last few incredible minutes.

'Just to be clear,' said Braedan thickly, 'I don't want to stop. But we must. I promised your father that I would protect you, and for us to go any further would betray his trust and my oath.'

'Yes,' she said again, because she didn't really know what else to say.

She hadn't seen her father in eight years. Sometimes it was difficult to remember what he was like. Mostly she relied on other people's reactions to the formidable man to form her memories. But right now the only man she could think about was the one half lying underneath her.

Despite his words, Braedan gently brought his mouth to hers again and kissed her softly. This time he trailed his hand back down her leg and gently rearranged her dress.

She almost moaned in disappointment when he finally took his mouth from hers. She only managed to stop herself by clinging to the last vestiges of her dignity.

'We should try and get some sleep,' he said softly.

She wanted to shout and scream at him. How could he be so calm? Wasn't his heart racing? Didn't he want to touch her all over, just as she wanted to touch him?

An icy chill washed over her. Perhaps he had just kissed her to be kind. After all, she had said how awful her life with Lord Swein had been and that she had enjoyed kissing Braedan. What if he'd just wanted to show her that being with someone could be pleasurable? He'd called their first kiss a mistake, after all.

She slowly removed her arm and her leg from his body. She kept the blankets over both of them and tucked herself as close to him as she could manage without actually touching him.

She didn't think she'd be able to sleep, but welcome oblivion fell upon her quickly.

Chapter Eleven

Braedan stared at the roof of their shelter. Light was coming through the fabric, which suggested morning had broken. Next to him Ellena slept soundly, her soft lips slightly parted.

He had barely slept at all.

He should get up and move away from the temptation she provided, but he couldn't. Although they weren't touching, he could feel the welcoming warmth of her body seeping across the small space between them. He wanted to tug her closer, so that she was half lying on him again. He wanted to feel the soft skin of her leg as he ran his hands along it, and this time he didn't want to stop when he reached her thigh.

In a day or two, unless any more disasters befell them, they would be back at Ogmore Castle and she would find out that the Earl of Borwyn was leading the race to become her next husband. She would also know that her father intended Braedan to take over the running of Castle Swein. She would hate him.

He swallowed. He wouldn't be able to bear it if her

large blue eyes, the only eyes that had ever seen him as more than The Beast, looked at him full of loathing.

She murmured something in her sleep and flung her arm around his waist. Awake, she'd probably prefer not to touch him. She'd certainly removed herself from him last night. But he couldn't bring himself to remove her touch. It felt so right to lie with her arms around him.

Even though he'd tried to tell her about his oath to Ogmore last night, she'd seemed to take his words as a rejection. If only she knew the truth. He wanted her more than he had any other woman. He'd faced death many times on the battlefield—so much so that he'd stopped fearing it—but he was afraid of the strength of his feelings for her.

He shifted and the movement woke her up. She snatched her arm back and pulled herself into a sitting position. Her expressive eyes homed in on the wound on his arm and a throbbing burning sensation flooded the forefront of his mind.

'How is your arm this morning?' she asked, her voice soft with sleep.

'It's fine,' he said, and was rewarded with a frown.

'It can't be fine. There was an arrow sticking out of it yesterday.'

He couldn't help but smile at her tone. He'd not had someone care about his wounds for as long as he could remember.

'It hurts a bit,' he conceded, and this time he was rewarded with a faint smile.

He was considering ramping up his response to claim that he was in agony, in order to see if that got him an even better reaction, but she beat him to it.

'You've had worse, though, of course?' She rolled her

eyes and flung back the blankets. 'We'd best get going. We're so close now I can almost smell the welcoming banquet my father is bound to insist upon.'

He almost believed she was really as cheerful about returning to her father's castle as she was making out. It was only the rigidity of her shoulders that gave her away.

She worked in silence, packing away the blankets and then unhooking their makeshift shelter from the branches. With only one arm he was useless in the folding of all the material, so he made his way over to Copsi's horse.

'What shall we call you, then, boy?' he said, stroking the stallion's long neck.

'How about Ffoi?' suggested Ellena from across the clearing. 'It means flee, which is something we've done a lot of in the last few days.'

He laughed. 'Ffoi it is, then. Let's hope he lives up to his name.'

'Is he rested enough for us to be going?'

'Aye, he's a good animal. Too good for the likes of Copsi. I think I'll keep him once this is all over.'

'Copsi certainly doesn't deserve him,' said Ellena as she attempted to tie a pack to Ffoi's saddle.

Braedan took the pack from her, his fingers brushing hers as he did so. He heard her quick intake of breath and longed to trail his fingers over the soft skin of her neck again. Instead he turned away and fixed the bundle to Ffoi's side.

By the time he turned back she was on the other side of the clearing, gathering up the rest of their supplies.

He made no attempt to get onto Ffoi. His arm burned and he thought the effort would make it worse.

'Shall I give you a leg up?' he asked her.

'Aren't you going to get on as well?'

'No, I'll walk alongside today.'

He hoped she wouldn't ask why. He didn't want to admit that his arm was hurting like the devil and show her just how weak he was feeling.

She nodded, but instead of accepting his proffered arm she led Ffoi over to a tumbled-down tree trunk and mounted the horse from there.

He sighed. From the set of her shoulders it was obvious she was annoyed with him again. Perhaps she thought his reluctance to get on the horse was because he didn't want to touch her, when nothing could be further than the truth.

'Do you have any idea where we are?' she asked as she nudged Ffoi into a slow walk along the narrow trail.

'Yes,' he said with confidence.

'You do?' She looked down at him with raised eyebrows.

'Yes, this is Hexham Woods. It's a two-day ride to your father's castle from here, depending on how fast we move. I've done several training exercises with my men along this path.'

'Oh,' she said, and the wind had clearly been taken out of her sails.

They walked for a while in silence.

'The second thing I'm going to do after I get to Ogmore is wash,' said Ellena eventually. 'I think I'll even burn these clothes—starting with this cloak. The fabric is so itchy.'

She scratched the skin of her arm irritably.

'What's the first thing?' asked Braedan, amused. 'No, don't tell me—the first thing you're going to do is eat.'

He grinned and she smiled in response. 'Yes, you've

guessed right. My mother's cook makes the most amazing seed cakes. I'm going to devour a whole trencher of them.'

She sighed in pleasure at the thought and Braedan's body tightened at the sound.

'What are you going to do?' she asked.

Braedan turned his head and looked deeper into the trees. He knew what he *wanted* to do as soon as he was back, but he also knew what he *had* to do.

'I expect I shall pay my respects to my mother and then I'll get back to work.'

He realised he sounded very dull in comparison to Ellena. Duty dictated that he must see his mother shortly after he returned, even though the meeting would be painful for both of them.

'You don't look as if you're thrilled by the prospect,' Ellena commented from high above him.

He thought about shrugging and ignoring the conversation, but within a couple of days they might never speak again, and there was something about her voice that soothed his soul.

He wouldn't tell her everything. His mother's increasingly erratic actions were something only his family knew about.

'My relationship with my mother is somewhat... strained,' he said eventually.

'You said as much before. Why do you think that is?'

Braedan kicked a log to move it out of the way, and watched as it disappeared into the undergrowth.

'I haven't lived with my mother since I was seven and started my knight's training. I only returned after my father's fall from grace. I think she was shocked by the way I'd turned out.'

'Are you referring to your scars again?' she asked, tilting her head towards him.

He shrugged. He didn't like to talk about his face. He hoped he wasn't a vain man, but he would rather look like Borwyn—the man intended for Ellena—than have his own battle-weary face. He rubbed his jaw. He'd never given much thought to his appearance before. Being with Ellena was making him want the impossible.

'I know you think she feels guilty, but I find that hard to believe,' he said, not commenting on his scars.

He didn't want to look as if he was fishing for compliments, even if everything in him ached to hear her tell him again that she thought he was attractive.

'My father's disgrace hit us all hard, but it hit her worst. She's used to a life of privilege—not being a poor dependant. She's constantly worrying that I'm going to dishonour the family name even further and that she'll be thrown out of your father's castle.'

He didn't want Ellena to know that his father's actions had sent his mother slightly mad, and that his sisters were suffering because without an estate he couldn't provide them with a suitable dowry. Without the money his stewardship of Swein would give him, there would be nothing he could do for them. If he told her that then he might end up telling her about her father's offer, and now was not the time he wanted her to find out.

He didn't know why he was telling Ellena any of it. He never discussed his family with anyone. But she was so easy to talk to. When he was with her his worries seemed to fade away until he wasn't The Beast any more. He was Braedan again. A young man who had been full of hope for the future before his father's actions had ruined his prospects and made him, in the eyes of the elite, no better than a rabid dog.

'Surely your actions over the last eight years have shown her otherwise?' Ellena commented primly.

Braedan smiled slightly, pleased she'd leapt to his defence. He'd often thought his deeds should have earned some merit with his mother, but nothing he'd done had improved their relationship or repaired the mind that his father had damaged. He'd given up trying to impress her.

'If I had a son,' Ellena continued, 'I would be proud of him no matter what.'

She would, thought Braedan. Ellena would make a good mother—protective, fierce and kind. He only hoped that Borwyn would be able to give her children she so thoroughly deserved.

He imagined a little girl with dark, rich hair and wide blue eyes like Ellena's...

It was only when his upper arm began to burn in pain that he realised he was clenching his fists. He slowly released his fingers. He was not going to be the man who gave her children and he needed to make peace with that fact. Even if by some miracle she wanted to marry him, she would quickly change her mind when she realised how badly he'd betrayed her. Besides, her father would never allow it, because Braedan had no useful land and was therefore useless.

He turned his head away from her and looked through the trees, as if he would find the answer to his problems in their gnarled roots. The wind picked up and rustled the branches, sending a shower of orange leaves to the floor.

A thought rubbed at the edge of his conscience. Perhaps he *should* tell her about her father's plans for her future. She would be angry with him for tricking her into leaving her castle, but it wasn't as if she could storm off back to Castle Swein by herself. They were so far away and the journey back would be fraught with danger.

If he told her the truth now she would have a few days to prepare for meeting her father. He owed her a fighting chance at least. He doubted anything she said would change her father's mind, so his future was probably secure. The Earl of Ogmore was a stubborn man. Once he'd made up his mind that something was going to happen he wouldn't veer from that path.

He turned his head to look at her and caught her gazing at him. Their eyes locked and the breath was knocked out of him. She was so beautiful, and the look in her eyes was unmistakable. The knowledge that his mother was repelled by him had upset her. She cared for him.

The thought almost brought him to his knees.

He couldn't tell her the truth.

He couldn't bear to see the light in her eyes die as she realised how he'd betrayed her. The knowledge that he'd tricked her into leaving her castle would be bad enough, but when she found out his reward was to be stewardship of Castle Swein she would truly hate him.

She'd find out once they reached Ogmore, but by then he would be busy with his own duties and their paths wouldn't cross. The fact that this was the coward's way out didn't sit well with him, but if it gave him a couple more days of her looking at him like that then he'd take it.

'Ellena, I...' He stopped. He had no idea what he was going to say.

She smiled softly at him. 'Would you like to stop and

rest? Your arm must be hurting you, even though you pretend otherwise.'

No one had ever cared about his welfare. He was always the one everyone else turned to.

He cleared his throat. 'I'm fine. I don't need to rest. Keep going.'

She frowned and turned away from him, and he instantly regretted his harsh response. But it was better to speak to her this way—better for her in the long run if she thought of him as The Beast, a cold, unfeeling brute of a man who didn't need or want people's compassion.

They passed the rest of the morning in silence, only stopping briefly to eat a few dry oatcakes before pressing on. He walked beside the horse, his throbbing arm not as painful as the thoughts continuously circling in his mind.

'I need to stop,' said Ellena abruptly.

He glanced at the sky. 'It's too early. We'll keep going for a while yet. If we keep up this pace we should be able to reach Ogmore by the end of tomorrow.'

'No,' she said, colouring slightly. 'I don't need to stop for long. I just want to…' She nodded to the trees.

'Oh, I see.' He felt his own skin heat and he frowned. He was a grown man and a hardened warrior; he shouldn't get embarrassed by bodily functions.

She pulled Ffoi to a stop and slipped quickly out of the saddle to the ground. 'I'll be quick,' she said, not looking at him as she handed him Ffoi's reins.

He watched as she disappeared into the dense forest. Should he have gone with her to check she wasn't going to run away? He shook his head. He was being fanciful. She didn't know what awaited her at her father's castle. Just because he was a bore to be around, it didn't automatically mean she would try and escape his company. She didn't give up that easily.

Ffoi snorted impatiently. It seemed he didn't like waiting even for a few seconds. It was a feeling Braedan could relate to. He led the horse a few paces further down the path until he reached a bend. He didn't like to wander out of sight from where Ellena had disappeared into the treeline, but Ffoi was reluctant to turn around. He tugged on the reins and clicked impatiently at the animal, but Ffoi couldn't be budged.

The silence of the forest pressed in on Braedan from every side. He shifted on his feet. The sooner they were off this path the better.

Something stirred behind him and the hairs on the back of his neck stood up. He dropped Ffoi's reins and rested his hand on the hilt of his sword.

'Well, well, look who it is,' came a sneering voice from behind him.

Braedan turned slightly to find two of Copsi's men silently making their way towards him. They must have been waiting up ahead, hoping he and Ellena would come this way.

His eyes quickly swept the area around him but nothing else moved. It appeared the men were alone, but he couldn't be sure. His heart began to slam loudly in his chest. What if their companions had already discovered Ellena? They could be doing anything to her while he stood here with the damned horse.

He forced his breathing to remain calm. He could do nothing until he'd dealt with these two.

The men before him were smug at having found him, but they weren't crowing about finding Ellena. If he was lucky then they had made a mistake in not waiting to see whether Ellena was with him. Hopefully she'd hear them talking and stay hidden in the forest until this was over. The last thing he needed right now was her stumbling into the middle of this.

'Where's Lady Swein?' asked the taller of the two.

His shoulders relaxed as they confirmed his theory. Ellena was safe for now.

'She's not with me,' he said, even as he observed the men, searching for their weak points.

They were wiry and muscled but unkempt and raggedy. They weren't soldiers, then. It wouldn't take long for him to defeat them both, so long as he kept them focused on him and not on Ellena's disappearance.

The taller man grinned. 'Of course she isn't. So it doesn't matter, then, does it? We can kill you and even if she's not hiding nearby then we've still done everyone the favour of getting rid of Ogmore's favourite guard dog. And if we kill you and she *is* hiding nearby... Well, Copsi doesn't mind what condition we return her in, so long as she's alive long enough to say her vows.'

He licked his lips suggestively and his companion grunted in amused agreement.

Braedan tightened his grip on his sword. He was going to enjoy running it through these two. Even with his injured arm, these goons were no match for him.

His opponents drew their swords. Even though he was more than capable of fighting them both at once, the path was too narrow for him to do so. He'd have to defeat them one-on-one: easy.

The taller man grinned and stepped forward. Before he had a chance to strike Braedan used his sword to knock the man's weapon out of his hand. Startled, the man leapt back and his friend took his place.

Braedan's wound began to burn as he thrust and parried, looking for a way to beat the second opponent, who was a worthier adversary than his companion.

Braedan nicked the man's jaw, but he retaliated and cut through Braedan's tunic. Sweat began to pool at the base of Braedan's spine. His weakened arm was making things harder, but he still wasn't worried he would lose. He did want this over with quickly, though, so he could get Ellena away from any danger.

He forced his opponent to stagger backwards a few steps and then followed up with several large strikes towards the chest. A look of fear crossed the other man's face as Braedan closed in on him.

From out of the forest a whirling blur rushed towards the fight.

Braedan's heart stopped as Ellena charged, a large stick clutched in her slender arms. She swung the stick at the man he was fighting and it connected with his head. The man crumpled instantly, leaving him with only one opponent.

Ellena whirled to face the remaining man, but then her fiery passion seemed to fall away and she hesitated. In that heart-stopping moment the man realised he had the upper hand and advanced towards her.

Moving more quickly than he'd ever thought possible, Braedan brought the hilt of his sword up against the side of the man's face. He staggered forward a few steps before collapsing next to his fallen comrade.

Braedan strode to them and relieved them of their swords, checking methodically for other weaponry as he did so.

'Did I kill him?' asked Ellena, her calm voice undermined by her trembling fingers and pale face.

'No, you merely knocked him unconscious,' said Braedan, straightening and marching over to Ffoi.

His arms were vibrating with barely suppressed anger. He led the animal over to Ellena and unceremoniously threw her up into the saddle. The pain in his arm dulled as adrenaline rushed through him.

'What the hell were you thinking?' he growled as he vaulted up behind her. 'What sort of imbecile attacks a sword-wielding man with a stick?'

He kicked Ffoi into a gallop and they thundered down the path.

'I was saving you!' shouted Ellena over Ffoi's hoof beats.

'*Saving* me? You nearly got us both killed.'

'I did no such thing. If it wasn't for me you'd be lying dead in a ditch—and where would that leave me? Stranded in a forest, goodness knows where, without any idea how to get to my father's home.'

His grip tightened on the reins. 'I'm sorry that my death would have inconvenienced you so much, but as it happens I had the situation under control.'

He felt her snort of disbelief.

'I was just about to deal a cutting blow when you erupted out of the forest like a madwoman. If that other man had been paying even the slightest bit of attention he would have cut you down like a twig.'

A wave of fear washed over Braedan as he imagined her pale and lifeless at the feet of those men. He knew then that he'd rather die than let anything like that happen to her. He groaned. This was a complication in his life that he did not need.

Ellena continued to argue. 'I was watching from the

wood. You weren't winning. You were tiring. You're injured. I wasn't going to let them gut you like a pig.'

'I was *not* tiring,' he ground out.

Not only had she put herself in unnecessary danger, she had also insulted him—and yet he still knew he'd risk his life a thousand times over rather than let her come to even the tiniest amount of harm.

He was a fool.

He felt her shrug against the fabric of his tunic and anger finally won out over his fear. He wanted to grab her and shake her and yell at her until she understood just how stupid her actions had been. But first he had to get her to safety.

He rode Ffoi hard, and as dusk began to fall he pulled the horse off the path and made his way to an abandoned crofter's cottage he'd used before while on training exercises.

He slowed Ffoi to a walk and led him over to a structure meant for livestock. Jumping from the horse, he loosely tied the reins to a post before pulling Ellena down to join him on the ground. Her body briefly brushed against his, but he stepped away before desire could take over. He needed to make her understand how much danger she'd been in today, and get a promise from her that she'd never put herself in danger again.

He strode into the cottage, tugging her along behind him and ignoring her muttered protests.

The single-room cottage had been swept clean since its last usage, but it still smelt of dust and old fires. He didn't care.

He strode to the centre of the room before turning to face her. 'Don't ever do something like that again,' he ground out.

'I will do whatever I want to keep myself safe,' she countered, thrusting her chin towards him and not backing down an inch.

He growled. 'You will promise me that you will not put yourself in harm's way again or I will tie you up and drape you over the back of the horse like a sack.'

She stamped her foot. 'I will not! You think you're so high and mighty, but you're not. You're nothing but a...'

She floundered and he took a step towards her. Her eyes were shining with anger and her hair was wild, with twigs and goodness knew what else stuck in it, and her cheeks were flushed with colour. She had never looked so magnificent.

'Nothing but a what?' he asked quietly, taking another step towards her.

'A...'

He raised an eyebrow.

'A foolish man,' she finished, and tilted her head up defiantly.

He barked out a laugh. 'That's rich, coming from someone without an ounce of sense in her.'

She spluttered indignantly. 'Do you know what your problem is?' she asked, prodding his chest with her finger. 'You're so used to having your own way you can no longer admit when you're wrong.'

'*You* were wrong today, not me—and stop prodding me!' He finished the sentence in a roar as her finger jabbed at his chest again.

She stared at him defiantly, and then slowly and deliberately brought her hand up and prodded him once more.

He snarled and grabbed her roughly around the waist, pulling her towards him.

She gasped in surprise and looked up at him, her

cheeks still flushed in anger. She opened her lips as if to protest and he swooped, bringing his mouth down to hers and silencing any further argument by kissing her.

All his anger and fear were poured into the action and she met his passion with a fervour of her own.

This was nothing like the sweet, gentle kisses they'd shared before. It was a blaze of lips and tongues and grasping hands.

Desire raged through him. He tugged off her cloak and it pooled by their feet. His hands swept down her back and over her rounded bottom. Her gasp of surprise whispered against his lips as he pulled her flat against his body, his desire evident against her stomach.

He didn't give her a second to think as he deepened the kiss further. Her fingers were in his hair and he growled in satisfaction. His desire wasn't all one-sided. He wanted to tear the clothes from her body and take possession of her, leaving her in no doubt as to whom she belonged.

He lifted his head to look down at her. Her eyes, half-closed, were glazed with passion, and her lips were plump and swollen from his kisses.

This was where he needed to stop.

The fingers in his hair brought his mouth back to hers and he was lost.

Gone were thoughts of his family's good name and his liege's commands. Gone was anything other than the feel of this woman in his arms right now.

He frantically pulled her dress over her head, keeping up a steady stream of kisses as he did so. The rest of her clothes went the same way. It said something about the power of her mouth that he didn't even raise his head to look at her naked body. Instead he allowed his hands to explore the soft skin of her back. She whimpered as his hands skimmed over the swell of her hips.

He nudged her over to the bed, her breathy moans filling his ears as he slowly trailed a hand over one peaked nipple and down over her abdomen until he reached the soft curls at the juncture between her thighs. It took all his willpower not to plunge his fingers into her, but even through the haze of his lust he remembered her comments about her late husband.

He would not be a brute.

He lowered them both gently onto the bed and she stiffened in his arms.

He softened his kisses and stroked her back in long, languid circles, until gradually her limbs relaxed against him again. Only then did he bring his hand to her breasts. Slowly he explored the sensitive skin. She arched against him as he swept his fingers across her nipples and he groaned.

He was lost for this woman. She was everything he'd ever wanted for himself. And if he couldn't have her forever then he'd at least have her for now.

His lips followed the trail his fingers had. Moving softly over the delicate skin of her collarbone and down over the swell of her breasts. She moaned as his tongue swirled around her left nipple while his right hand pinched the other.

Her fingers stole once more into his hair and held him in place and he groaned against her skin.

Slowly and tenderly his lips explored the rest of her body. She shuddered as he traced the curve of her ribs and ran his hand down the length of her leg.

A small scar crossed her left hip and he ran his tongue along its seam. He wanted to know every part of her body. He wanted to know what would make her sigh with pleasure and what would make her laugh out loud. He wanted everything.

'I…' she murmured, but whatever else she had been going to say was lost in a breathy moan as his fingers began to journey back up her leg, tickling the inside of her thigh.

She tensed as he brought his head lower, but he continued with gentle kisses across her skin.

Then his tongue licked her sensitive bud and her whole body arched off the bed.

'Oh!' she cried. 'What…?'

His tongue swooped and whirled and her fingers tightened in his hair. He smiled against her core as he did it again.

'Braedan… I… Oh…'

The warrior in him roared with the success of her surrender.

Her cries became breathless as his fingers joined his tongue in bringing her pleasure, gently at first and then with increasing pressure as she writhed across the bed, murmuring incoherently.

He stayed with her as she fell over the edge. And as the tremors gradually faded from her he trailed his lips back up her body until he pressed a gentle kiss against her mouth. Then he turned her slightly and tugged her back against him, so that his arms became a protective cocoon.

'What has happened to me?' she mumbled sleepily.

He kissed the soft skin of her neck. 'That's what it should be like between a man and a woman.'

'Now I see what the fuss is all about…' she muttered, her eyes closed and her body limp against his.

He huffed out a laugh. 'Indeed.'

'But what about you?' she asked, her eyes fluttering open. 'Don't you want…?' A delicate flush swept across her neck and face.

He gently stroked her arm. 'Sleep, my love. I'll be here when you wake.'

A small crease appeared between her eyes and he leaned over to touch her mouth with his once again.

'Don't worry about anything,' he said. 'You're safe now.'

He settled behind her and brushed her hair away from her face.

Her slow breathing gradually dropped into the heavier sound of a deep, dreamless sleep.

Braedan lay quietly next to her, his body screaming for release. A large part of him demanded that he wake her and finish what they'd started, but he knew that would be wrong. This had been for her. He'd wanted her to know the joy she could experience if a man cared for her pleasure above his own.

He hoped she would remember how he'd made her feel, when she learned of his betrayal…

Chapter Twelve

Ellena woke gradually. Her body had the boneless quality that came only after a particularly good rest. She stretched, and coarse blankets moved against her skin. She froze as memories came flooding back. Memories of delicious lips and tender hands, exploring her body and making it sing in a way she'd never imagined possible.

She turned and her eyes confirmed what she already knew.

She was alone in the bed.

She reached up and touched the pillow next to her. It was cold. Braedan must have left her some time ago.

Did she want to see him right now, with the memory of what he'd done to her body so fresh in her mind? Or would it be better if she was dressed when he returned? If he'd wanted a repeat of what had happened yesterday surely he'd have woken her with more of those luxurious kisses.

Her body tingled as she thought about what his mouth had done to her. She hadn't known such a thing was possible, but now that she did… Shamelessly, she wanted more. More of his mouth and his clever tongue.

Her nipples peaked against the rough cloth as she remembered how his fingers had played with them until she'd been all but senseless.

She listened for his returning footsteps. At first all she could make out was the call of the birds, twittering loudly in the trees surrounding the cottage, but as she strained to hear more she made out the low rumble of nearby voices.

She sat bolt upright, all thoughts of lovemaking fleeing. Someone could be out there, hurting Braedan, while she lay there doing nothing.

She slipped quickly out of bed and donned her clothes. Braedan's sword lay abandoned on the floor of the cottage and she picked it up, nearly dropping it under its surprising weight.

She hefted it over her shoulder and slowly opened the door to the cottage. It squeaked slightly on its hinges, but the noise became easily lost in the birds' early-morning chorus. She would still have the element of surprise.

She tiptoed down the steps and edged along the side of the cottage, keeping its wooden wall to her back.

She stopped to listen when she reached the corner.

She realised the voices were nearer than she'd anticipated. The deep tenor of the speech suggested a group of men, but it was hard to make out any words. She thought she caught 'two days' and 'enough food'. No voices seemed to be raised in anger.

Her heart raced anyway. What if the two men from yesterday had followed them and brought reinforcements? If they were talking so calmly then it probably meant Braedan had already been taken out of the picture. He might have thought he hadn't needed her help against those men but he'd been wrong. With a wound as serious as his he was not as strong as usual—although he was too stubborn-headed to realise it.

She edged forward, praying that they had left Braedan alive. She knew then that she would sacrifice herself for Braedan's safety. If the men wanted to take her to Copsi she would allow it if it meant Braedan could walk free.

She tugged the sword from its scabbard and slowly edged around the corner. What she saw made her drop the weapon in surprise.

'Careful, Ellena—my lady,' said Braedan, taking a step towards her.

She took a moment to acknowledge that he was fully dressed before her attention turned to everyone else.

'You're all alive,' she whispered. 'I thought…'

She was looking at the full company of Braedan's men. Even Eluard, pale and bandaged, sat atop a horse, smiling shyly at her.

Merrick jumped from his horse and bowed towards her. 'We're all very pleased to see that you are safe, my lady. We hoped you and Sir Leofric would come this way, and we've had patrols scouting the area for days. Walden found you this morning, and we've arrived to escort you to your father's castle.'

He moved to stand next to Braedan, who didn't say a word, his gaze fixed on a point somewhere behind her head.

She glanced at his face, willing him to look at her, but he didn't. His expression was stony and gave no hint as to what he was feeling.

A fine trembling started in her fingers and quickly spread to the rest of her body. She tried to hide her shaking hands, but everything suddenly seemed too much. She let out a sob, and was embarrassed when she couldn't contain it. She slammed a hand over her mouth and backed away towards the comfort of the cottage, tears streaming down her face.

Aldith dropped down from her horse and hurried towards her, surprising her by muttering, 'Hush, my lady. Everything is all right.'

Ellena allowed Aldith to pull her into her arms, but her whole body protested in confusion. Why wasn't Braedan comforting her? Why hadn't he moved from his position beside Merrick? Had the last week meant nothing to him? Now that he'd had her in his bed had he lost interest in her? And why was Aldith being so kind and gentle when she had only been surly before?

It was as if the world had gone mad in the last few moments.

Aldith tugged her into the cottage, rubbing her back sympathetically while she did so.

Ellena stumbled into the room and stopped.

Right here she'd found bliss with a man she'd never imagined liking. Had it meant anything to him at all or had she simply been a convenient body? Someone to relieve his pent-up frustrations? But he hadn't taken his own pleasure. It made no sense.

The rumpled bedcovers would tell anyone who cared to look exactly what they'd been up to the night before. Tactfully, Aldith made no comment, only going over to the bed and fetching a blanket and wrapping Ellena tightly in it.

'I'm sorry I wasn't the best maid to you before,' said Aldith as she bustled about the room, looking for firewood. 'I've had much time to think on this journey and my behaviour has been awful. Merrick gave me a fine roasting after we were separated. I was so worried that we wouldn't find you alive and I'd never get the chance to apologise. Please say you'll forgive me.'

Ellena hadn't the energy to work out what had caused this shift in behaviour, although it fleetingly crossed her mind that her new maid wanted to stay with her because it would mean contact with Merrick. She didn't care—nothing really mattered any more.

Aldith looked so contrite as she bent to light the fire, and Ellena realised she didn't have the energy to question her maid's change of heart. It only mattered that she had a friendly face near her.

'Did you encounter much trouble on your journey, Aldith?' she asked, in the calm voice she'd perfected over years of hiding how she really felt.

She held her hands out to the tiny flames and saw Aldith's body sag in relief; she'd obviously feared Ellena's rejection. Aldith began to describe the encounters they'd had with some of Copsi's men, none of which seemed as serious as her own run-ins with the man himself.

Despite the direness of the situation, Ellena's mind began to wander. Braedan hadn't been next to her when she woke and she was still wondering why.

Maybe he'd heard the voices and gone to investigate. But surely he would have woken her first? It wasn't like him to leave her vulnerable and alone, or to dress himself carefully before rushing towards danger. He'd have wanted her to run if the voices had turned out to be Copsi and his men.

The only conclusion she could reach was that he'd left before she'd awoken in order to get away from her.

Last night had meant something to her. The feel of his lips and tongue running over her skin had unlocked long-repressed desire. For so long she'd thought her body was a thing to be ashamed of and that it was next to useless. Lord Swein had taught her that lesson over and over again. She'd believed that only pain could be experienced for a woman when it came to bedding.

Braedan had shown her differently. The care he'd taken of her and his obvious delight in her pleasure had thrilled her. But he was obviously regretting his actions this morning. The connection she'd thought they'd formed was not real, and only served to highlight her naivety. Bed-play obviously meant something very different to men than it did to women.

She twisted the blanket around her fingers and tried to concentrate on what Aldith was saying.

'I'll fetch some water, my lady. You can have a wash and we'll tidy your hair.'

Ellena touched her shortened locks as Aldith bustled from the room. She'd forgotten how different she must look now. Her head was lighter without the burden of all that hair falling from it, but it wasn't the way a lady should look. No matter. Her veil would cover what was left, and no man would see her without it ever again.

Aldith had kept Ellena's personal bags. After she'd fetched some water they spread her clean clothes over the bed and she picked a simple deep red dress to change into. After Ellena had washed her body, Aldith helped her to step into the dress. Ellena thought about destroying the dress she'd worn for days, but for some reason she wanted to keep it, so she folded it neatly into her saddlebag.

While Aldith put her hair into a simple braid Ellena slipped Braedan's signet ring off her finger and placed it into the purse dangling from her belt. She rubbed the finger where the ring had sat and blinked back tears at the sight of her bare hand.

Once her hair was in place, she and Aldith attached her veil. Finally she smoothed down her cloak and exited the cottage without a backward glance towards the bed.

She was so pleased to be reunited with Awen that for a few minutes she forgot about everything else as she stroked her horse's long neck. But once they were moving again reality came flooding back. She would be seeing her father very soon. And the one man she'd thought was her ally could not even bring himself to look at her.

She was alone once more.

Braedan barely spoke to her for the rest of the day. When he did he was all formality, calling her 'my lady' and all but bowing to her whenever he left her company. If it hadn't been so depressing it would have been funny. He showed her far more deference now that they'd been intimate than he had at any point during their acquaintance before.

With nothing to occupy her mind as they travelled through Hexham Woods, she couldn't stop an endless debate with herself as to why their passionate encounter in the hut had happened.

She tried to convince herself that his blood had been up after the fight in the woods and he'd used her body as a way to slake his lust. But no sooner had she decided that this was fact than she remembered he hadn't actually spent his desire during their encounter. It had all been about her.

She was bewildered and angry and a little bit lost. If his intent had been to distract her from Copsi then he had succeeded completely.

She longed for him to take her in his arms again.

Her mind continually tormented her with visions of his strong hands roaming over her body.

After they'd set up camp for one last night she lay awake, hoping he would come to her after Aldith had fallen asleep, but he didn't.

The following morning they emerged from the protective confines of Hexham Woods and she allowed herself to be cocooned in the middle of Braedan's riders—much as she had been when they'd first started out all those days ago. This time she didn't complain. She was desperate for this endless journey to be over and yet equally keen for it never to end.

From her position in the pack she could watch Braedan as he rode out front. His eyes constantly swept the horizon but they never turned to her. He hadn't looked directly at her since they'd left the cottage, preferring to look over her shoulder whenever they spoke.

She shook her head irritably. All her thoughts were centred on this man and he obviously wasn't thinking about her at all. She needed to pull herself together and plan what she was going to say to her father. Her future happiness depended not on Braedan's kisses but on whether her father believed she was competent enough to run Swein's castle by herself. She must forget all about the distracting knight and concentrate.

But no matter how hard she tried her gaze kept wandering back to him. It was incredibly frustrating.

Chapter Thirteen

Ogmore's formidable fortress walls came into view early the following day, but it took a whole morning of hard riding to reach the impenetrable castle. Merrick carried her father's standard so that they would be identified by the soldiers guarding the walls, although Ellena doubted anyone would mistake Braedan, even from a distance. His chain mail glinted in the autumnal sun and his broad figure sat unmistakably self-assured atop his horse.

They slowed to a walk as they approached the large stone gatehouse. Ellena shivered, despite the warmth of the sun warming her back. Ogmore's great castle had been built to intimidate and repel potential invaders, and it had worked. There wasn't a hint of welcome in the imposing walls.

'The Earl will come to great you,' Braedan said, and his words were clearly meant for Ellena, despite the fact that he didn't turn in his saddle to look in her direction.

Ellena doubted her father would bother; she wasn't that important to her family. She was the only girl in a gang of more useful boys—a pawn to be used in her father's complicated game of chess. She knew her mother loved her, but she'd been busy producing boys through-out Ellena's childhood, and hadn't had a great deal of time for her only daughter.

Ellena was an afterthought for everyone. For once she wished somebody would put what *she* wanted first.

She glanced at Braedan and then away again.

She knew that was a young girl's dream. *She* had to be the one in charge of her own destiny, and the next few days would be critical in achieving that.

As the horses slowed to a stop, silence descended on the group of riders. All Ellena could hear was the creak of saddles and the soft clink of chain mail as the war-riors shifted in their seats. Guards stood at either side of the open gateway. No one moved to block their path, but no one moved to welcome them either.

She let out a long, slow breath.

'We might as well...' she began—and then stopped as the sound of many approaching feet reached her.

Instinctively she leaned back in her saddle, her heart pounding. The urge to flee pressed upon her but she held her ground. This was her parents' fortress; there would be no trouble from Copsi here.

Even as she told herself it would all be all right her fingers trembled against the reins and her eyes sought out Braedan's reassuring presence. His hands were re-laxed, but she noticed that one hovered near the hilt of his sword. Obviously he was braced for trouble.

Finally her father appeared, surrounded by his per-sonal guards and other hangers-on. He was greying at the temples, grizzlier than when she'd last seen him, but he still towered over his compatriots.

But although he commanded attention by his very

presence, Ellena barely had eyes for him. Next to his imposing figure was a tall, slender woman she'd recognise anywhere. With eyes just like her own, her mother stood smiling, her expression full of love.

Without conscious thought, Ellena jumped down from Awen and ran.

'Mama!' she cried as she threw her arms around her mother's neck.

The slender woman laughed and hugged her daughter in return. 'Ah, my darling girl, it is good to see you. You have grown even more beautiful.'

'Of course she has,' came her father's gruff voice. 'She takes after her mother.'

Tears gathered at the corners of Ellena's eyes and she squeezed them tightly shut. Her father wouldn't want her to show an excess of emotion in front of all these people, but she didn't think she'd ever heard him say anything so positive about her before.

Maybe he'd mellowed over the years. If so, perhaps there was some hope that he would be lenient towards her request after all.

'Let's get you inside,' said her mother, relaxing her hold. 'I ordered a bath to be prepared as soon as you were spotted from the battlements. I'm sure you'll want to get clean after your long journey.'

Ellena allowed herself to be tugged along in the maternal warmth, promising herself that she wouldn't turn around and look at Braedan, but the temptation was too great.

Just before they disappeared from sight, she turned. He was looking straight at her, his expression unreadable.

Braedan watched as Ellena was taken away from him and into Ogmore's fortress. He rubbed his chest, where an uncomfortable ache had taken root since his men had arrived yesterday morning. It had grown steadily worse as they'd ridden relentlessly towards Ellena's destiny.

He caught a last glimpse of her cloak as she disappeared around a corner and out of sight. This was it; the last time he would be in her company had come and gone.

He tightened his grip on his reins to stop himself from charging after her. He wanted to grab her and take her to a place far away from here—a place where they could both forget their responsibilities and think only of themselves.

He shifted in his saddle; he knew he couldn't do it and he'd never hated his circumstances more.

'You and I have much to discuss,' said the Earl of Ogmore, breaking into Braedan's thoughts and reminding him of where he was.

He tore his gaze away from the spot where he'd last seen Ellena and turned his attention to his liege. Ogmore was studying him intently, and Braedan instinctively gripped the hilt of his sword. He wasn't used to being on the receiving end of such a look, and it wasn't a comfortable sensation to find the hard stare aimed at him.

'Of course, my lord. Would you like to speak with me now?'

'Yes. Have your men stable your horse and join me in the solar.'

Braedan nodded to Merrick, who had heard the exchange. Without a word Merrick took Ffoi's reins as Braedan jumped down from the horse's back. Braedan had been right about Copsi's horse. The animal would be a fine addition to their stables and Braedan would enjoy riding him—not just because of the physical pleasure but also because he'd always know he'd taken Ffoi from his despicable owner.

He fell into step beside Ogmore and the Earl's personal guards followed them into the highly fortified building. Ogmore didn't speak, and Braedan didn't volunteer any information. He was used to Ogmore using silence as a way of breaking his adversaries. He'd long since learned not to say anything if this tactic was used against him.

Many a man had spilled their secrets to Ogmore in this way, and now Braedan had more secrets than most.

He knew that Ogmore would have no compunction about running him through with his sword if he so much as suspected Ellena had been naked and willing in his arms only two days before. Hell, he should run *himself* through for the liberties he'd taken. She could never be his, so why had he acted as if she was?

Any woman of high birth would expect a marriage proposal after the way he'd acted, and Ellena deserved such an offer from him. Even if she'd ultimately turned him down he should have got on his knees and asked her that night. But in the end he'd prevaricated, and fate had dealt him an untimely blow with the arrival of his men. Their appearance had put an end to their privacy and to his secret hopes.

As he'd lain awake, with Ellena soft and pliant in his arms, he'd come to the decision. He would tell her everything. Tell her that her father planned to marry her off once again and that he, Braedan, had been offered the stewardship of Castle Swein.

If, by some miracle, she still allowed him to speak at the end of his declaration, he would ask her to be his wife.

In the darkness he'd almost convinced himself that it could happen. If she agreed, they would find a little village, with a priest willing to marry them, before they returned to Ogmore. The Earl would be presented with a *fait accompli* and there would be little he could do about it.

He'd fallen asleep, his arms wrapped tightly around Ellena, believing in the impossible.

Morning had brought reality crashing down upon him. Ogmore would never accept their marriage and Braedan couldn't expect Ellena to live in poverty with him once her father turned them away from his castle. He owed his sisters more than that as well. Without his good name he'd have nothing to support them, and he wasn't so selfish that he'd ruin their futures for his own pleasure.

He'd staggered from the bed, unable to bear the comfort of her arms while knowing he'd never be able to do so again. He'd leant against a tree and fought a battle with his body, which had urged him to go back inside and wake Ellena, so they could finish what they'd started the evening before.

His body had just begun winning the argument over his conscience when Walden had appeared silently from the woods and all hopes of being alone with Ellena again had faded into the morning mist.

It was just as well. Ellena could never be his, and tormenting himself with visions of her as his wife was a waste of time. A fact that had been brought home to him when she'd emerged from the hut dressed in clean clothes and no longer wearing his ring. He still felt the pain in his stomach that had hit him when he'd seen her bare finger.

She hadn't given the ring back to him, and he hoped she would keep it as a token of their time together. Although it was more likely that she would throw it in his face when she learned of his betrayal.

Despite the warmth of the day outside, the inside of the castle was cool. The fire which burned continuously in the large hearth warmed the solar. As they stepped into the high-vaulted room Braedan was hit by the smoky scent, but even though it was reassuringly familiar he couldn't allow himself to relax.

His years as a page and then as Ogmore's most trusted knight had taught him to read his liege. It was a fact he'd kept to himself and one which had served him well over the years. The Earl was up to something, and until Braedan knew what it was he couldn't let his guard down.

'Where's Stoirm?' asked Ogmore as he lowered himself into his chair—the largest and most comfortable in the solar.

Braedan remained standing. He would only sit if asked.

'Stoirm is dead, my lord,' he stated calmly, even as his heart twinged.

Ogmore nodded. 'And my daughter has arrived looking less than pristine. I think you'd better sit and tell me what has happened.'

Braedan sat down opposite Ogmore. His chair wasn't cushioned, but he didn't mind that. Softness made people weak, and he needed all his strength right now. If Ogmore thought Ellena looked bad now, it was a good job he hadn't seen her two days ago.

Behind him he heard members of Ogmore's court

filing into the room, talking in low voices, probably hoping to hear what passed between Ogmore and his head guard.

He rubbed his beard. 'Lord Copsi presented us with some problems.'

Ogmore raised an eyebrow and glanced towards his personal guards. 'You may leave us for the moment.'

The two men faded away, but they would remain nearby. Braedan knew this because he had trained them himself, and they were amongst the best. He didn't doubt they would turn on him if given the order by Ogmore. He'd expect no less of them.

As succinctly as possible he ran through the events of the last week, avoiding any mention of sharing rooms with Ellena and passing as quickly as he could over the fact that they'd been alone for some considerable time.

'You were alone with my daughter for nearly ten days,' Ogmore said calmly, once Braedan had finished his report.

Braedan curled his fist against his thigh. Yes, it was true he'd been alone with Ellena for that time, but surely Copsi's actions should be Ogmore's first concern. Copsi had threatened Ellena's safety over and over again; that was an insult which would need addressing.

Braedan knew better than to question Ogmore. Ogmore would be looking for the detail in everything Braedan said, and for him to show a marked interest in Ellena would go badly for both of them.

'I was alone with Ellena, but I swear on my honour that I treated her with the respect she deserves,' he said solemnly.

Beads of sweat formed on the back of his neck and

he was glad Ogmore's guards had moved away, so there was no one else to spot his discomfort.

'Will she say the same?'

Ogmore's look was piercing, and Braedan shifted in his seat. Despite his resolve not to show any emotion he was quickly becoming undone under Ogmore's scrutiny.

He paused for a moment while he mulled over how best to answer. He was sure Ellena wouldn't want what had transpired between them in their most private moments to become common knowledge, but she might mention that he hadn't allowed her as much freedom as she was used to.

'Occasionally,' he said eventually, 'Ellena may have felt I was a little harsh on her. But I only ever acted in her best interests.'

Ogmore nodded thoughtfully, an expression Braedan couldn't read crossing his face.

'And yet if it becomes common knowledge that you were alone together the chance of her making a good match will be gone.'

Braedan's wound burned as he tightened his clenched fists. Why was Ogmore focusing so much on this? He must know that Braedan could be trusted not to gossip after all their years together. Braedan had kept far greater secrets than being alone with a noble-born woman.

'My men will not tell anyone,' he ground out.

Ogmore nodded. 'See that they don't.'

'Is that all, my lord?'

Braedan wanted this interview to end, before he punched the Earl for focusing on Braedan's actions rather than on Copsi. Clearly Braedan would have to make sure the insult to Ellena was repaid by himself, because it didn't look as if Ogmore was going to do anything about it. Hitting Ogmore would be satisfying, but it wouldn't do him any good in the long run, so he managed to restrain himself.

'That's all for now,' said Ogmore, a look close to amusement crossing his face. 'In two days' time there'll be a feast to celebrate my daughter's return home. There'll be a jousting competition in the afternoon. I'd like you to oversee it. The men will all be vying to impress me and Lady Swein, but no one will cheat if they know you are looking over their shoulders.'

Braedan nodded briskly and stood. 'I'll speak to my men. We will ensure everything runs smoothly.'

As they always did.

'I know I can count on you, Braedan,' said Ogmore softly.

Braedan began to move away.

'Oh, and Braedan…?'

Ogmore's voice still had that silky, soft tone to it. Braedan stopped in his tracks, the hairs on the back of his neck standing to attention.

'Copsi has been spotted in the town. I fear your men didn't do a good enough job of scaring him off. I want him watched at all times, but don't approach him.'

'What?' growled Braedan, unable to hide his shock at Ogmore's words.

Ogmore raised an eyebrow at Braedan's tone, but Braedan didn't apologise. This surely had to be Ogmore's idea of a joke. There was no way that man should be allowed to roam freely in the nearby town. It presented a terrible threat to Ellena's safety.

'I want Copsi to show his hand in front of me. If I'm lucky he'll do something so outrageous I can be rid of him forever.'

It took all Braedan's years of training for him not to seize his liege by the throat and squeeze the life out of him.

'Copsi isn't just your enemy. He is someone who has threatened your only daughter,' he spat out. 'You cannot seriously be considering letting him stay so close to Ellena. What if the rash thing you are hoping he will do is to kill your daughter? Is your petty feud really worth that?'

Ogmore stood slowly and stepped towards Braedan. The Earl was tall, and often used his height to intimidate people, but Braedan was taller. He pulled himself up to his full height now, so that Ogmore had to look upwards to meet his eyes.

'How interesting that you call my daughter by her given name,' said Ogmore smoothly.

Braedan shook his head. He refused to be distracted.

'Lady Swein was kind enough to grant me the use of her name during our journey together. It won't happen again,' he ground out. 'But Copsi, my lord—he cannot be trusted to be within the same county as your daughter, let alone in the nearby town.'

For a long moment Ogmore only looked at Braedan. His steely gaze seemed to be trying to penetrate Braedan's soul to see what secrets were hidden there. Braedan fought to keep his expression blank.

'Why don't you leave Lady Swein to me and worry about your own role in this castle instead?'

Ogmore turned away from him and beckoned to his steward.

Braedan was clearly dismissed.

He turned on his heel and swept down the length of the solar.

Ogmore might think Braedan was obedient to his commands, but he wasn't going to blindly allow Ellena to be so close to a monster without his men's complete protection.

He would sacrifice everything to make sure she had the future she deserved.

Chapter Fourteen

'Your father wishes to see you,' said Aldith as she bustled into Ellena's room, carrying a bowl of warm spiced water.

Ellena couldn't fault Aldith's attention to her since they'd been reunited. Perhaps it was the thought of staying close to Merrick, or maybe it was her father's impressive wealth that was influencing her behaviour. Whatever the cause, it was very pleasing. Even in the warmth of her mother's welcome she was still feeling more alone than ever before, and Aldith's company was reassuring in a world where everything seemed to be running away from her.

In the two days since she'd arrived at her father's fortress she'd seen Braedan only once. He'd been her anchor during some terrifying times and without him she was adrift.

As she and Aldith had walked across the courtyard yesterday afternoon she'd caught sight of him, striding along the battlements high above her. He'd frozen, as if he'd sensed her gaze on him, and then he'd turned to look down to where she'd been standing. For a long moment their gazes had held, and then he'd turned, striding away from her as if nothing had happened.

Aldith had tucked her arm through hers and tugged her along, chattering about the braid she wanted to try out on Ellena's shortened hair. She'd not commented on her mistress's strange behaviour, and Ellena was grateful for her discretion—whether it came about from loyalty or was because Aldith didn't want to serve a lady mired in scandal.

Whatever it was that had caused Aldith's behaviour, Ellena was thankful; she didn't think she'd have been able to come up with any kind of conversation at that point.

Just one glance at Braedan had set her heart racing and her body awash with unfulfilled desire. Desire she'd had no idea she could feel until Braedan had awakened something inside her. Now she could no longer sleep at night, because she was so tormented by dreams of soft lips and sure, caressing fingers.

From that brief sight of him it had been clear he wasn't being tortured in the same way.

Ellena had allowed Aldith's words to wash over her as her fingers had trembled against the folds of her dress. She'd stumbled back to her room in a daze and let Aldith begin to dress her hair. But the smooth action of Aldith running a comb through its length had reminded Ellena of Braedan's strong fingers gently tugging at the strands…

That had taken her right back to the questions that had been revolving around her head for the past few days.

Had the time they'd been together meant nothing to him? While he'd slowly but surely taken pieces of her heart, had he remained completely unmoved? Perhaps all their shared companionship had been a ruse to keep her calm and contained throughout the journey. That must be the case, because why else would he now be acting as if they were strangers and not two people who had spent some of the most exhilarating hours of Ellena's life together.

Although all logic argued against it, she wanted to speak to him again.

If she could only see him alone... But Aldith accompanied her everywhere.

The only place she might have been able to approach him without censure was during the evening repast, but he was avoiding mealtimes even though the rest of his men were attending. She wanted to ask Aldith if she knew what he was doing, but she didn't dare draw attention to the fact that he was in her every thought.

'Shall I get you ready, my lady? I don't think we should keep your father waiting.'

Aldith's words brought Ellena back to the present and she realised she was just standing next to her bed, staring into the distance. This really wouldn't do.

'Yes. I'll wear the blue dress with the embroidered hem,' she said decisively.

This was the moment she'd been waiting for. The chance to talk to her father about her future. She needed to push all thoughts of Braedan out of her mind and concentrate. Her freedom depended on how well she played this meeting. Her father was always one step ahead of everyone else, so she needed to keep her wits sharp and focused.

Aldith helped her to wash and together they pulled on Ellena's gown. It was one her mother had given her as a present. She was touched that her mother had remembered her favourite colour and had had the dress specially made up for her.

Flung in the corner of her room was the dress she'd worn on her frantic flight from Castle Swein. She didn't know if the gown could ever be repaired, and she wasn't even sure she wanted it to be. It was a visual reminder of everything she'd gone through, and eventually would be the only thing she had left of that intense week.

Her fingers fluttered over the purse which was tied to her belt. She really should give Braedan back his ring, but she couldn't bear to part with it just yet.

Her footsteps echoed loudly on the stone staircase as she made her way to her father's private room. He did a lot of his work in there but he rarely used it to meet people, preferring to display his authority in the solar.

Only his family were allowed in this private sanctuary, and a visit was rarely a pleasure. She squirmed as she remembered several disapproving lectures from her father which had taken place there. Ellena didn't know if he'd chosen a small room specifically so his large presence was able to dominate the space, or whether she'd been so in awe of him as a child he'd only seemed to fill the chamber.

Hopefully today it would be different. She would hold her own against her formidable sire and prove that she was a worthy steward for Castle Swein.

The door to his room was slightly ajar, with his two personal guards flanking either side.

'I won't need you here, Aldith. You're free to do as you please this morning. We'll meet back in my room before this afternoon's entertainment, so you can help me get ready.'

'Very well, my lady,' said Aldith, dropping a small curtsy which made Ellena smile before walking away.

Ellena ran her hand down her dress, smoothing out any creases, and then reached up to check her veil was still in place. Everything was perfect. Now all she had to do was remain calm, whatever her father did to throw her off course. She'd already planned what she was going to say—she just had to persuade him that she was right.

She took a deep breath and pushed open the door.

The Earl of Ogmore was sitting behind a large, wooden desk, his fingers pressed together as his elbows rested on the surface. He didn't move as she stepped into the room, his gaze fixed somewhere to her left.

She turned to look at what held his attention and gasped.

Braedan was standing next to her, his intense gaze fixed on her father.

He was looking neater than she'd ever seen him, with a smart clean uniform and his dark blond hair brushed away from his face. His beard had been neatly clipped, and she resisted the urge to reach over and gently feel the bristles.

She tapped her foot on the stone floor.

The sound seemed to snap the two men out of their silent stand-off and they both turned to look at her.

'Lady Swein,' said Braedan, bowing slightly in her direction. 'I hope you have recovered from the ordeal of your journey.'

She had felt amusement at Aldith's formality but her heart throbbed at Braedan's. All familiarity had gone from his tone of address.

'I am well, thank you, Sir Leofric,' she said quietly. 'How is your arm?'

His eyes flickered at her question, and for the first time since she'd entered the room he met her gaze.

'My arm is fine, thank you, my lady.'

His lips twitched slightly and she wondered if he was remembering how annoyed she'd been at his continued insistence that his arm was 'fine', despite the arrow that was wedged in it.

'I am glad,' she said, trying to inject some of the warmth she was feeling towards him into the tone of her words.

For a brief moment he held her gaze, the look in his eyes unreadable, and then he turned away from her.

'I'll leave you to your discussion,' he said.

'No, I'd like you to stay,' said the Earl.

Ellena jumped. She'd almost forgotten her father was in the room and watching the whole exchange. Heat flooded her face as she wondered what her father must be thinking. Had she been over-familiar with Braedan?

She looked at her father's face but could read nothing from his craggy features. But wait... Had he just asked Braedan to stay for their discussion? What was about to be said between her and her father should surely remain private?

The look on Braedan's face suggested he shared her confusion.

'This concerns you too, Sir Leofric. Please, sit, both of you.'

A short bench ran along the wall opposite her father. It was the only seating in the room, so Ellena lowered herself tentatively onto it. After a moment's hesitation Braedan joined her.

His body took up most of the bench, and although they both held themselves tightly the top of his thigh brushed hers. The brief contact sent an unwanted bolt of desire through her. As surreptitiously as she could, she moved away, but when she glanced at her father she saw he was watching her every move.

Heat washed over her face and she resisted the urge to squirm. She was a fully grown adult and not a naughty child any more.

'As you know, Ellena,' her father began, thankfully ignoring her blush, 'we are holding an afternoon of entertainment today, to celebrate your return home.'

Ellena nodded uncertainly. She'd expected to talk about her future, not about the festivities this afternoon.

Next to her, Braedan's hands curled into fists, and her heart began to slam painfully in her chest. There was more at play here than she'd first thought. What was her wily father planning—and why did she get the feeling that Braedan knew more than she did?

'I understand that you had a problem with Lord Copsi on your way from Castle Swein. And now I'm afraid to inform you that he has been spotted in town. But Sir Leofric has assured me that his best men will watch him at all times, and I'm sure he won't try and attack you while all our guests are here. He wants to be seen to be good in all of this, after all. We won't let the man spoil our enjoyment.'

Ellena twisted her fingers into the folds of her skirt. She'd had years of practice at hiding her emotions, but it took all her effort to say calmly, 'Lord Copsi tried to kill Sir Leofric and take me prisoner, in order to force me into marriage so that he could take my land. I would call that more than "a problem".'

'Aye,' agreed Braedan. 'The man's a maniac.'

Ogmore glanced between the two of them. 'Even so,

we cannot move against him if he has done nothing wrong.'

Ellena felt Braedan's muscles tense on the bench next to her. Like her, he must be thinking of all Copsi had done over the last ten days. That didn't count as 'nothing wrong' in her eyes. But from the look on his face she could tell there was no point arguing over this with her father—especially when there were far more important things to discuss.

'The Earl of Borwyn will be here,' continued the Earl. 'I think you'll agree, when you meet him, that he'd be a most suitable husband for you, Ellena.'

Braedan's hands were now so tightly clenched the white of his knuckles was pronounced against his dark skin.

Ellena cleared her throat. She'd been expecting something like this, but would rather not have had any audience when she replied—even if it was Braedan, who already knew her thoughts and feelings on taking another husband.

Perhaps her father had decided to raise the subject in front of Braedan thinking that his presence would stop her fighting back.

He was wrong.

'I am not going to marry again, Father,' she said calmly.

Her face heated as her father laughed.

Braedan shifted next to her but said nothing.

'Nonsense,' said the Earl. 'You're a young woman who has been raised to be mistress of a great residence. Borwyn's estate is huge, and it's situated near the Wye Valley—a very favourable spot. I'm told he is a handsome and charming man. He will make you a good husband and me a strong ally.'

White-hot rage pulsed through Ellena, but she forced herself to remain calm. 'I am not interested in moving. I like the home I have.'

Ogmore leaned back in his seat. 'You'll be bored here. Your mother runs this place like clockwork, and when your oldest brother marries there'll be far too many women in the place. No, you'll be better off being mistress of your own home.'

'I am already mistress of a castle. Castle Swein is my home. Ever since Lord Swein became sick five years ago the estate has prospered under my guidance. You must see that...'

Ogmore shook his head. 'No, it's not safe for you to run Swein by yourself. A woman on her own is seen as defenceless. There has already been talk of rival lords moving against you. In a couple of months you'll be overrun, and I can't have that. Swein is one of my most strategic outposts. We'd be cut off from the sea without it. Later you'll meet with Borwyn and you'll be pleased by my choice.'

Ellena glanced across at Braedan. All through this exchange she'd hoped he would say something in support of her, but he was so still it was almost as if he wasn't breathing.

'No,' she said firmly. 'I won't be pleased with Borwyn because my future is in the stewardship of Castle Swein. The estate has already prospered under my guidance. If you're worried about me being attacked then you could send me more guards, or have my men trained by yours. There is no reason why I cannot continue as I have for the last five years.'

Ogmore leaned forward in his chair. 'Ah, but there is *every* reason.'

Beside her, Braedan inhaled sharply.

'Sir Leofric is going to take over the stewardship of Castle Swein, so you cannot return there. Isn't that right, Braedan?'

Chapter Fifteen

'They are rather magnificent, aren't they, dear?' asked Ellena's mother, trying to engage her daughter in conversation.

Below their raised seats, knights competed in friendly but fierce competition. It was all for their entertainment, but Ellena was far from amused—particularly as Braedan and his men were among the contestants.

'Mmm…' she murmured in response.

Her mother sighed softly and turned to one of the other guests, sitting on her left. A pang of remorse at the way she was treating her blameless mother stirred Ellena, but she refused to be drawn into conversation with anyone.

She hadn't said a word since her father had revealed the depth of Braedan's betrayal and the extent of how alone she really was.

Her reaction in her father's study had disappointed her. For months she'd planned her response to her father's manipulative ways, but instead of standing up to him today she had swept from the room without further comment.

She had returned to her bedchamber, escorted by guards, her mind feeling peculiarly empty. Aldith had been waiting for her and had tried to encourage conversation while she'd chosen a dress for her to wear at the afternoon's celebration. Ellena had only stared blankly at the choices, and eventually Aldith had picked a dark blue dress edged with a jewel-studded neckline.

Ellena hadn't cared. She could wear a sack and she would feel the same. She had felt so cold on the inside—as if her heart had stopped working. She might even have believed that was possible if the thing hadn't been hurting with every beat.

But as Aldith had arranged a golden embroidered tunic over her dress she'd realised she needed a plan for her future—a solid one which her father couldn't break. And now she was completely alone in the world she knew she needed to do it by herself.

Unfortunately her brain refused to settle on practicalities, preferring to remind her again and again of how Braedan had taken her trust and completely destroyed it. And she hated it that despite her anger towards Braedan she couldn't take her eyes off him now, as he fought at the centre of the group of men.

She couldn't understand why, despite her all-consuming rage, she still wanted to run her hands over the muscles that flexed so effortlessly as he disarmed his opponents. She was annoyed at the flicker of worry that flared when she thought about his injury and wondered whether he was making it worse through his actions.

He'd been right to tell her he hadn't needed her help that day when she'd fought those men in the woods for him. She'd underestimated his prowess. He was clearly a lethal warrior who was able to take down his opponents easily despite an injury.

She'd underestimated a lot of things about him. She had thought him straightforward and honest, but all the time they'd been together he'd been plotting to take over her castle. No, he hadn't been plotting; he had already known he was getting the stewardship of Castle Swein. He hadn't needed to form any argument because the deed had already been done—probably months before she'd even met him. She'd been such a fool to tell him of her hopes... How he must have laughed at her.

The ladies around her began to stir, but she didn't turn her head to see what was bringing about the commotion. She couldn't tear her gaze away from Braedan, damn him.

'Ellena,' said her father, obviously the cause of the disturbance as he joined them on the stand. 'I'd like to introduce you to one of our guests.'

She didn't want to look at her father. Right now her anger with him was second only to the rage she was feeling towards Braedan. But she'd been too well-trained to ignore him in public. Besides, although she'd not yet formed a plan, she knew that openly rebelling against her father would not help her at this stage. It would be better if he thought she was compliant; he would have her watched all the time if he suspected she might defy him.

She tore her gaze away from the fighters below and stood, coolly nodding her head towards her father by way of greeting.

'Borwyn, may I present to you my daughter, Lady Swein? Ellena, this is the Earl of Borwyn.'

Borwyn took her proffered hand and bowed over it. 'It is a pleasure to meet you, Lady Swein.'

'Why don't you sit next to Lady Swein so that you can get to know one another?' suggested her mother, standing and moving away.

Ellena smiled blandly up at the Earl, who lowered himself into her mother's recently vacated spot. It really didn't matter to her family whether she liked this man or not. They would still believe she should marry him. But she had no intention of doing so, so there was no point in her getting to know him.

Up close, she could see that his handsomeness had not been exaggerated. His light blond hair, so different from Braedan's unruly locks, framed piercingly blue eyes, an unblemished face and high cheekbones. In another lifetime she might have been tempted by his fine features, but as it was he left her cold.

'I trust you are enjoying the festivities, Lady Swein?' he said.

'Indeed,' she said, sounding croaky as she used her voice for the first time in hours.

'Your father's guards are among the finest in the land.'

'Indeed,' she said again, turning her attention back to where the fight was drawing to a close.

There were only three men left now: Braedan, Merrick, and one of her father's personal guards whose name she didn't know.

She opened her mouth to ask the Earl something innocuous, but nothing came out so she closed it again.

Below her Braedan moved, dodging a blow from Merrick and causing the audience to gasp with delight.

'I understand that there is a little awkwardness attached to our situation,' said Borwyn. 'But I hope that we can be honest with each other. I have approached your father because I want to gain an alliance with him. He has suggested a union between us, and for my part it sounds like an eminently sensible proposition.'

Ellena watched as Braedan easily disarmed Merrick, eliminating him from the competition. Now there was only Braedan and the guard left. The two men circled each other, testing for weaknesses.

'Indeed,' she said to Borwyn—because what else was she to say? She would never marry him, but he wasn't to know that.

Borwyn surprised her by throwing his head back and laughing. She turned to face him, one eyebrow raised.

'I must confess I'm really rather conceited,' said Borwyn. 'I expected any proposal of marriage I made to be greeted with enthusiasm. I've always believed I'm considered quite a catch.'

Ellena smiled at the good humour she saw in his eyes, 'I'm sorry,' she said. 'I'm rather distracted.'

'I understand. Your father mentioned you had had a difficult journey from your home. Maybe I shouldn't have mentioned our union, but I always feel it is better to speak bluntly. That way there can be no misunderstandings.'

Ellena nodded emphatically. 'I agree that is a good idea to have complete honesty between two people. Lies destroy trust.'

Borwyn smiled, and Ellena could see that for the right woman that smile would be devastating. She was unmoved.

'You and I will do very well together, I think,' said Borwyn, and, taking her by surprise, he clasped her hand in his.

His skin was warm, and surprisingly callused for an

Earl who was more likely to have people under him to do physical work. Before she could remove her hand he raised it to his lips and brushed the lightest of kisses on her knuckles.

All around her the crowd gasped and she snatched her hand back. But no one was looking at her. Everyone's eyes were on the events going on below the stand.

Ellena turned to see what held their attention.

'I can't believe The Beast has fallen,' said a woman's voice to her right. 'He's never lost his concentration before.'

'He's down—but he's not out yet,' said another voice.

Below them Braedan rolled from his prone position on the ground and jumped up into an attacking stance.

'What can have caused that to happen?' murmured someone else. 'It's not like The Beast to show any weakness.'

Ellena watched, transfixed, as Braedan advanced on his opponent. His fall seemed to have galvanised him and he attacked the guard with ferocity.

Murmurs of shock ran through the crowd and Ellena held her breath. It almost appeared as if Braedan would kill the other man as he continued to rain down blow after blow, without giving his opponent any time to respond.

A crushing swipe caused his opponent to stagger and allowed Braedan to rip the man's sword from his grip. He held it aloft for a moment, while the audience cheered, then flung it down next to the defeated man and stalked away.

'He's quite a warrior,' commented Borwyn, as Braedan disappeared from sight and the crowd began to settle down for the next round of entertainment. 'I wonder if your father would be open to lending him to me for a while. My northernmost borders have been troubling me for some time, but a man like that would soon put an end to it.'

'I believe my father has other plans for Sir Leofric,' said Ellena, her voice coming out cool despite the white-hot rage flooding through her.

'Of course he does. A man like that is a valuable asset. Are you feeling quite all right, Lady Swein? You are suddenly looking very pale.'

Ellena raised the back of her hand to her forehead. Inside she felt as if she was burning, but her skin was cool to the touch. Nevertheless, her paleness was a good excuse for her to leave the stand for a while.

'I think I have been sitting in the sun for too long. If you will excuse me I think I will take a short break.'

'Of course,' he said, standing when she did so. 'May I accompany you?'

'Thank you, but my maid will be waiting for me at the bottom of the steps. She can escort me back to the castle for a moment. I will return shortly—watching the jousting is a particular favourite of mine.'

She smiled reassuringly at him and made her way past the other ladies enjoying the day of sport.

Aldith wasn't at the bottom of the steps, despite having promised to remain there waiting for her. She'd probably taken a moment to see Merrick.

Ellena didn't care. She would far rather be alone.

She ducked under the stand and stood in the shade for a moment. She had no intention of returning for the jousting. She needed to plan for the future, and being surrounded by all those people wasn't helping. But if she headed back to the castle she would be found easily enough, and would be forced to watch the rest of the afternoon's entertainment. It was supposed to be for her benefit, after all.

She tapped her fingers against a wooden pillar and thought. The riverside was the best place to be alone. She'd often escaped down there as a child, when being around her brothers had been too much. She would wait here until the jousting began and then, when everyone's attention was engaged, she would sneak off.

She settled down on the ground to wait.

Two maids carrying trays of food for the guests above approached the stand, their footsteps clattering heavily on the wooden steps. The sound of laughter filled the air as the guests began to pass the food among themselves. Ellena rubbed her stomach. She hadn't eaten anything today, but for once she wasn't hungry.

She heard the maids make their way back down the steps, but instead of moving away they stopped at the bottom, probably waiting to take the empty wooden trenchers away when the guests had finished eating.

'Did you see The Beast fall earlier?' asked one.

'No, I missed it. But Maud told me it happened at the same time the Earl of Borwyn kissed Lady Swein's hand.'

The two maids giggled.

'Have you seen the way The Beast looks at Lady Swein? It's as if he wants to consume her.'

Ellena's heart skittered. She'd not noticed Braedan looking at her at all, and surely his gaze would hold only contempt.

'Do you think The Beast fell in love with her during their journey together? I heard a rumour that they were alone for over a week!'

Ellena sucked in a breath. No one was supposed to know they'd been alone together. As for Braedan being in love with her…she could believe he desired her, but, no, he didn't love her. He wouldn't have betrayed her if he did.

'I doubt it. To do that he would have to have a heart… But perhaps something *else* transpired during their time together!'

The two maids giggled again.

Ellena raised trembling fingers to her cheeks and realised they were wet. She was crying and she hadn't even realised it.

Was everyone gossiping about her like this? Her good name would be ruined—and, really, her name was all she had left. She willed the girls to move away, or to stop talking, but it seemed they weren't finished yet.

'Those scars of his are disgusting. No woman in her right mind would want to kiss that face.'

The woman's clear disgust made Ellena's skin crawl. Braedan might be deceitful, but there was nothing wrong with his face—the fact that she still wanted to feel his lips on hers was testament to that.

'I don't know…' The other woman leered. 'There doesn't always have to be kissing, does there? With a body like that I can think of many things he'd be good for.'

Their sniggering began again and a flush rose up Ellena's neck. How dared they talk about Braedan like that? Her fingers flexed with the desire to scratch their eyes out for their impertinence.

This time their giggling was cut short by a cool voice. 'I think that's enough gossiping, ladies. Return to your duties.'

Ellena was surprised to hear it was Aldith. She had imagined her maid to be at the forefront of any gossip, and she was rather ashamed to have thought badly of her.

The two maids scurried off and Aldith took her position at the bottom of the steps.

Ellena shrank back into the shadows. She was grateful to Aldith for stemming the tide of gossip, but she would still prefer not to be seen. She desperately needed time alone, and she knew that Aldith would cling to her like a burr if she discovered her hiding place.

After what felt like an eternity the jousting began and Ellena could see that Aldith had turned in the direction of the competitors. She slid out from her hiding place and crept behind a bush. Being careful not to be seen, she hurried away from the sound of voices before reaching the cool of a small copse of trees.

She took a deep breath of the fresh pine-scented air. The smell took her back to a more innocent time, when her only concern had been avoiding her brothers—not fighting for her freedom. It didn't quite relax her, but it did ease some of the muscles in the back of her neck.

The path she'd used to follow down to the river was overgrown. She used her boots to trample over the brambles, relishing the ache of stretching her muscles for the first time in days. Eventually she reached the river and stopped to watch as it rushed and gurgled over stones; little fish were darting out from behind the shadows and then back again, as if they could sense a predator looming over them.

A rough hand grasped her arm and spun her around.

'What the hell do you think you are doing?' growled Braedan, his face white with fury.

Her rage matched his. 'Get your hands off me!' she yelled, struggling to get out of his grip.

He only tightened his hand further.

'Are you so spectacularly cavalier about your own safety that you deem it safe to wander unaccompanied in your father's grounds when you *know* that Copsi is nearby?'

'I am safe because I am *in* my father's grounds. Copsi will not harm me while he knows I'm protected by Ogmore guards,' she protested as she tried to use her own fingers to peel his off her.

'I thought you were less ignorant than that,' hissed Braedan. 'He will be looking for any opportunity to snatch you. He has spies everywhere in your father's court and you're quite alone out here. After all that we've been through I thought you'd acquired a grain of sense. It appears I was wrong.'

'Not as wrong as I was about your good character,' she replied, giving up trying to peel his fingers away and giving herself the satisfaction of poking him in the chest.

'This isn't about me,' growled Braedan, capturing her fingers in his iron grip.

Desire flooded her as the warmth of his hand encased her skin.

'It's about you and your safety. Something you don't seem to care about.'

She pulled her fingers free. 'I care about my safety and my freedom far more than anyone else.'

An emotion she couldn't read flickered in his eyes. She thought he might say something, but he didn't. Instead he began to tug her back in the direction of the castle. She tried to dig her heels into the muddy ground, but he was too strong and she had to skitter along after him.

'Let go of me!'

'No.'

'I can't be seen in your company,' she snapped. 'There are already rumours.'

He stopped abruptly and she cannoned into him.

He let go of her arm and held onto her waist to steady her. She could feel the warmth of his hand through the fabric of her clothes and she hated her traitorous body, which wanted to lean into the comfort of him. She watched the rise and fall of his chest as his breath came quickly, almost as if he'd been running.

'What rumours?' he asked quietly.

'Rumours that are unfortunately accurate,' she said, stepping out of his hold.

This time he let her go, but she could tell from his stance that he would grab her again if she tried to get away from him.

'Explain.'

'I overheard two maids talking. It's known that we spent time alone together and it's being suggested that we...'

Suddenly she was back in the hut, his lips on her body, his hands awakening sensations she'd not known existed. From the darkening of his eyes she knew he was thinking along the same lines.

'Aldith must have said something. My men know when to keep their mouths shut,' he said huskily.

Braedan's body seemed to be exerting some sort of pull over hers. She wanted to sway towards him, to lean her head on his solid chest and allow him to hold her as he protected her from the world. But it was a feeling she couldn't trust, and so she folded her hands behind her back before they could reach out and touch him.

'I don't think it was Aldith. I heard her scolding the maids. And she didn't know I was there, so she wasn't saying it for my benefit.'

He scratched his beard and Ellena noticed the purple shadows beneath his eyes. He'd obviously been working hard since he'd returned to Ogmore and not had much sleep. No doubt he had his successor to train, she thought bitterly.

Her heart twisted and she stumbled away from him.

'Ellena, wait...'

She shook her head. She didn't want to hear what he had to say. If he tried to explain his actions her heart might believe him, and he didn't deserve forgiveness.

'I don't want to hear any more from you,' she snapped.

'But I have things I need to say,' he said, moving so that he was walking next to her.

'You have nothing to say that I want to hear. You're right—I should head back to the festivities.'

'So you can get back to Earl Borwyn?' he sneered, his lips curling in disgust.

'Yes, so I can get back to him,' she said angrily.

'I see he's as handsome as the rumours suggested.'

'I think he's more attractive than the rumours claimed,' she ground out.

Braedan didn't respond. His scar pulled tight around his angry mouth. She almost wished he would say something. She wanted to argue with him.

He reached out and pulled aside a thick bramble which blocked her path.

She mumbled her thanks as she stepped through the gap. She didn't want to feel grateful to him for anything. His ring still rested in her purse. She knew she should return it to him, but for some reason she didn't mention it.

'Do you know what Borwyn said to me earlier?' said Ellena, stopping to look at Braedan, whose lips were twisted into a tight grimace. 'He said that honesty between two people was important. But *you* wouldn't know anything about that.'

'I never lied to you,' he snarled, taking a step towards her.

'You lied by omission, which is the same thing. I'll never forgive you for that.'

He stepped back as if she'd slapped him and she took the opportunity to dart away. After a moment she heard his hurried footsteps coming after her. She made it to the edge of the copse and burst into the sunlight.

'There you are, my lady,' said Aldith, scurrying towards her. 'I was out of my mind when I realised you weren't on the stand any longer. I've been searching for you all over.'

Behind her, Ellena heard Braedan emerge from the woodland. Aldith kept her eyes on her mistress's face and didn't turn in his direction. At that moment she could have flung her arms around her maid for her loyalty and discretion.

'I'm sorry to cause you concern, Aldith,' she said. 'I wanted a little time on my own. I'd like to return to the festivities now.'

'Of course, my lady. The jousting is going well, and I believe the Earl of Borwyn is going to have his turn soon.'

'Let's go and support him, then,' said Ellena, linking her arm through Aldith's and walking away from Braedan without a backward glance.

Chapter Sixteen

Braedan ran his hand over Ffoi's fetlock. The horse had been limping earlier, but he hadn't found anything to suggest the cause. He suspected Copsi of foul play, but he could find no evidence that the man had left the town, and he had not approached Ogmore's fortress since he'd arrived. Braedan was having him watched constantly, and so far he was doing nothing more offensive than harassing serving girls.

The sound of footsteps sounded down the stable and he froze until he recognised Merrick's distinctive gait.

'Find anything?' asked Merrick as his head appeared above the stable door.

'No. What's Copsi up to?'

Merrick sneered. 'He's got his eyes on the new barmaid at The Swan. Tanner and Walden are keeping an eye on him. I've got the rest of us watching his men.'

Braedan straightened. 'And who's watching Lady Swein?'

'Aldith.'

'Are you sure you can trust her?'

'I know she didn't get off to the greatest of starts

with you, but she's going to be my wife. I'd trust her with my life.'

'I hadn't realised things had gone that far,' said Braedan, stepping out of the stall and closing the stable door behind him.

Ffoi nickered as he left, and he leaned over to rub the stallion on the nose.

'Aye,' confirmed Merrick, and Braedan's heart thudded with something akin to jealousy.

He didn't want Aldith for himself, but he wished he could find a wife as easily as his friend. As it was, his heart appeared to be tied up with a woman who hated him.

Braedan gave Ffoi one last pat. Merrick might trust Aldith with his life, but Braedan wasn't going to trust her with Ellena's. If he had to stand watch on her bedchamber all night then so be it.

Merrick followed him as he strode out of the stable and back towards the entrance to the solar.

'With your permission, I'd like to go with Ellena and Aldith when they move to Borwyn's lands.'

Braedan stopped abruptly.

'Sir?'

Braedan sucked in a breath. Ellena was going to marry Borwyn, the lucky bastard. He needed to get used to that. She hated *him*, and he needed to accept that too.

'Of course you can go, Merrick,' he said thickly.

He resumed his walk towards the castle but changed direction. He didn't want to enter the solar and find Ellena deep in conversation with her intended. He didn't think he'd be able to stop himself from leaping across the room and tearing the man's head off.

He'd grab something to eat from the kitchens and then

find somewhere from where he could watch the door to Ellena's bedchamber. He would only believe she was safe once Copsi was far away from Ogmore—preferably in another country altogether.

'Of course, Ellena *could* return to Castle Swein,' said Merrick conversationally.

Braedan growled. What must he do to get rid of his irritating friend?

'She cannot return there. Her father will not allow her to run it by herself. She'd be too vulnerable,' he snapped.

Braedan entered a narrow corridor and quickened his pace. Perhaps Merrick would get the message that he wanted to be alone and disappear off to find Aldith.

But Merrick refused to take the hint and followed closely on his heels. 'There is one way she could return to Castle Swein,' he said.

Braedan stopped. 'What are you talking about, Merrick?'

Merrick shrugged; there was a look of innocence on his face that Braedan didn't believe was genuine.

'Perhaps the new steward of Castle Swein will want a wife. If that man did, then Lady Swein would be the best choice. We both saw how well the estate was prospering under her hands. Aldith tells me she is very highly regarded by everyone who depends upon Swein for their livelihoods.'

Braedan turned on his heel and strode away from Merrick without commenting. This time his friend didn't try and stop him.

Rumours must be swirling, saying that he was taking over the stewardship of Castle Swein. Either that or Ellena had vented her wrath at the news to her maid, who had told Merrick. However word had got out, it now appeared that Merrick suspected Swein's management would fall to Braedan. Merrick wouldn't have come up with that suggestion otherwise. He was singularly un-interested in politics, preferring a simpler life behind a sword.

Nobody stopped Braedan when he stomped into the kitchens. Serving lads scurried out of his way as he took some hunks of meat and strode back out again, all the while with Merrick's words bouncing around his head and tormenting him with thoughts of a life that he couldn't have.

Ellena's bedchamber was at the top of the east tower. It was meant to be the safest room in the castle and it would be difficult for an intruder to reach.

Braedan believed otherwise. The room didn't give her any escape route if someone did try and attack her. He had wanted to move her elsewhere, and had made his case to her father. He'd been overruled.

He clenched his fists at the reminder of Ogmore's dis-regard for the seriousness of the situation. If Ogmore re-fused to take the necessary precautions Braedan would have to protect her himself.

He bounded up the steps of the east tower and fol-lowed the narrow corridor which led to Ellena's bed-chamber. He moved past her door and further down the corridor, into the shadows.

The evening meal would be coming to an end soon, and he knew from his men who kept an eye on her that she didn't linger long after it had finished.

Sure enough, he soon heard her light footsteps com-ing towards him and his heart rate increased. He roughly rubbed the skin above the sensation. This was getting ridiculous. He wasn't some young girl with her first crush. He was a grown man and a seasoned warrior.

He'd meant to stay hidden from view. She was already angry with him. If she knew he was hanging around trying to protect her she would be furious. She was as wilfully stubborn about her own safety as her father. But as she rounded the corner he realised that once again she was alone and he snapped.

'Why in God's name are you not with Aldith?' he roared, striding towards her, stopping when he was within a few paces away.

'You again!' she snarled. 'Why can't you leave me alone?'

'I'll leave you alone when you finally understand what level of danger you are in.'

She raised an eyebrow and said, in the frustratingly calm voice she used whenever she wanted to put him in his place, 'I'm in my father's fortress. I am perfectly safe. The only danger I appear to be facing is from The Beast, who is lurking outside my bedchamber.'

All the anger and frustration he'd been carrying around with him for days suddenly fractured. He closed the remaining gap between them and pulled her roughly into his arms. He thought she'd fight him, but her arms came around him and her fingers stole into his hair. Their lips met in a savage kiss. He groaned as he pushed his tongue into her mouth and she met him with a passion of her own.

His hands found the door to her bedchamber and he pushed her out of the corridor into the room, his lips never leaving hers.

'Marry me,' he ground out against her mouth.

'*What?*' she snapped, and pulled herself out of his arms, moving away from him.

'Marry me and return to your castle. It's the perfect solution.'

He hadn't meant to say it. He'd never really believed it possible. But her kiss suggested she didn't hate him as much as she'd like him to believe.

Her face was frozen with wild fury. 'I've told you before I will not marry again, and I certainly will not marry *you*.'

'Why not?' he ground out.

'You betrayed me.'

He snorted. 'You had to return to your father whether you liked it or not. I protected you.'

'*Protected* me!' she yelled. 'I was shot at, dragged through woods, and I nearly drowned in mud. My hair has been hacked off and then there was that night in the cottage when you...when you...'

'When I what?' he asked, taking a step towards her.

'You know exactly what you did to me.'

'I know you enjoyed it,' he said, his body tightening at the memory of her breathing out his name on a sigh of pleasure.

'Why, you arrogant...'

He raised an eyebrow. 'Deny it.'

'I don't deny it,' she said, tilting her chin defiantly at him. 'You're a very capable lover. And I won't object to you coming to visit me in *my* castle when I've returned there.'

'You little...'

He reached out a hand and pulled her to him. She fell against his chest with an *oomph* and he brought his mouth down on hers, pressing her lips apart and sweeping his tongue inside once more.

He tugged at the edges of her veil, desperate to run his fingers through her hair. Her fingers joined his, and for a moment he thought she was fending him off, but when her hair fell free he realised she was helping him and he growled in satisfaction.

The silky locks fell over his hands and she moaned as he threaded his fingers through the strands.

'So beautiful…' he whispered against the skin of her neck as he trailed his lips along her soft skin.

'Don't lie,' she whispered, tilting her neck to allow him better access.

'I'm not,' he said, returning his mouth to her lips. 'You are exquisite. Your long, graceful neck…' He ran his fingers along its length. 'Your body…' His hands traced the outline of her figure through her dress and she shuddered against him. 'Your beautiful, elegant legs…'

He kissed her again. This time without the fury but with all the longing he'd been feeling for days. She kissed him back and he forgot about duty, forgot about his father's treason and all the reasons he had to stay away from this lady. She was his, and he was damned if he was going to leave this room without her knowing it.

He gathered her up in his arms and strode over to the bed. Remembering just in time that she was still scared of what happened between a man and a woman, he sat down on the edge and pulled her gently but firmly onto his lap.

Her soft whimpers filled the room as his hand stole beneath her dress and her thin chemise. He'd believed he'd never have her in his arms again, and now that she was here he was going to savour every touch of her soft, delicate skin.

He trailed his fingers up her calf and over her knee. She shifted on his lap as his hand reached her thigh, rubbing her bottom against his length.

He groaned. 'I've dreamed of you like this,' he murmured as his hand travelled up past her hip.

'You have?' she whispered.

'Aye. All during those long horse-rides with your thighs between mine I imagined you soft and pliant in my arms, your body mine to explore.'

Her breath came out in a wispy moan as his thumbs skimmed the underside of her breasts.

'But you're even better than my imagination,' he said as he pulled her dress and chemise over her head in one movement.

He didn't dare raise his head to look at her in case he broke the moment and gave her time to think. He wanted her senseless with desire...desire that was all for him.

His lips kept on moving across her mouth and down her neck as he explored her body with his hands, tracing the curve of her back up to her shoulders and along her collarbone.

She sucked in a breath as his hands traced the outline of her breasts, his fingers brushing over her taut nipples, and he smiled against her lips. Slowly, so as not to frighten her, he eased her back onto the mattress, stretching out so he was lying next to her.

'Ellena...' he murmured as her lips travelled down the length of his jaw.

'I want to see you,' she whispered as her fingers stole beneath the top of his tunic.

'It's not a pretty sight, my love—not like you,' he said as his own fingers resumed their journey down her back.

She tugged harder at the fabric and he smiled slightly. He'd never really cared before what women thought of the many scars that crossed his body, but he didn't think he could bear it if the lust in her eyes was replaced by repulsion.

He stood and disrobed quickly, joining her back on the bed before she had the chance to change her mind.

'Let me see *all* of you,' she demanded, pushing gently on his shoulder.

Ellena watched as Braedan reluctantly obliged by rolling onto his back. He propped his head up on one bent arm and looked at her as she studied his body.

'I'm sorry I'm not beautiful like you,' he murmured as her gaze took in the hard planes of his chest, where the solid muscles were crisscrossed with many scars.

She looked up at his face, surprised to see vulnerability in the depths of his eyes. Her heart tugged; the arrogant warrior was worried.

Her blazing anger at him had been consumed by the desire pulsing through her. It was as if the last ten days had been leading to this point.

She glanced down at his magnificent body and bit her bottom lip. If this was the only time she was going to have with him then she wanted to savour it. She wanted to touch every perfect inch of him, to learn what made him shudder and cry out with desire as she'd cried out to him.

Her fingers traced the muscles on his arm, up and over to his hard chest. One hand brushed over his nipple and she squeezed it as he had done to hers. He gasped, so she brought her mouth to his other nipple and licked.

He groaned deep in his throat and his arm moved to pull her to him.

'No,' she said, before he could take over again. 'This time it is for me to explore *you*.'

'You're going to be the death of me,' he ground out as her fingers carried on their journey over his abdomen.

'Possibly,' she agreed.

He huffed out a laugh. 'Well, there are worse ways to go.'

She continued downwards, past the hardness of his impressive length, which strained towards her, and over his hips. Up close, she could see thin scars littering his body. She brought her mouth to him and kissed each one, her hair brushing over his skin.

His breathing was coming heavily now, and his eyes were hooded with desire, but he still kept himself in check and she knew he wouldn't move until she told him he could. In that way she knew she could trust him. Unlike her late husband, he would never hurt her physically.

'Ellena, I…'

Her fingers traced his length and he bucked off the bed, a deep groan breaking free from his throat. She pressed her lips to its base and his hands tightly gripped the bedcovers. Using her tongue, she travelled up the solid length of him. Another groan ripped out of him as her lips slipped over the head and she sucked him into her mouth.

'Ellena…please… I can't…'

Her tongue swirled and his groans became even more incoherent as she explored him with her mouth.

'Stop…' he groaned. 'Please, I'll… This will be over before…'

She raised her head and looked at him. His fists were bunched so tightly the veins stood out against his skin.

'Make me feel the way you did before,' she breathed.

'Oh, thank God—yes,' he said, and before she knew what was happening he'd flipped her onto her back and his lips and tongue were everywhere, kissing and licking as if he were devouring her.

Then it was her turn to writhe against the mattress as his mouth settled at the juncture between her thighs. She cried out as his tongue teased her sensitive skin, her world narrowing to the single point where their bodies connected.

'Ellena…' he growled against the skin of her thigh. 'I want you so badly.'

'Yes…' she whispered, her hands tugging ineffectively at his shoulders.

She felt his laugh against her stomach and she wished she'd seen it. He hardly ever smiled, and he never laughed.

'Are you certain about this?' he asked as he moved up the mattress to join her.

'Yes, I'm sure,' she said.

She knew Braedan's body would help remove the nasty memories she had of bedding. It was as if his body had been made especially to bring hers to ecstasy.

'I'll try to be gentle,' he said as he placed a feather-light kiss against her lips.

'I don't need you to be gentle,' she said against his neck. 'I only need you to be *you*.'

He moved, and she felt his hardness press against

her entrance. She braced herself for the intrusion, her muscles clamping involuntarily.

'Ellena, look at me.'

She opened her eyes and looked into his warm gaze.

'I won't hurt you, my love. There is nothing to be afraid of.'

He lowered his mouth and kissed her once more, his lips soothing and caressing against hers. She turned boneless again as the power of his kiss relaxed her. Slowly he eased himself into her body. There was no pain, only pleasure, as he gradually filled her.

'Oh...' she gasped as he reached the hilt.

'Aye,' he murmured, and he pulled out again, only to slide slowly back in.

'Now I see...' she breathed as he did it again.

She felt him smile against her lips and she couldn't help but smile back.

He deepened the kiss as he began to rock into her, building a steady rhythm. Her hands skimmed over the muscles in his shoulders and down over his back as new, thrilling sensations built at her centre and spiralled through her.

As the pace quickened she wanted him deeper and harder. She dug her fingers into the base of his spine and pulled him tight against her.

'God, Ellena,' he ground out.

He increased the pace, his tongue delving into her mouth and driving her to that edge she now knew existed. He pushed into her once more and she called out as wave after wave of sensation washed over her.

He groaned as he followed her over the edge. Both of them were lost in an unending moment of intense pleasure.

He continued to kiss her softly as the world returned to normal, the sensations slowly dying away and leaving her with a bone-deep contentment.

'Are you all right?' he asked softly as he rolled onto his side, bringing her with him so that her head nestled in the crook of his arm.

'Yes.'

'It didn't hurt?' he asked, and the tenderness in his voice was unmistakable.

'No, it felt… Words can't really describe it, but it didn't hurt.'

'Good,' he said, as he brought his hand up to run his fingers lightly over the skin of her back.

For a long moment they lay in each other's arms. Ellena wanted to prolong this moment, to hold on to it before real life intruded once more. Only a tiny gap of air separated them but it seemed too much, so Ellena shuffled forward until they were skin to skin.

Braedan responded by hooking one of her legs around his waist and pulling her tight against him. 'It won't be easy,' he said into her hair.

'What won't?'

'Persuading your father. But if we come up with a plan together, and we present it in a favourable light, then maybe it won't be so bad.'

'What are you talking about, Braedan?'

'Marriage.'

'Marriage?'

'Yes,' he said. 'Marriage to me. You didn't think I would do this and not want to marry you, did you?'

Her heart stopped. Did he really think that this one act of passion would wipe away his betrayal? They'd both been angry, and then half-mad with desire. But that didn't change the fact that he'd deceived her so completely.

She unhooked her leg and scooted away from him, cool air washing over her body and making her shiver.

'Braedan, you've not been listening to me. I'm not marrying again. Not you. Not anyone. I won't be owned by a man—especially by one who has no respect for my hopes and dreams.'

'Ellena, if you think your father is going to let you get away with not remarrying then you are sadly mistaken.'

Ellena pushed herself off the bed. 'And this brings us right back to the fact that you lied to me.'

'I did not lie,' he ground out, following her off the bed and coming to stand before her.

'Yes, you did. You implied that I would be able to negotiate with my father, all the while knowing full well that you had already been promised the stewardship of my castle. That, Braedan, is a lie.'

He blinked at her, and then bent to pick up his clothes, pulling them on roughly. 'I did what I needed to do to survive.'

She nodded. 'And I'm doing what I need to do to survive.'

'Did this mean nothing to you?' he asked, gesturing to the bed.

'Yes, it meant something to me, Braedan. But it didn't mean enough for me to give up my freedom to a man who has lied to me since the day I met him.'

He stepped back from her as if she'd slapped him.

'If that's the way you feel, I won't insult you with my presence any longer,' he said stiffly.

She nodded, even though her heart was hurting so badly it felt as if it had split in two.

She turned and pulled on her clothes, so that she didn't have to watch him leave. Shortly she heard the creak of the door as it opened and closed sharply behind him.

She waited until she heard his footsteps stride away before she crawled into the centre of her bed and began to cry.

Chapter Seventeen

The air of the solar was grey with smoke as a fierce autumnal wind blew down the chimney, disturbing the logs in the great fire. But the revelry was undimmed by the weather. If anything, it only served to heighten the enjoyment of Ogmore and his guests. They were all together on an evening when it was better to be inside than out. Food, ale and rich wine were being served in abundance, and the insistent babble of voices was intermingled with the fiddlers' playing to entertain them all.

Ellena watched the proceedings dispassionately; she was the only one not partaking in the laughter and camaraderie that flew around the hall. She took a long sip of fruity red wine and looked around her. But perhaps it wasn't true to say she was the only one not enjoying herself.

Braedan sat among his men, a deep scowl lining his forehead, his lips twisted into a sneer. Conversation flowed around him but he ignored it all.

Ellena wished she wasn't aware of his every move. She wished she wasn't even aware he was in the room. But that was proving impossible.

Every bite he took, every drink he gulped, every person he glowered at—she observed it. From her position on the raised dais at the front of the room she could see him clearly, and she was hypersensitive of everything he did.

'Would you like some lamb, Lady Swein?' asked Borwyn, who was seated to her right.

Ellena's only consolation in her unending fascination with Braedan was his obvious awareness of everything *she* did. And the fact that every time she interacted with Borwyn his frown became deeper.

'Thank you, my lord,' said Ellena, bestowing a smile upon him—a smile that was not meant for her suitor but for the man who couldn't keep his eyes off their exchange. 'Tell me,' she said, taking a small bite out of the proffered meat. 'How close is your land to Swein?'

'My nearest border is a day's hard ride away.'

Ellena smiled again—not because his response was amusing, but because even from a distance, and through the smoky air, she could make out the whiteness of Braedan's knuckles as he gripped his tankard of ale.

She turned her gaze away from him and tried to concentrate on what Borwyn was saying. Over the last few nights she'd been gathering information from him about the land between Ogmore and Swein, mining him for any facts he could give her. She wanted a mental map of the most direct route between the two estates. She would never be dependent on someone else knowing the way again.

While her father was insisting he was too busy to meet with her, she was busy plotting. And if he kept prevaricating any longer she would send to Swein for her own men. True, they weren't as ferocious as Braedan and his soldiers, but they were loyal and would defend her if necessary. She would travel back to Swein with them and stake her claim to the castle. It might finally wake her father up to the fact that she was serious: she would not give up Castle Swein and her independence without a fight.

Finally the long meal drew to a close. The rest of the guests showed no sign of rising to their feet, but Ellena had long since had enough. She rose to her feet. Aldith, who was sitting next to Merrick further down the hall, reluctantly rose to join her.

Ellena didn't want Aldith to follow her. She wanted some time to herself—time to think about the events of yesterday evening—but Aldith must have been told to follow her closely because she'd not left her alone all day.

Ellena bade goodnight to her parents and dropped a curtsy to Borwyn before sweeping from the solar, aware of Braedan's stare following her the whole time.

Aldith bustled into Ellena's bedchamber the following morning carrying a tray of seed cakes—Ellena's favourite delicacy.

'I've brought you these, my lady,' she said, placing the tray on the dressing table in front of Ellena.

'How kind of you,' said Ellena.

Aldith smiled and busied herself by straightening out the objects on the table in front of her.

Ellena forced herself to pick up a cake and take a bite. When she could chew no longer she managed to swallow past the lump in her throat. She had no appetite, and not even her favourite food could tempt it to come back. She hadn't wanted to eat anything since Braedan had left her room less than two days since.

She closed her eyes. Only a month ago they'd never met, and now he was occupying almost her every thought.

She'd half expected him to renew his attempts to get her to marry him, but he'd not approached her since she'd rejected him. She was glad and heart sore in equal measure. She didn't know whether she would be able to refuse him if he asked her again.

She'd started to fantasise about dark-haired sons with rich brown eyes and little daughters with thick hair running to their father when they were hurt. Braedan would be a good father, protective and kind. And he'd be a caring husband, who'd never lock her in a room when she displeased him.

While she lay tangled in her sheets at night, remembering the way his body had awakened hers, she longed to run to him, to beg him to make her his wife. A lifetime without him stretched before her and her heart ached with misery. It was only the reminder of his betrayal that held her back. If he'd betrayed her once, what was to stop him doing something similar in the future?

Besides, he always thought he was right, and he would expect his orders to be followed even if she suggested something better. She would not be able to run her castle as she saw fit and the feelings she'd developed for him would be squashed as he lost her respect.

It was far better to have fond memories of the time they'd shared. Thanks to his care, she now knew that there could be mutual passion between a man and a woman. She now knew that a man's body wasn't designed to hurt a woman. She'd be grateful for ever for the memories Braedan had created. She would turn to them whenever thoughts of Lord Swein threatened to overwhelm her.

Her fingers fluttered over her abdomen. His babe could be growing inside her... But, no. She mustn't think like that. She hadn't fallen pregnant during her married life—no matter how many times her husband had forced himself upon her. She was unlikely to be carrying a child now, after only one encounter with Braedan.

She picked up her mirror and held it to her face. Tired eyes looked back at her. She picked up her tweezers and plucked out a few stray hairs in her eyebrows. It didn't make things better.

'Shall we go for a walk, my lady?' suggested Aldith. 'It is looking fine out.'

'Very well,' said Ellena, putting the mirror and the tweezers down. 'I'll wrap these in a cloth for later.'

She folded the seed cakes into some material and set them to one side, glad not to have to force them down any longer.

The two women stepped outside. A brisk autumnal breeze greeted them, ruffling Ellena's veil and making the skirt of her dress wrap tightly around her legs.

They made their way towards the Countess of Ogmore's private garden. Inside it was a peaceful haven away from the main business of the fortress, somewhere only the noble ladies could come to get away from the bustle of the castle. Men were not permitted within its walls.

Aldith stopped as they reached a stone bench. 'My lady,' she said in a rush. 'You do know that you can turn to me if you have a problem? I'll support you, whatever it is.'

Ellena looked into Aldith's wide eyes. She wanted to

trust this woman who'd been her near constant companion for the past days, but knew that she couldn't. Ultimately Aldith's loyalty rested with Merrick. The man she had agreed to marry was Braedan's man through and through.

'Thank you, Aldith, I'll remember that,' she said, gently touching Aldith's sleeve.

Aldith nodded and they started walking again. The wind scattered petals across their path as they rounded a corner. In front of them a young woman Ellena had never met before was attempting some needlework.

'Bother!' said the stranger as she held up her stitching to the light.

Even from a distance Ellena could see it wasn't a very good attempt.

Just before the woman moved to unpick her mistake, she spotted Ellena and Aldith. 'Oh, sorry—I didn't realise I wasn't alone.'

The woman stood up quickly and curtsied deeply to Ellena. Her clothes were neat, but old-fashioned and faded, as if they'd been left in the sunlight for too long. Long dark blonde hair was tied back in an elaborate braid which looped about her head in a style that didn't flatter her face.

'I'll leave,' she said, and made to scurry past them.

'There's no need,' said Ellena.

The woman's cheeks flushed a deep red, 'Oh, my lady, you are very kind but I must go.'

She darted past them and hurried out of the garden, her dress flapping in the wind.

'Who was that?' asked Ellena, bemused by the exchange.

'That was Katherine—Sir Leofric's sister,' said Aldith, folding her hands over her stomach.

'Why was she so eager to get away from us?' asked Ellena, puzzled.

'Her mother keeps her and her sister confined to their rooms in the castle. They are virtually prisoners.'

'Why ever does she do that?' asked Ellena.

Aldith shrugged. 'She feels the taint of her husband's treachery deeply. She believes her daughters should be isolated from other people so that no further scandal can be attached to them. She wants them to be pure, and to make good marriages, but I don't know how they are going to meet husbands while their mother allows them so very little contact with the outside world. It's rumoured that their mother has been touched by madness. She is said to have wild tantrums if the girls displease her.'

Ellena gazed at the spot where Braedan's sister had been sitting. Up high, a blackbird trilled in the afternoon air. 'This isn't their home, though, is it?' she said softly.

She moved quickly away from Aldith before she could hear her maid's response. Sensing that she wanted to be alone, Aldith kept a respectful distance as Ellena moved restlessly beneath the shady pergola, the wind rustling the leaves above her.

Braedan had talked about his mother, but she'd assumed the woman's behaviour was motivated by love for her son and embarrassment about the predicament in which the family now found themselves. Ellena hadn't realised Braedan's father's treason had made her unhinged.

She touched her stomach; a strange unsettled feeling was churning inside her. She wanted to hold on to the blazing anger she felt for Braedan. It was the only thing getting her through these long, lonely days. She needed to keep it in order to justify her plans to escape.

But how could she remain angry with a man who only wanted to put his family first? With the stewardship of her castle he would gain a home for his sisters—two women who were currently trapped in a life of isolation through no fault of their own.

She tried to hold on to the knowledge that he'd betrayed her trust, but a little voice in her mind argued that Braedan had made his deal with her father before they'd even met. How was he to have known they would become friends? *She* certainly hadn't expected it. And when she'd found out the truth she'd not given him a chance to explain himself.

She closed her eyes at the memory of the way she'd treated his marriage proposal. If she was looking at her own behaviour she'd have to admit that it hadn't been exemplary.

She stopped and ran her fingers over the fading petals of a rose. It was still soft, despite its browning edges.

Perhaps she should engineer a meeting and talk to Braedan. If she reasoned with him he might agree to give up the stewardship of Castle Swein. She would tell him she'd be willing to take his sisters with her and help arrange good matches for them. Maybe he would even be glad of her suggestion. She couldn't imagine him sitting down with a ledger and working through the estate's accounts. He was too elemental. And of course he would want to visit his sisters...

Her heart fluttered. This need not be the end for them...

She rounded a corner, still lost in thought.

'So we meet again, Lady Swein.'

Ellena gasped. Lord Copsi stood in front of her, out in the open, in her mother's garden, as plain as day.

She spun and darted back around the corner.

Aldith was lying crumpled on the ground, with two of Copsi's men standing over her, grinning.

She skittered to a stop, inhaling sharply as thick fingers encircled her right arm.

'You've caused me no end of trouble, Lady Swein,' growled Copsi, close to her ear, his fingers digging into her skin. 'But don't worry... I'm going to enjoy myself as you repay your debt.'

'You'll never get out of the fortress grounds,' she said, pleased that her voice came out calm, despite her knees shaking violently.

Copsi laughed. 'I can assure you that I will. Not all of your father's guards are as loyal as he believes.'

She felt a heavy blow against the back of her head.

Her world turned black in an instant.

Chapter Eighteen

Ellena woke slowly. All around her was darkness. She blinked. Her eyes were gritty. She blinked again but she still couldn't see anything. She turned her head but was still none the wiser.

She appeared to be lying down and yet the floor beneath her was swaying violently.

She licked her lips and tasted the metallic tang of blood.

She swallowed; she was so thirsty.

She tried to roll over but her back hit something solid. Where *was* she?

She blinked again and sucked in a sharp breath as she remembered. Copsi had come for her—and this time he'd succeeded.

Sweat broke out across her forehead as she tried to gather her thoughts. The throb in her head was making it virtually impossible.

Her upper arms screamed in agony. She tried to move, to relieve the tension, but found her hands were bound tightly behind her back.

Her heart sped up until it was beating painfully fast.

She took a deep breath and filled her lungs with stale air. She coughed, remembering at the last minute to keep the noise down.

Her eyes still hadn't adjusted to the darkness and so, shifting slowly, so as not to hurt her arms too much, she managed to roll onto her back. Beneath her fingertips she could feel rough cloth. She tilted her head and felt the same material against her cheek.

Her hands trembled as she squirmed frantically, trying to get the cloth off her face. She only pulled it tighter.

She kicked out her legs, but the cloth must be surrounding her completely because her feet hit a barrier.

Her breathing came faster as her heart rate kicked up another notch.

Tears pricked her eyes and she scrunched them shut, willing herself not to cry. Crying wouldn't solve anything, and showing weakness to Copsi could be fatal.

Despite her resolution, she felt water leaking over her cheeks. She bit her lip until she tasted blood again. She couldn't even wipe away the evidence of her distress.

She took a few shuddery breaths.

She had to call on the resolve which had got her through all those years with Swein as her husband. She hadn't fallen apart then and she wouldn't fall apart now.

She had to assume that Copsi had taken her out of her father's castle. The rocking motion of the floor beneath her had to be from some sort of cart. She listened carefully and could just make out the muffled sound of hooves against soft ground.

She didn't know how long she'd been unconscious. It could have been minutes or hours. If Aldith had been found then Braedan would know something was seriously wrong. He could be following her right now.

Her heart clenched at the thought of Braedan. He'd warned her so many times to be more careful and she'd ignored him, imagining herself safe within her father's walls. How naive she had been.

There was nothing she could do to free herself until the cart stopped moving. Until then she needed to conserve her energy, because when the moment presented itself she needed to run. She had to hope that when she did Braedan and his men wouldn't be far behind. If she could get to them she would be safe.

Her throat constricted. She couldn't begin to contemplate her future if Braedan *wasn't* following her. She'd only survived running from Copsi the first time because of him.

Her head felt heavy, and pain pressed down on the top of her skull. She closed her eyes and her surroundings slowly faded away...

When she woke again the ache in her head had dimmed a little and the world didn't seem quite so hazy. Over the noise of creaking wood and the clomp of horses' hooves she could hear the faint rumble of deep voices.

The swaying beneath her appeared to be slowing, and then they seemed to turn sharply. She held her breath as the cart gradually came to a stop.

She forced herself to relax her muscles as the voices came nearer. She heard the sound of material being untied, before rough hands dragged her from her resting place and she was thrown unceremoniously over someone's shoulder.

Even through the thick cloth she could smell the scent of an unwashed body. She retched, unable to keep her body from the violent spasms that gripped it. Her captor paused for a moment, before adjusting his grip so that he held her tightly across the legs. The throb in her head returned as she dangled upside down and another wave of sickness washed over her. She swallowed convulsively.

A door creaked open and the rumble of several voices grew louder. It was difficult to isolate one voice, but her scrambled brain calculated that there must be at least five men nearby—possibly more. She squeezed her eyes tightly shut as visions of Swein's rough treatment of her pushed into her mind, forcing her to imagine the horrors that might be inflicted upon her by her captors.

Suddenly she was dumped roughly on her side, and she bit her lip to stop herself crying out in pain.

'Get her out of the sack,' came Copsi's voice from quite close to her. 'If she's still unconscious throw that water on her. I want her awake for this.'

The men around her laughed and she trembled, instinctively curling herself into a protective ball. A dull light reached her eyes as the material holding her was untied at the end nearest her feet. She whimpered as coarse hands grabbed at the bare skin under her skirts. Her legs were pulled from where she'd tucked them under her stomach and she was yanked out of the sack into a dully lit timber room.

Seeing she was awake, the man pulled her roughly to her feet and spun her to face Copsi. She stumbled and fell to the floor, her knees jarring without her hands to break her fall.

The man cursed and set her on her feet once more. She staggered, and then righted herself before she could fall again.

The smell of unwashed bodies was even stronger now, and she retched more forcibly as her empty stomach spasmed in pain. Slowly the cramping subsided and she forced herself to stand straight and look around her.

She was standing in a low-ceilinged barn, with only one entrance and no windows. Her fingers curled as it quickly dawned on her that escape from here would be virtually impossible. No light seeped from the edges of the door. She'd been unconscious for most of the afternoon.

Her heart stopped as she realised no one had come to rescue her in all that time.

She was alone.

'Ellena, you'll be pleased to know we have just been married,' said Copsi, stepping towards her.

Her head swam. 'No...' she muttered. 'Impossible.'

'Ah, yes, I thought you might say that—but you see we're surrounded by witnesses who all saw it happen.'

Her head lolled onto her chest and she forced it upwards. 'No one will believe you. My father...'

He laughed. 'Some peasants from the nearby town will also confirm they were witnesses. They will happily tell anyone who asks how you entered into the union of your own free will, glad to be out of the shackles of your meddlesome father. What better way to repay the manipulative bastard than by marrying his biggest enemy? I've paid them handsomely for their trouble.'

'No.' She shook her head again, the motion making the room spin.

'Of course,' he said, stepping towards her, 'no marriage is properly legal until it's consummated...'

The men around her leered and grunted in agreement. Ellena's fingers trembled behind her back.

'I can't decide,' said Copsi, sliding a hand up her arm, 'whether we should have an audience for that too.'

A chorus of approval ran through the group.

'No!' she gasped, stepping backwards into the man who had dragged her from the sack. His stubby fingers dug deeply into the tops of her arms and she flinched away from him.

'If you're good I'll send my men outside, but if you try and struggle… You decide. I hear you've already experienced the attentions of Ogmore's hideously disfigured knight. If you've rutted with *that* animal you'll enjoy what I have to offer.'

Ellena couldn't speak. Terror clogged up her throat until she couldn't breathe. Then everything turned black again.

Cold water being flung over her face brought her coughing and spluttering back into the world.

She was lying on the floor, her hair tangled with the straw that littered the barn's insides. She shivered as the icy water seeped into her dress. Her hands chafed against the rough ground, but they were still tied behind her back and she couldn't move enough to release them.

Copsi stood over her, an empty water skin in his hands and his lips twisted into a smile that made her shiver.

'Good, you're awake,' he said as she blinked the water out of her eyes. 'Now, enough of this nonsense. You owe me for the amount of trouble you've caused.'

He knelt down next to her, his bulbous nose looming over her, and fumbled with the hem of her dress, trying to drag it up her body.

'No!' she screamed as she tried to wriggle away from him, feeling the skin on her hands scraping across the rough floor. 'Stop! I won't!'

He backhanded her across the face and she cried out in pain.

'We will be consummating this union right here and now,' he yelled, grasping her face in one hand.

The men around him jeered in approval.

She shook her head and the room swam. 'Please, don't do this...'

'It's too late. I'm already doing it. Swein's lands will become mine and every advantage of its strategic position will increase my prosperity. You can either fight me on this or submit to my will.'

'I'd rather be dead than be married to you.'

He barked out a laugh, his foul breath brushing across her face. 'That can be arranged as well—but not before I've ridden into Swein with you as my wife. I want there to be no doubt in everyone's minds that you and the lands are mine. I intend to enjoy myself too, but when the enjoyment runs out...'

He grinned, and Ellena cringed as low, masculine laughter rumbled around the room.

Copsi's hands resumed their struggle with her clothing. And as Ellena was plunged back into the horror of her marriage bed the remembered pain and humiliation paralysed her with fear.

Her skirts were over her knees when a high-pitched scream rent the air.

Chapter Nineteen

Copsi froze.

'What was that?' grunted the man who had pulled Ellena from the sack.

'A vixen,' barked Copsi, but his hand on Ellena's leg stopped moving nonetheless.

Ellena breathed out slowly.

The barn descended into silence.

A muffled thud sounded outside.

'What was that?' the man asked again.

Copsi's men started to shift on their feet, a low murmuring breaking out among them.

'It's nothing,' snapped Copsi, his small eyes narrowing in anger. 'Yates, go and check with Ulmer. I want to know that everyone is still awake and watching out for anything suspicious.'

The man Yates tugged at his belt. 'I'm sure it's nothing, my lord.'

Another thud sounded—this time much nearer the barn's walls.

'Yates…' warned Copsi.

'What if The Beast has followed us, my lord?' asked

Yates, sounding a lot less confident now that he was expected to go outside alone.

'That's impossible. No one followed us from the fortress.'

'Then what's making those noises, my lord?' Yates's eyes were darting from side to side and sweat was beading across his brow.

'It's only the wind!' roared Copsi. 'Now, get out there and check that everyone is awake. I don't want anything to disturb me while I enjoy myself with my new wife.'

Yates unsheathed the dagger he carried at his side and made his way over to the barn door. He stepped outside into the darkness, the door creaking shut behind him.

Then there was only silence.

'Now, where were we?' said Copsi. 'Ah, yes—I was about to make you my wife in every way possible.'

Copsi laughed and the men around him relaxed too.

Ellena squirmed frantically against her bonds, serving only to scrape some of the skin off her fingers as she rubbed them against the barn floor.

She gritted her teeth against the pain. Then Copsi's grasping hands reached her thighs and she cried out as his fingers bit into her flesh.

Moments later something heavy slammed into the side of the barn, shaking the timber frame and causing Copsi to jump to his feet.

Ellena scrambled onto her side, gasping for breath.

'Wylie!' he barked. 'Stay with Ellena—make sure she doesn't try and run for it. The rest of you come with me. Swords out—expect trouble.'

Ellena rolled onto her knees as the men traipsed outside, with Copsi staying towards the back of the group. Before Wylie could reach her she was able to stagger to her feet. The room swayed alarmingly, but she managed to stay upright.

'Don't come any closer,' she slurred as the short, bald Wylie swaggered towards her.

He laughed. 'How do you plan to stop me, hey? It doesn't look to me as if you're in any position to be giving orders.'

She skittered backwards, her heart hammering in her ears. 'Just don't…' she whispered hoarsely as her back hit a wall.

There was nowhere else left for her to run.

He sniggered and, reaching out a hairy arm, easily pulled her towards him.

'Copsi will be back soon,' she croaked.

'I can be quick.'

Ellena closed her eyes. Her worst nightmare was coming true and there was nothing she could do to stop it.

Outside metal clanged and shouting suddenly filled the air.

Her new assailant laughed. 'It looks like Copsi will be a while after all!'

He wrapped his arms tightly around her waist and Ellena's instincts took over. She brought her knee up sharply and hit the man hard between the legs. He instantly let go of her and crumpled to the floor.

She stepped over him, just managing to dodge the flailing arm which reached up to try and stop her.

She stumbled to the door, hearing Wylie cursing her from his prone position. She toed it open and slipped outside.

She screamed as a body flew past her and hit the wall of the barn.

'Ellena!' called a voice which caused her knees to weaken in relief.

Braedan was here.

He had come to get her.

Her head swam as she tried to find him in the melee.

'Get away from the barn!' shouted Braedan.

She twisted and turned as she tried to pick out his familiar body. But her eyesight wasn't working properly. Everything seemed hazy. Men were moving in all directions and she couldn't tell the difference between friend and foe.

Braedan had told her to get away from the barn. She stepped forward and the world tilted. She retched as nausea swept through her. She was so tired. All she wanted to do was lie down and rest her eyes...

She took another step and slipped in the mud.

'Keep moving!' yelled Braedan, somewhere to her right.

She tried to get her legs underneath her once more but they kept sliding away, and her dress was becoming heavier as wet mud soaked into it.

Swords clashed against swords.

A body fell next to her.

She saw Yates's eyes, wide and unseeing. Relief swept through her. Perhaps Braedan and his men were winning. Maybe this nightmare would end.

She heard a low, keening noise and took a moment to realise it was coming from her. She shuffled forward on her knees, trying to put as much distance between herself and the hateful barn as she could.

When she twisted backwards to see how far she'd come she realised she'd only managed a few steps. The man she'd hit would be able to get up and come after her soon.

She started shuffling forward more quickly.

A hand reached out to grab her, but a sword swooped and the hand disappeared.

'Please...' she muttered. 'Please, let this be over.'

She screamed as someone grabbed a handful of her hair and pulled her up out of the mud. All around her the sound of fighting stilled. Heavy breathing sounded in her right ear.

'Tell your men to back off, Braedan!'

Ellena whimpered as the grip on her hair tightened.

'I'm warning you, Braedan,' Copsi growled. 'If your men don't back off right now then my new wife is going to meet an untimely end.'

'You can't win, Copsi. You're outnumbered and out-classed.'

Copsi responded by brandishing his dagger in Ellena's face. 'Shall I give her a scar to match yours?' he taunted Braedan.

In the sudden silence Ellena could see Braedan, his muscles tightly bunched as if he was ready to spring into action, mud streaked across his face.

'All right...all right,' said Braedan. 'My men are backing off.'

'No...' whispered Ellena as Braedan's men slowly moved away from their opponents.

'It seems we've reached an impasse,' said Copsi.

Braedan said nothing. Ellena willed him to look at her. If these were her last few minutes on earth then she wanted her vision to be filled with the image of him.

But Braedan didn't heed her silent pleas, keeping his

gaze firmly fixed on Copsi. 'Let Ellena go and I will let you live,' he said huskily.

'Let me ride off with Ellena and I will let *her* live,' responded Copsi.

Ellena's vision swam. 'I would rather be dead than leave with Copsi,' she rasped.

Braedan nodded, and in one swift movement he brought his dagger up and flung it at Copsi. It flew straight and true towards its intended victim.

Ellena heard a grunt, and then the arms holding her so tightly fell away. She staggered, but Braedan reached her before she could fall again and gathered her in his arms.

'Ellena, my love,' he said as he held her close to his chest, his hands quickly untying the cords that bound her.

She flung her aching arms around his middle and held on tightly. He became the centre of her world as all around her everything swooped and swirled.

'I'm sorry,' she sobbed against his chain mail. 'I'm sorry...'

'Hush, my love. Everything is all right. You're safe now.'

His hands stole into her hair and he tenderly stroked the strands away from her face.

'Is he dead?' she asked.

Braedan glanced away from her and towards the body on the floor. 'Yes.'

For some reason her tears came harder at the news, and she clung to Braedan, who still held her tightly.

She was vaguely aware of people moving around them. There were grunts, and the sound of bodies being dragged through mud mixed with the sound of chains being fixed around wrists. But for the most part she was only concerned about Braedan: his familiar scent, the rough stubble of his chin against her hair and the reassuring pressure of his arms around her.

She never wanted to move.

'I'm sorry,' she said again, when she could speak.

His arms only tightened around her. 'Hush, my love. You've got nothing to be sorry for.'

'You were right. I was foolish to assume I was safe in my father's grounds.'

She heard him sigh. 'You should have been safe. It's me who's sorry that you were taken from right under the nose of my men. When I think of what could have happened...'

She felt a shudder run through his whole body. 'He didn't... I mean, there was only...'

'Aye, I know, my love. We weren't far behind you. We only lost you when Copsi's cart turned off the track unexpectedly. We found you quickly enough, but I'm so sorry for those moments you had to endure while we took Copsi's guards. I wanted...' He heaved a sigh and tightened his grip even further. 'But Merrick was right. It was best not to storm in there, no matter how much I wanted to. You could have been killed in the confusion. I am sorrier than you will ever know that you had to face that unpleasantness.'

He leaned a little away from her.

'I wish I could kill him all over again for the pain he's caused you.'

He reached up and lightly touched his fingers to the place where Copsi had hit her.

'It's fine,' she said, smiling shyly up at him.

He smiled, and then he brought his lips gently down to hers.

Their kiss started off softly, but it quickly built in intensity. All her worry and fear poured into him and he took it, replacing it with wild desire.

Around them his men continued clearing the area, but neither of them paid any attention. All that mattered was Braedan's mouth on hers. She was safe once more and it was all because of this man.

Eventually there was the sound of shuffling feet, but Braedan still didn't raise his head.

Merrick cleared his throat. 'The bodies are buried, Sir.'

'Good,' murmured Braedan against her mouth.

'The Earl will be worried about his daughter.'

Braedan sighed softly and raised his head, tucking Ellena to his side. 'Then we'll return to Ogmore.'

His men remained silent as Braedan led Ellena over to Ffoi. The only sound came from their horses, snorting impatiently into the cold night air. He helped her into the saddle and then swung up behind her, using one arm to pull her flush against him.

She didn't resist. Here in Braedan's arms she was at her safest.

He kicked the stallion into motion and his men fell in around them.

She smiled slightly, remembering how closed in she had felt riding at the centre of them only a few weeks ago. Now she felt protected and cocooned, and she knew that these men, with this leader, would always come for her.

The rocking motion of the horse lulled her and her eyes drooped. Before she could succumb to sleep she murmured, 'How is Aldith?'

'She has a sore head, but she will live,' Braedan rumbled behind her. 'Now sleep, my love. You'll be home soon.'

She must have dozed off, because the next thing she knew was the sound of many voices, and then she was being handed to her mother, whose soft, flowery scent had her crying again.

'She needs rest.'

Braedan's voice came from high above her.

'No…' she mumbled, her fingers stretching towards the sound of his voice.

There was something very important she needed to say to Braedan, but she couldn't remember what it was. If she stayed with him then perhaps it would come to her. One thing she was certain about was that they mustn't be separated. Bad things happened to her whenever he left her side.

But she wasn't strong enough to stop the tide which swept her away from the dark courtyard and into the warm candlelight of Ogmore Castle, up and away from the only man she trusted to keep her safe.

Chapter Twenty

Days passed. Ellena drifted in and out of consciousness. She was aware that her mother only left her side to eat, and heard the soft sound of Aldith's voice as she came and went from the bedchamber. Gradually she felt able to sit upright and take some food, with her mother spooning broth into her mouth as if she were a babe.

A few more days passed in a hazy blur of broth and sleep until finally one afternoon she felt strong enough to sit up in bed and feed herself.

'What happened?' she asked Aldith, who was sitting nearby, her head bent over her sewing.

Aldith didn't need her to explain what she meant. The two women had become close in the aftermath of their shared experience, and Ellena finally felt able to call the woman her friend.

'I'm afraid I don't remember much myself,' Aldith said, looking up from the hem she was mending. 'I only know what I've been told. Apparently Sir Leofric was having you watched all the time, but there was a late change of duty. One of the new recruits got lost on his way to your bedchamber and missed us leaving the room. It took him a while to work out that we were no longer in there. He raised the alarm straight away, but no one knew where we had gone, and because we were in the Countess's garden, where no man is allowed…'

Ellena tapped the bed next to her and Aldith moved to sit next to her, gently patting her outstretched hand as she did so.

'It was Katherine Leofric who told her brother where she had seen us. I don't know how long I had been lying on the ground before they found me, but by then you had already disappeared.'

'How did they know I'd been taken out of the castle?'

'They didn't. Braedan had all his men, and every man, woman and child who wasn't part of his guard, searching Ogmore's grounds for you. Nobody denied him; apparently he was like a man possessed. He even yelled instructions at your father, and the Earl did what he was told. Apparently no one has ever seen *that* happen before.'

Aldith raised her eyebrows and Ellena felt heat wash over her face. She could well imagine Braedan in full warrior mode. His anger at her disappearance must have been terrible to behold.

'What happened next?' she asked.

'Braedan split his men into teams, and each one set off after a different carriage of the two that had been seen leaving the castle during the day. Braedan chose the one he thought most likely to be carrying you, and it turned out his instinct was right.'

Aldith picked at a thread that had worked its way loose from Ellena's blanket. 'You know the rest,' she said quietly.

Ellena did know the rest. Braedan had found her before any real harm had been done. Copsi and his men had been killed and she had been returned to her father's castle. Her father was no doubt pleased that his greatest enemy had been destroyed. She wondered if he'd thought about *her* at all.

What she didn't know, because she couldn't ask, was what had happened to Braedan since. She'd asked Aldith casually, but all she'd said was that he'd returned to his normal duties. She couldn't believe that he'd kissed her like that in front of Merrick and then carried on as if nothing had happened.

As the days passed, and he still didn't come to see her, she convinced herself that he had only kissed her because his bloodlust had been up. The fight with the two men in the woods, the demand for marriage and then her rescue had all been moments of high tension, and now that she was lying in bed like an elderly invalid he wasn't interested.

She closed her eyes. The pain in her heart was worse than any physical damage she'd sustained. She wondered if she would be told one day that he had left for Castle Swein. If she couldn't get up soon then that particular fight would be lost before she even got to say her piece. Not that she wanted to fight with him any more. Her anger had died and all she wanted was for them to talk about the estate in a rational manner and hope that there was a solution that suited them both.

Several more long, restless days passed. Ellena felt ready to go out into the world, but despite numerous pleas to her mother she was ordered to remain on bed rest for at least a week. No matter whom she appealed to, everyone had the same response.

More days passed and it was as if the walls had started to close in on her.

Her desire to see Braedan became frantic. She needed to speak with him about her castle. She wanted to explain that she understood why he'd acted in the way he had. She needed him to know that she forgave him for his decision, even if she didn't agree with it. She wanted to tell him of her offer to take in his sisters in return for his taking back his claim. But most importantly she wanted to know whether he felt the burning passion for her that she did for him, or whether he had only ever been acting in the moment.

He didn't come.

'If you're well enough,' said Aldith one morning, when Ellena felt as if she would burst if she didn't feel the sun on her skin for another day, 'then your father would like to see you.'

Ellena's heart skipped a beat. 'I'm ready.'

She was going to tell her father that she refused to marry Borwyn, or anyone else her father might try and throw her way. While she'd lain in bed with nothing to do, and thousands of hours to think, she'd come to a decision to speak plainly with her father. He might be a master of games, but she refused to play any more. She wanted to use honesty and pragmatism from now on. She would never say the words that would bind her in marriage to a man she didn't love.

She didn't know what would happen after their meeting. But she wanted time to speak with Braedan before she brought up the issue of Castle Swein with her father once more. She had to hope that the man who'd carried her around on his shoulders when she was little wouldn't be cruel enough to force her into marrying. He might try

and manipulate her, but she knew she was strong enough
to resist whatever he threw her way.

She'd survived much worse, after all.

Aldith arranged her hair in a neat braid and helped
her to don a rich purple dress with a gold embroidered
tunic over the top.

'My lady?' said Aldith, just as they were about to step
outside her bedchamber.

'Yes?' said Ellena.

'I hope I don't speak out of place when I ask you not
to be too harsh towards Sir Leofric.'

Ellena tilted her head to one side. 'What do you
mean?'

'It's my fault we were in the garden that day,' said
Aldith, looking guiltily towards the floor. 'I wanted you
to see Sir Leofric's sister, so you would know what it is
that motivates Sir Leofric. I thought you might look more
kindly on him and not judge him so harshly.'

Ellena tapped her foot against the floor. 'I don't judge
him harshly, Aldith. I was only cross that he'd lied to
me. He had plenty of opportunity to tell me about my
father's plan but he didn't mention it once.'

The familiar tug of anger she'd thought long since
disappeared stirred inside her.

'We all make mistakes, my lady,' said Aldith softly.
'I've made more than others and yet you've managed
to forgive me.'

'That's different,' said Ellena gruffly. 'You were
merely guilty of being a bit sullen. Braedan lied to me.
I do forgive him, but I can't forget it.'

Aldith's skin burned red under Ellena's scrutiny. 'Everyone knows how he feels about you, my lady. It would
be foolish to turn away from love that strong.'

Aldith turned away from her mistress.

Ellena was rendered speechless. *Love?* No one had mentioned love to her.

She touched her hand to her heart. Was the strange feeling that fluttered there when she thought of Braedan *love*? She knew she had many complicated feelings for him. Anger, frustration, longing and an all-encompassing desire all warred within her. But did she love him? Could she imagine a life with him?

Her heart skittered. What about a life without him?

Her chest tightened, but before she could get her thoughts in order a guard arrived to escort them to her father.

Her mind whirled as thoughts and images tumbled through her brain. Braedan keeping her warm when she thought she would die from the cold... Braedan blinking like an owl whenever he woke... The way he'd always insisted she take the bed... The way he'd kissed her... The look on his face when she told him she wouldn't marry him...

She stumbled and Aldith caught her arm, throwing her a look of concern. She shook her head and Aldith gave her a small smile before dropping away. They carried on through the twisting corridors of the castle as Ellena's stomach whirled.

People bowed respectfully towards her as she passed, but unusually nobody stopped to speak with her, and she began to feel a tightening of her breath.

Did people believe she had been violated by Copsi while in his power? Had she fallen from grace? Or were people gossiping about her and Braedan?

It was impossible to tell.

They paused outside her father's private room. 'You

may take some time off, Aldith,' said Ellena. 'I will be here awhile.'

'Very well, my lady. Send a guard when you want me to return.'

Ellena nodded and stepped into the room, relief seeping through her as she moved away from prying eyes.

Her relief was short-lived.

Her father was standing behind his large desk, the book she used for recording housekeeping at Swein Castle open in front of him.

'How did you get that?' she asked, without bothering with a greeting.

'I asked for it to be sent to me. I thought you could talk Sir Leofric through it before he takes over the stewardship.'

The scuff of a boot drew her attention to the fact that they were not alone in the room.

All her senses flared to life when she turned to see Braedan glaring at her father. A look of contempt crossed his hardened features.

Her heart raced and her legs itched to cross over to him, so she could burrow her face into his strong chest. She fancied she could smell his unique woodsy scent from where she stood.

He didn't turn to her.

'I thought,' continued her father, 'that now you are well you could talk him through the figures you've recorded.'

Ellena wanted to stamp her feet. Her father kept wrong-footing her. She'd been expecting to talk about Borwyn. She knew what she was going to say about that. But this... This was an unexpected blow which left her feeling winded.

She opened her mouth to say something.

'No.'

She snapped her mouth shut. That word hadn't come from her.

'What's that, Sir Leofric?' said Ogmore.

'I said, no. This is wrong.'

'What's wrong?' asked her father, one eyebrow raised.

Ellena's heart began to beat wildly.

Braedan kept his gaze locked on her father.

'This.' Braedan gestured to the book on Ogmore's desk. 'Taking Castle Swein away from Lady Swein is wrong. She is more than capable of running the place. She has done for years. One glance at those records will be enough to reassure you on that front. When I visited I could see how smoothly everything operates there and how prosperous the estate is. She will provide you with excellent stewardship.'

'And the fact that she is a woman…?'

'Merrick wishes to marry Ellena's maid. I suggest he becomes head guard at Swein. He's ideal for the job. Not only is he a fully trained knight, he is also excellent at training young men to become guards. Ellena will be fully protected and she need not marry for protection. You'd be a fool to take Swein away from her.'

'And what of yourself?'

'I no longer want the stewardship of Castle Swein,' said Braedan, his eyes hard, his posture resolute.

For a long moment her father held his gaze and then he nodded. 'Very well—then you are dismissed. Return to your normal duties.'

Braedan nodded and swept from the room, closing the door behind him. Not once did he look in Ellena's direction.

Ellena's father sank slowly into his chair. 'Well?' he asked.

'Well, what?' croaked Ellena.

She couldn't believe that Braedan had done that for her. Sacrificed his freedom and the restoration of his family's good name all for her.

'Aren't you going to chase after him?'

'Wh…?'

Ellena's head whipped towards the door and then back to her father.

'Isn't that what young lovers do?' asked Ogmore, his forefinger tapping against the top of Ellena's record book.

'We're not…'

Her father raised an eyebrow. 'Are you telling me that Braedan has just given up everything he's been working towards for years because you happen to be good at running a castle?' He held up one finger. 'And before you argue, I know you are. I've read your accounts.'

'Oh…' said Ellena, the wind completely taken out of her sails.

'Ellena,' said the Earl, leaning his elbows against the desk. 'A man only gives up his life's dream for the woman he loves.'

'I…'

'For a woman who likes to argue, you're not saying very much,' he said, a small smile tugging at the corner of his lips.

'I don't…'

Ogmore stood and came to stand in front of her.

'I owe you an apology,' he said, taking her hands in his. 'Actually, the truth is I owe you several. I didn't realise what manner of a man Swein was until it was too late. After his death I invited you home so that you could meet Braedan. He's a strong, principled man, and I knew he would take care of you in the way you deserved, but you kept thwarting me. In the end I realised you were stubborn—a trait you must have inherited from your mother.'

Ellena harrumphed and her father smiled softly. There was a look on his face she hadn't seen for years.

'Well, perhaps I can be a bit stubborn sometimes too... Maybe that trait *does* come from me. The point is I sent Braedan to you, hoping you would see what a good match you would make together.' He took a deep breath. 'Your mother always tells me not to meddle so much with our children's lives. It's advice I should take more often. My biggest regret—the one I cannot forgive myself for—is not having Copsi drummed out of town as soon as I knew he was there. I can never apologise enough to you for what you went through—all because I didn't listen to your mother or to Braedan.'

Ellena was shocked to see the glimmer of water in her father's eyes. She had never seen him express remorse or show distress before.

He blinked and the moisture was gone.

'Why didn't you send Copsi away?' she asked.

'Because sometimes even I make mistakes.'

Ellena laughed, despite herself.

'I didn't send him away for two reasons. Firstly, his interest in you seemed to send Braedan a little crazy with protectiveness. I hoped it would push him over the edge and force him into asking you to marry him.'

Ellena flushed.

'Ah, I see...' said her father. 'But I have to confess that wasn't my only reason. The main one—and for this

I will always feel guilty—was that I wanted to catch Copsi trying to take you. I hoped he would hang for his crime. I knew that Braedan was having you watched constantly, so I didn't worry enough about your security. It is entirely my fault that you were taken from here and subjected to that awful ordeal.'

Ellena looked down to where their hands were still clasped. His hands, once so sure and firm, were gnarled and weather-beaten.

She squeezed his fingers. 'The ordeal was only for a short time, and I was unconscious for the most part. Braedan saved me before anything terrible happened.'

'Ah, you are being kind to me, but you must allow me to wallow in my guilt for a while. Your mother tells me it will do me good. Now, on to the subject of Braedan... While I can see he's fallen so deeply that he's acting completely unlike himself, I'm not sure about *you*. Despite your sweet blushes whenever he is around, you have become better at hiding your feelings from me. I'm sure you're pleased about that, but I am your father and that makes me sad.'

'I... What about Borwyn?' Ellena hedged, not willing to admit yet that she had any feelings for Braedan one way or another.

'He's a fine man, and if you tell me you'd rather marry him then I will happily accept that. Either man would make an excellent son-in-law.'

'And if I don't want to marry at all?' asked Ellena softly.

'I think that would be sad,' said Ogmore. 'You are a young woman with plenty of years ahead of you. I know that I am difficult, and a trial for your mother, and that my recent actions have made her wild with anger at me.

But our years together have mainly been happy, and I know that having her by my side has helped me enormously through difficult times. I only want the same for you.'

'Will you force me to remarry?' Ellena persisted.

'I doubt I could force you to do anything you don't want to,' said Ogmore, releasing her hands and returning to the other side of his desk. 'Having said that, I do really think you should put Braedan out of his misery. I hear he is taking the pain of his unrequited love out on the new recruits, and they are all terrified of him.'

Ellena stood staring at her father, completely dumbstruck.

'But please take your maid with you when you search for him. I don't think your reputation can withstand another scandal.'

For several long moments she didn't say anything. Then she turned away from him and ran out of the room.

Chapter Twenty-One

For once, Ogmore's guards weren't standing outside his room, guarding either side of the entrance. Ellena debated waiting for Aldith, but the thought of staying there even a heartbeat longer before looking for Braedan was too much to bear.

She hurried through the twisting corridors, her father's words swirling around her head. Once again he had manipulated events, twisting everything to his satisfaction. But for the first time in a long time, she didn't care. If Braedan did truly love her it would change everything.

She paused. Where would he be now?

She'd never seen him mingling with the other men of her father's court—not for him, the constant bickering of internal politics. He was more likely to be training with his men, out in the elements.

She stepped out of the castle and ground to a halt.

A soft autumnal breeze brushed over her skin for the first time in days. The crisp fresh air hit her lungs and she tilted her head towards the golden sun.

In the distance a bevy of maids wrung out washing,

talking animatedly among themselves. None of them were looking in her direction, so she scurried across the small courtyard and hid in the shadows, her heart racing wildly.

She slipped through an archway and peered round a corner. From her vantage point she could make out the width of the training grounds, but she couldn't see Braedan's tall body among those practising there.

The stables were empty apart from the stable boy, who looked at her wide-eyed and staring. She backed out quickly, before he could spot that she was alone. She darted into an alcove and waited for a group of giggling children to pass.

Of course Braedan could be in his bedchamber...

Should she try it? Did she dare?

She knew where it was. As head of her father's guards he was afforded the luxury of his own room, away from the soldiers who shared their quarters.

If she was caught in his room, or anywhere near it, she knew the scandal would be enormous. Her newfound accord with her father would be broken only moments after it had begun.

She twisted her hands together.

She needed to see him before she lost her nerve.

Glancing around to check again that no one was looking at her, she stepped into the part of the keep that housed the guards. Moving quickly but cautiously, she darted down several corridors until she came to the room she knew to be his.

Without stopping to knock, she pushed open the door and stepped inside.

Braedan was stripped to the waist, his muscles bunched as he bent over an open chest. He looked up, his eyes widening when he saw who had barged unannounced into his bedchamber.

'Ellena…' he breathed, striding over to her and grabbing hold of her upper arm. 'What are you doing here? Did anyone see you arrive? You'll be ruined if you're caught.'

Despite his angry words she saw the look in his eyes and it gave her courage.

'I needed to see you,' she said simply.

'And it couldn't have waited until later? Talking to me in the solar in front of everyone wouldn't be scandalous, whereas this could ruin you!'

His grip remained tight but he didn't attempt to throw her out.

'You don't ever come to the solar. Besides, this is private.'

She reached up and touched his face, her fingers trembling against his skin. His beard tickled the palm of her hand and he turned into her touch, placing a gentle kiss against her skin.

Hope flared in her heart.

'What is it that you wanted to see me about?' he asked softly, all the anger seeping out of his stance at her touch.

'I wanted to know why you changed your mind about Castle Swein.'

He sighed and let go of her arm, stepping away from her.

Her hand fell to her side. She immediately missed the warmth of his skin. She wanted to touch him again. But it would be better to hear his answer when desire wasn't muddling her senses.

He rubbed his forehead. 'When your father mentioned the stewardship I was thinking only of what it would mean to my family. Your thoughts and feelings didn't matter to me. After we met, however...' His gaze flickered up to meet hers and then moved away again. He took a deep breath. 'Since then I've realised what the place means to you. It's somewhere you can be yourself. It's your home and you've worked hard to make it prosperous and safe. I can't take that away from you.'

Ellena's heart thudded in her chest. This was everything she wanted to hear—and yet it wasn't enough. Was her father wrong? Was it only honour that drove Braedan?

'You need to leave now,' said Braedan, straightening his shoulders. 'Be careful not to be seen.'

Despite his words he'd stepped closer to her, and now he delicately took her face in his hands, brushing his thumbs over her cheekbones. He gently pressed a soft kiss against her lips and then moved away from her once more.

'Goodbye, sweet Ellena,' he said softly, smiling sadly at her.

She inhaled sharply. 'Braedan, you know I'm against marrying again?'

'Yes.' He nodded, pain flickering across his features. 'I know and I understand. There's no need for you to explain any more.' He sighed. 'I don't wish to be rude, but I would prefer it if you left now.'

'But I have one more thing to say,' she protested, taking a step towards him so that only a whisper of air separated them.

'I'm not sure I'm strong enough to hear it,' he admitted.

This close she could see that his eyes were filled with sadness, and her heart ached for him.

'I want to tell you that I'm only against being forced into marriage for alliance purposes. I'd quite happily marry for love.'

Braedan froze. Only the steady rise and fall of his chest showed he hadn't turned to stone.

She waited.

'Say something…' she whispered eventually.

'Ellena…' he murmured, pulling her towards him and brushing her jaw with his lips.

He shivered as she ran her fingertips over his chest.

'Something else…' she breathed as his fingers stole into her hair and down over her back.

She felt his laugh whisper across her cheek.

'I love you,' he said, as his fingers found the ties to her tunic and began to pull them free.

'Really?'

She gasped as he pulled the tunic from her body and dumped it on the ground.

'I am amazed you even have to ask,' he said, and laughed as he nudged her towards his bed.

Her fingers traced the contours of his chest, doubt rushing through her despite the physical evidence that he desired her.

'I'm Ogmore's ugly daughter…tall and reedy like a sapling. I'm only useful for making good alliances and that's if you can ignore the fact that I'm headstrong and opinionated.'

'Don't forget bossy,' said Braedan as he pulled her dress over her head, throwing it in the direction of her abandoned tunic. 'And stubborn. And lacking even a grain of sense.'

Laughter gurgled out of her. 'I am amazed that you could love such a harpy.'

Braedan stood back to look at her and she fought the urge to cover her naked body with her hands. He'd said he loved her and she believed him. It shone fiercely from his eyes, making her knees tremble at the enormity of what was happening to them both.

'You are so beautiful,' he said. 'You're tall, yes. But I could hardly love a short woman. I wouldn't know what to do with her. As for reedy...' His hands traced the outline of her body, leaving her skin burning with desire. 'Once you may have been, but now you have a figure to make men weep.'

He pulled her towards him and brought his mouth down to hers, kissing her deeply and thoroughly, leaving her in no doubt that he believed what he was saying even if no one else could see the beauty he described.

'As for your personality,' he said as his lips left hers and travelled down her neck, 'you are kind, passionate and thoughtful.'

His stubble brushed the sensitive skin of her breast and she moaned softly.

'You're forgiving and ferociously intelligent,' he said as he continued his journey down her body.

Her knees turned liquid as he knelt before her, and it was only the strength of his arms wrapped around her waist that stopped her from sinking to the floor.

'And if you sometimes rush headlong into danger without a second thought, it's only because you care so passionately.'

His words whispered against her thigh.

Her body quivered with anticipation.

She hadn't come to his room for this. She'd come to find out whether he really did love her. But now that she was here, in his arms, she knew she couldn't leave until he'd made her body sing with desire once again.

He placed the softest of kisses against her centre and she moaned.

He smiled against her. And then she could only feel as his lips and tongue moved against her sensitive skin. The pressure building within her took her by surprise with its intensity. She called out his name as pleasure shot through her, starting at her centre and travelling through her whole body, leaving her breathless.

He stood and lifted her into his arms. She fell against his chest, limp and boneless.

He laid her reverently on the bed and stood gazing down at her, a soft smile playing over his lips. She held out a hand to him and he took it, before joining her on the bed, lying next to her and gently trailing his fingers down her neck and over the swell of her breasts.

'I'm not afraid,' she whispered.

Whatever expression he saw on her face must have reassured him, because he brought his mouth down to hers and began to kiss her once more. She ran her hands over his chest, desperate to touch every inch of him.

Her fingers tugged at the material at his waist. 'The rest of your clothes…' she murmured as his lips travelled along her jaw.

He huffed out a laugh and quickly shrugged off his braies, throwing them to the floor and pulling her tightly towards him so that every inch of her body was against his.

He pressed another kiss to her mouth as he moved over her, his solid weight pushing her into the mattress.

'I need you,' she said, squirming beneath him as his tongue teased her nipples.

'I love you,' he said, and groaned as he entered her, slowly filling her up. 'I love you,' he said again as he began to move, slowly at first but with increasing urgency as she responded.

She pushed her fingers into his hair and pulled his mouth down to hers. His tongue swept into her mouth, plunging in and moving in a steady rhythm that matched his hips.

She held on to him tightly. Her movements became frantic and jerky. Desperate moans fell from her lips. He pulled her arms above her head, lifting his own head so that he could look into her eyes.

'You're so beautiful,' he ground out.

She shattered again, crying out as her world fell apart in an instant.

He followed her on a growl, collapsing against her as shudders ran through him.

They lay like that for an unending moment, their heavy breathing filling the air. Then his head settled against her breast as he pinned her to the bed with his weight.

'I should move,' he said eventually.

'Don't. I like feeling you there.'

She stroked her fingers through his hair and felt a shudder run through him.

'I love you too,' she said.

He planted a soft kiss between her breasts, his beard tickling her soft skin.

'Despite your stubbornness and your arrogant belief that you're always right,' she went on.

His laughter rocked the mattress and made her smile.

'I love your bravery, your loyalty and your innate nobility.' Her fingers traced the path of his scars. 'And I love your face,' she said softly.

He kissed her fingers as they skimmed his lips. Then he heaved himself off her and curled his large body around her.

'It's just as well. This whole encounter would be awkward if you'd come to tell me you'd decided to marry the Earl of Borwyn.'

She threw back her head and laughed, pleased to see the answering grin on his face.

As her laughter died away his expression sobered. 'But we still have to tell your father that we are going to marry. It won't be easy, my love. I'm not the man he would hope for you. But I will have you—with or without his consent. Now that I know you love me I feel able to conquer the world.'

Ellena smiled and touched his face. 'We don't have to worry about that. We already have his approval.'

'What?' he demanded, sitting bolt upright.

She laughed at his comically wide eyes. Joy bubbled up within her. 'My father has already given his permission for us to marry. Apparently all those times he demanded I come home it was with the express intention of introducing us. He thought we would suit, and for once I have to admit that he was right.'

'What?' said Braedan again.

'It turns out he's a romantic at heart, although his practical nature is never far from the forefront. He wants his best warrior looking after his furthest outpost—and, although he didn't say it, I'm sure he wants me to carry on looking after the accounts.'

Braedan raised an eyebrow and Ellena laughed. She was sure there would be plenty of arguments in the future about who was really in charge. She'd only have to make sure he *thought* it was him while doing everything her way. She was fairly sure she knew the way to wrap him around her finger.

'What about the handsome Earl of Borwyn?' asked Braedan, a frown crossing his face.

'If I didn't fall in love with you, then Borwyn was his alternative plan.'

'The manipulative, underhand…'

'Quite,' she said, reaching up to tug him back down to her.

'I suppose,' he said, as he dropped another kiss on her mouth, 'we could let him win just this once…'

Epilogue

'That's a big horse,' said the small boy standing next to Braedan.

'Aye.'

'Is it yours?'

'Aye,' said Braedan, eyeing the young stallion which had yet to be broken in but was already showing a great deal of promise.

'Can I ride him?'

'Not until you're bigger,' said Braedan, the thought of the small body on such a gigantic beast making his knees weak.

'How long will that take?'

'Another six summers, I should think.'

'But that's *ages*,' said Garrick, his slender shoulders slumping forward in disappointment.

'It will go in a flash,' said Braedan. *But hopefully not too quickly*, he thought. 'In the meantime, you've got Beadle to ride.'

'But he's a *baby's* horse. Hunter could ride him.'

Braedan laughed. 'I don't think so; he's only six days

old. Speaking of which—it's high time we went to see him and your mother.'

'But we've only just seen them. And the *girls* will be there.' Garrick's shoulders slumped even further.

'I don't see what's wrong with that,' said Braedan, reaching down and lifting his son onto his shoulders. 'You love your sisters and they love you.'

He felt Garrick shrug. 'They love Hunter more.'

Ah, so that was the problem. His eldest son was experiencing his first taste of jealousy.

'They do not,' said Braedan. 'Give it a few days and they'll be back to causing mischief with you again. They're just excited to meet Hunter after such a long wait.'

'The babe *was* inside mother forever,' said Garrick, resting his chin on the top of Braedan's head. 'I thought she was going to go bang.'

Braedan chuckled. 'Aye, I think she would have done if he'd been in there any longer.'

He ducked through a doorway, making sure Garrick didn't bang his head on the stone entranceway, and climbed the steps that led to his bedchamber.

Inside, his wife lay at the centre of the large bed, his two daughters sprawled across it, all of them gazing at the newest member of their family, who was curled up in his mother's arms and twitching in his sleep.

'There you both are,' whispered Ellena, smiling up at them. 'Would you like to hold Hunter, Garrick?'

'Can I?' said Garrick, his voice full of awe.

Braedan smiled and tugged his son down from his shoulders.

'Climb up next to your mother,' he said. 'Then she can pass him to you.'

Garrick scooted across the bed and curled up against his mother's side. When he was sitting securely, Ellena handed over the baby.

Braedan watched as his two sons met properly for the first time. His older son grinned as his younger brother wrapped his tiny fingers around Garrick's slightly bigger ones.

'Come and join us,' Ellena said softly, holding out her hand towards Braedan.

Careful not to disrupt the bed too much, Braedan stretched out next to Ellena. His two daughters clambered on him, using him as a mattress.

'How are you feeling, my love?' he asked Ellena as she settled her head against his shoulder.

'I'm fine,' she said, grinning.

He kissed her forehead. 'You'll never let me forget that, will you?'

'No, my love, but I am lying to you. I'm not fine.'

Braedan's body tightened. This last pregnancy had been hard for Ellena, and the birth had been long. Every time she fell pregnant he worried that he would lose her, and every time she amazed him with her strength. Four children would have to be enough. He couldn't go through the worry again.

'What's wrong?' he asked, sitting up slightly and examining her.

There were dark smudges underneath her eyes, and more wrinkles gathering at their corners than there had been eight years ago, but she was still the most beautiful woman he had ever seen.

'Nothing's wrong, my love,' she said, reaching up to touch his face. 'I'm not fine. I'm *perfect*. I have everything that I've ever wanted right here in this room.'

He hid his face against her hair, inhaling her soft lavender scent as tears pricked his eyes.

He felt laughter gurgle through her. 'Ah, you soft-hearted man.'

He laughed too. 'Don't tell anyone,' he murmured.

'No one would believe me if I told them that The Beast gets emotional around his family,' said Ellena, giving him a playful nudge.

He put his arms around her and held her tightly. Ellena was right. Everything was perfect.

* * * * *

K